MW00941440

Unwrapped

A SOUTH POLE SANTA ADVENTURE
Book 4

BY

JINGLEBELLE JACKSON

Copyright © 2015 JingleBelle Jackson
All rights reserved.
ISBN: 1517008069
ISBN 13: 9781517008062

For the students in the Redwood classroom at Valley Montessori School in Livermore, California. Thank you for your love of Sandra, love of books and love of great ideas!

And to Judy and Ryan, my favorite grandma/granddaughter team who have loved Sandra and her pals from the beginning, made great suggestions for plot twists, and cheered me on. Thank you!

Choose Kindness!

Character List:

- **Santa** – The main man, the big guy, the elf in the red suit
- **Cassandra Penelope Clausmonetsiamlydelaterra…** -- South Pole Santa
- **Cappie** – Also known as Captain Margaret Richmond. Sandra's legal guardian since her parents disappeared when she was eleven.
- **The *Mistletoe*** – The tugboat Sandra and Cappie call home
- **Squawk** – Sandra's beloved talking macaw
- **Rio** – An emerald-colored dolphin that is loved by and travels with Sandra and Cappie
- **Ambyrdenna "Birdie" Snow** – Sandra's best friend, daughter of a water wizard and African princess mother. Birdie can talk to birds.
- **Spencer Mantle** – Sandra's super smart best friend, son of two humans
- **Sanderson "Sandy" Claus…** -- Sandra's dad, of elf and human descent; tragically lost at sea **Cassiopola "Cassie" Claus…** -- Sandra's mom, of human and royal elfin descent; tragically lost at sea
- **St. Annalise** – A remote island in the Caribbean Sea that is home to St. Annalise Academy where Sandra attended school.
- **Christina Annalise** – The head mistress of St. Annalise Academy and mother of Jason Annalise

- **Jason Annalise** – Adopted son of Christina and purported King of Fairies
- **Gunderson "Gunny" Holiday** – A runner-up for South Pole Santa from the great state of Texas. Now assists Santa and keen on Sandra.
- **Thomas Jackson** – A retired St. Annalise Academy professor living on the island and a friend of Sandra and Cappie's.
- **Crow & Ghost Holiday** – Gunny's twin brothers
- **Zinga** – An elf and executive assistant to Santa
- **Breezy** – An elf in charge of weather reporting and friend to Sandra. She, like many elves, can read thoughts.
- **Emaralda "Em"** – A bright green "delgin elf" with special talents who assists Sandra as her transportation
- **Wistle** – A Shan fairy
- **Nuka** – An Icelandic elf
- **Redwood** – A very tall elf, new to the North Pole
- **Reesa** -- The Shan fairy ruler apparent
- **Quisp** – A tiny Shanelle fairy
- **Nicholas Navidad, Redson O'Brien, Klondike Tannenbaum, Rollo Kringle** – Runner-up competitors for South Pole Santa
- **Grander** – A helpful spire
- **Thogo** – A monument held prisoner by the drags
- **Danger** – A drag held prisoner by the drags

- **Beatrice Carol** – A World Wide News TV reporter from London England
- **Calivon, Laile, Grosson, Zeentar** – Members of the Esteemed High Council of Magical Beings

Prologue

Sandra sat in the sand admiring the busy beach where she had landed. She didn't know where she was but she could see a big city in the distance. She had used her locket to "take her to a warm beach where she had never been" to get away from the joyous chaos of the North Pole for a few minutes of quiet time. The elves had woke up from Slumber Month and were all aflutter.

She didn't want her sadness and frustration to take away from their joy on wake-up day. It had been a little more than a month since she had received the news about Jason missing and Gunny being held by the fairies and nothing had changed. Not one single thing.

A little boy came and sat next to her on the beach. "Hi," he said to her shyly but boldly.

"Hi back, Desmond," she said, grinning. There was no chance at all her day could not be brightened up by a curious child. She glanced down the beach and saw Desmond's parents checking to be sure everything was alright. She gave them a smile and a wave to assure them.

"You know my name! I knew it!" the little boy said. "I think you're Sandra Claus!"

"Well then, you are almost right," Sandra said smiling at him. "I am Sandra Claus dot dot dot." "Oh yeah," said the little boy. "I like the dots but I don't really get the long name. Too hard to spell. No offense."

"Ha!" Sandra said laughing so loud people turned to look and see what the fun was about.

"What's the deal with that anyways?" he asked her.

"Well the deal is that when I was your age we lived on a tugboat."

"The Mistletoe!" Desmond grinned.

"That's right," said Sandra, enjoying this well-informed child, as other children joined them at their spot on the beach. One little girl sat down as close as she could to Sandra and held her hand.

Sandra was in her glory. Gone and forgotten was her sadness.

"So, as I was saying, when I was little we lived on a tugboat and traveled all around the world," she said to the group of attentive children. "We saw many wonderful things."

"Is that when you got your special parrot, Squawk?" asked the sister of the little girl holding her hand. Sandra knew her name was Savanna.

"It is!" said Sandra, so impressed the children knew so much about her. "And Rio, too."

"Rio is her dolphin friend," Desmond said, with authority, as all of the children nodded their heads knowingly.

"She is indeed, and she is really spectacular. Squawk and Rio were my very best friends growing up and still really are."

"You're lucky," said a little girl named Leonie.

"You are too, Leonie! I know your best friend Avery Cate loves you, too."

Leonie's eyes got wide with surprise that Sandra knew so much.

"Well, back to my whole name now, okay?" The group all nodded. "Do you all know it?" she asked, thinking it was unlikely but, in unison, some louder and faster than others, they all shouted it out:

"CASSANDRA PENELOPE CLAUSMONETSIAMLYDE LATERRA DOT DOT DOT!"

How could any person on the planet be as lucky as me? Sandra thought at that moment, smiling till her jaw began to hurt.

"You are all so smart!" she exclaimed, clapping her hands with applause for them all. "My last name, as I bet you all know already, started out as just 'Claus.' As we left each place we lived, my parents added something on to it to honor the country and to add some fun, I suspect, to a little girl's imagination and our grand adventures at sea. So, when we left France they added on 'Monet.' When we left Thailand, they added on 'Siam.' Then we spent time in Vietnam and they added on 'Ly' and finally we got 'De La Terra' after we spent time in some Latin America countries. And because my last name isn't done yet, it has the dot dot dots on the end."

"You're lucky," said a little boy named Joe. "My last name is Donut."

The kids all laughed. Donut was a funny last name. Sandra didn't laugh though. "Donut is one of the best last names I've ever heard of," she said. "It's short and sweet, and you could draw it if you wanted and people would still know who you were."

Now the children were staring at Joe Donut like he was the luckiest of them all. He beamed at Sandra.

"I want a good last name," wailed the little girl holding her hand. A lot of the children were starting to tear up. Sandra had to keep from smiling. She had been teased many times about her name and now here were children loving it.

"Now, now, everyone, remember it is very long and sometimes easy to forget how to spell. Even I go by Sandra Claus dot dot dot most the time."

"I'll add dots to my name," Savanna said and the others nodded at her. "I'm going to be Savanna dot dot dot." Sandra laughed with delight. The other children started adding dots to their names too. All of them to their first names.

"Yeah, I'll be Desmond dot dot dot."

"Trinh dot dot dot!"

"Leonie dot dot dot!"

"Ryan dot dot dot!"

"Cole dot dot dot!"

"Your mom and dad are fun, Sandra," said Joe Donut. "I wish mine were more fun."

The mention of her parents in that way gave a tug on her heart and a catch in her breath. "Well Joe, I think you are very lucky to have parents who love you so much that they brought you to this beautiful beach today. My parents," she paused to know what to say next. "My parents were the very best for me but I lost them when I was just a little bit older than some of you. Now they live with me right here." She tapped her fingers on her heart. The children said nothing but gave her little nods of understanding. A tear rolled down Leonie's face and Sandra quickly changed the topic before one rolled down her face, too, and turned the day upside down for them all. "Now listen! I love all of your dot dot dot names and I love you all," Sandra said, standing up and meaning every word. "But you really must head back to your parents and I must get back to the elves and the others. We have lots to do you know, even now, to be ready for next

Christmas."

The group of children all jumped up and down at the mention of Christmas. "You are all wonderful and I can see you are all kind. Thank you. Be sure to send me your lists of kind things you are doing this year so I can share them with the elves. You can get a chance to win a trip to visit one of the Poles! Twelve children are coming this year and you could be one of those selected for next year!"

The children hugged Sandra all at once before they went running off to tell their story about who they had met. Sandra hoped their parents would believe them. She knew some would and she knew some wouldn't. Believing in Santa magic was up to each individual no matter their age.

Leonie and Savanna held back.

"Sandra," Leonie said shyly, now speaking for both the sisters. She almost whispered the next part afraid perhaps that someone would hear her. "Don't tell Santa, but we love you best."

Sandra was both touched and shocked to hear the words. Desmond was also still there and had heard Leonie as well.

"Me too," he said as he gave Sandra a quick hug and dashed down the beach. "Remember me,

Sandra Claus... I'm Desmond dot dot dot!"

CHAPTER I

A Long List of Troubles

Location: St. Annalise

Sandra's list of troubles was a mile long.

"It is not a 'mile long'," Cappie, her treasured guardian who had raised her after her parents were lost at sea, admonished. "It really only has three things on it."

"Well, they are really big things, Cappie, with loads of little things under them which leads to it feeling like it's a mile long. Maybe two miles long." Sandra added the last part with a bit of defiance. At the moment, she didn't like having her troubles downplayed.

Cappie just sighed at her. "Let me hear them again then."

Sandra plopped in a seat at the table in the galley on the *Mistletoe* and began to recite her list using her fingers for drama.

"First, of course, is Jason. We've been looking for him for more than a month. And not just us. Every single fairy in the seen world and the unseen world has been instructed to find him and, so far, not a single real clue has turned up."

". . . *squawk*! . . . tired of Jason . . . *squawk*! . . . heart breaker . . ."

"Squawk!" Sandra said to her talking parrot. "You can be naughty sometimes and I'd still come look for you if you were missing."

Squawk flew out the door to perch on the tugs rail in protest of her calling him "naughty." *Of course she'd look for him,* he thought, but squawked out nothing. It was a totally different matter.

He was insulted she had compared the two. He hadn't liked Jason when he was Sandra's boyfriend and started taking up all her time and he really didn't like him after he broke her heart by breaking up with her. Now that he was missing and taking up all their time for fun thinking about where he might be, Squawk was really, *really*, not liking him. Not to mention, it seemed Jason was the king of fairies and Squawk, like many, did not care for fairies.

"Yes," Cappie was saying. "Jason is a huge concern. But not your concern alone as you have pointed out. His mother is actually in charge of that search and you need to let her be the lead."

Christina Annalise was the headmistress of St. Annalise Academy on the island of St. Annalise that Sandra and Cappie called home. Jason was Christina's adopted son and had not told even her what route he was going when he had left to join the fairy realm to learn more about who he really was and what it meant to be the apparent king of fairies. No one had heard from him in months. Both Christina and Sandra had assumed it was because he was busy with his new role and had chosen to break, at least for a while, from his life with all of them. While it seemed outrageously rude, to both of them, not to write or call, it wasn't out of Jason's character and definitely not out of the character of a fairy. Generally speaking, Shan fairies, the ruling party and haughtier side of the fairy realm, felt no need to keep anyone apprised of any of their comings and goings. Most beings that were not fairies were simply beneath them.

"I'm so worried about him, Cap. I can't have him be gone in the same kind of way mom and dad were gone. One minute they're there and the next they just aren't and no one has ever been able to figure out what happened. That's how it's going with Jason and that's hard."

"Oh, sweetheart," Cappie said, pulling her beautiful Santa girl over and hugging her. "I understand. I just hate to see you so troubled. What else is on the list?"

"Gunny, of course," Sandra said, standing up and pacing again. "The fairies are still refusing to give him up until they know where Jason is, which is absolutely ridiculous since not only did Jason break up with me, he didn't even want me to know where he was going. So, obviously, I'm not the one hiding him." Her voice got loud with frustration. She was beyond annoyed that the Supreme Esteemed Fairy Council refused to release Gunny still. Santa had thought he had successfully negotiated his release a couple of times but it fell through for no valid reason both times.

Sandra missed him. Gunny was not the easiest person in her life but he was one of the most important. Their relationship had been complicated from the start. They met competing to be South Pole Santa and when she was selected over him, Gunny had, at first, rebelled. To put it more accurately, he had sulked. Then he had Santanapped her last year which had not endeared him to her at all. It had taken a lot of effort, but their fragile relationship had seemed on the cusp of something more than friendship when the fairies had whisked him away, and held him for ransom, in exchange for Jason.

Sandra missed them both, which was a complicated mess all on its own.

"Third big item," she said out loud to help dismiss that uncomfortable topic in her head. "I have twelve very kind children whose names have been drawn from nearly a million entries. A million, Cappie!" She repeated that last part because she still could not begin to believe it. Kind acts were washing over the world thanks to her request for children to help her perform random acts of kindness - RAKS as they were often known as - and then send in what they had done. From those lists of kindnesses, twelve children were going to get to visit the North Pole and she had ideas brewing in her head for making it even bigger in the future.

"I know they will like getting to meet the elves and Santa, but I just want to make sure it is an extra special time for them."

"Sandra, really. That is hardly worth worrying on since no children have ever been so lucky and these children are nice to begin with! Of course they are going to love it - even if they do nothing at all."

Sandra just frowned at her. She knew she had time to figure it out since she wasn't planning on them visiting until later in the year but she loved to plan early and it was really important to her that it be "just right."

"What is item number four?" Cappie asked a little too sweetly suspecting there wasn't more than three items on Sandra's "mile long list."

"Four is that no real progress has been made now for months on getting the South Pole Village barge finished. Not through the Christmas season, of course, and not since Gunny has been gone. Spencer and Birdie, and even Crow once in a while, have been trying to help with it but they just aren't the same as having Gunny managing it all. Cappie, they put up two walls in the wrong place! How is that even possible?"

"Walls can come down," Cappie said assuredly. The South Pole Village barge was Sandra's new love. She had always lived on the *Mistletoe* and loved it, and always would love it, but her new responsibilities as South Pole Santa meant she would need to leave the *Mistletoe* for a new home in her new role. Working with Gunny, they had figured out that a large barge could be built to duplicate North Pole Village. It could be towed by the *Mistletoe* all around the seas if necessary and that would be South Pole Santa's new home. She loved the most that the barge, dubbed South Pole Village, meant she could work from anywhere and still be South Pole Santa. Spencer and Birdie, her very best friends, had been trying to keep some work on the barge happening without Gunny, and using Gunny's brother Crow, but none of them really understood construction.

"Okay, any items past those four?" Cappie asked politely.

Sandra looked at her and flashed her first smile since they had started their chat. Talking things out with Cappie always made her feel better. "Not really. Just stuff. Okay, the list isn't a mile long."

"Ahoy!" a voice called out from the deck and Cappie leapt up, smiling. She knew the voice of their neighbor, long-time friend and now Cappie's official boyfriend, well. Thomas Jackson, had his arm around Cappie by the time Sandra joined them on deck. Despite his show of affection for Cappie, he was clearly there for Sandra, this visit, as he looked directly at her.

"There's news," he said. "Rio has found us a way in."

CHAPTER 2

Jason

Location: Somewhere Unknown

Jason, by his count, had been held by the drags, the "evil little bird beasts" as he had taken to calling them, for somewhere around nine months, judging by his scribbled marks on the bars. It was already late February at home. The scratches looked just like he'd seen in movies. Four strokes with a line through them to mark five days passing. "This is not the kind of movie I would have picked to star in," he mumbled to himself.

"What'd ya say?"

He had started out in a cage in a room all by himself but in the last two months he had been joined by two other captives locked up in their own cages. There were bars and space between them all but no walls. He had never seen beings like either of them but somehow they all new English and could communicate – English, it seemed, was not just the

International language but a Universal language. Thankfully, they could talk without any interpretation needed.

The big guy, who had just asked what he had said, was called Thogo. Thogo wasn't human. He was a monument, which he explained was similar to being a granite except they were bigger and slower and not as smart. Granites and monuments all looked like big, walking rocks. Walking rocks with eyes and a mouth. Thogo talked the most and snored something awful at night. Jason found himself sleeping away his days at times because he couldn't sleep at night with Thogo's loud snoring echoing around the barred room.

The other guy was always quiet. Curiously, he was a drag himself. Jason and Thogo had only recently learned his name. He called himself Danger but Jason suspected it was a made up name intended to scare them. He had heard one of the drags call him Jeezer once. Jason had said nothing but was pretty sure that was Danger's real name. He didn't care either way. In fact, wanting to find out his own real name was part of what had gotten him into this whole mess.

Jason Annalise. He'd always known he was adopted. Christina Annalise, his adopted mother, had been completely upfront about that as soon as he was old enough to understand it. She had never married, barely dated that he could recall, so he'd never had so much as a stepdad in the picture. He had literally floated to St. Annalise in the bottom of a dinghy with a blanket and a note asking whoever found him to take care of him. So Christina had, with joy and pride.

Shamefully, he realized now, he had never treated her as well as he should have. But then, truthfully, he had never treated anyone as well as he should have. When he felt people got too close he always tended to back them off a bit by being rude and aloof. He'd never had many real friends, found relationships to be challenging, and had done poorly in school, even when, with just a little bit of effort, he could have done well. The one thing he excelled at was every sport he tried. Put it all together and he felt like he had never really known himself, which he blamed on being adopted. When it finally became painfully obvious that he was indeed a magical being – a fairy apparently, which seemed unbearably cruel since he could hardly abide most of them – he realized there was a reason for why he never felt like he fit during his first eighteen years of life.

He was on a quest to meet the real him when these nasty drags had snagged him.

They had been horrible about it all. He had felt certain that by entering through the cave he had found to wait out a rare big storm, he would be in magic-filled middle earth and able to make his way back to fairy central. No, he had no idea where "fairy central" really was, but in his mind all the magical realm lived inside the planet. That was based on no actual understanding as he had slept through his "Magical Beings" classes. It was simply his own idea. After months imprisoned by the drags, it seemed ridiculous to think he had ever believed that but at the time it had made perfect sense in his own mixed-up head.

"Would have made it just too easy to have asked for any help," he muttered out loud. Now it seemed preposterously stupid. The "unseen world" was indeed the world of magical beings but that didn't mean it was in the middle of the earth. Yes, there were beings living in Middle Earth - most seemed to be quite creepy - but many magical beings lived in unseen spaces with magical ways of getting there. "Duh," he said out loud again, fighting back the anger he felt for himself as he reviewed his own actions for the ninth time that day alone.

"Quit thinking about it," Thogo called over. Thogo knew that times like these were the worst for Jason as he spent hours churning on things with regret and pain showing on his face, uttering only the occasional word.

Jason ignored him as he continued to berate his own decisions and behaviors. Not only had he selected to go through the cave, he had ignored the warning the drags had given him the year before to stay away, had told absolutely not one single person of his plans, and had, perhaps most stupidly, thought his new found clout as fairy king and the powers that came with it would somehow magically make any troubles go away.

He knew within three days of entering the cave it wasn't the way to anywhere he wanted to be. He had turned around to head back out but by then the drags had picked him up against his will and dragged him to their bleak "home away from home" as they called it, for no legitimate reason. He'd been there ever since. Nine months. Making it all even more frustrating was that none of his powers worked at all. He couldn't even orb which he had only done a couple of times before his quest began. In fact, his powers had barely worked as soon as he entered the cavern and gotten weaker and weaker the deeper in that he went. Somehow, the drags were able to completely block them. The one and only power he had maintained was that he could see a long distance away. Sadly, there was really nowhere to look. He closed his eyes and leaned back on the hard bars staying sane only because he could think of Sandra and know there was love in the world.

As bad as I was to her and just about everyone I met, he thought, *I belong here.*

"No you don't," Thogo said. "No you don't. None of us do."

Jason bolted upright and stared at Thogo. He hadn't said those thoughts out loud. Thogo could hear thoughts. Even in here. Thogo just grinned. It was actually a common feature for many magical beings. Some of the elves could do the same.

Breaking out never left Jason's mind. He knew it was unlikely but it kept his mind busy thinking about it. Now, he realized, they had a new "tool." They had his eyesight and Thogo's mind reading on their side. Their resources were growing.

CHAPTER 3

Gunny

Location: Unknown to all humans

Gunny's accommodations were luxurious in comparison to Jason's. He was under watch at all times and was restricted as to where he could go, but he was able to wander freely in the large building where he was being kept. The fairies showed no fear that he would break out. He was constantly watched by orbing fairies, however, that no matter how many times he swatted at them, threw things at them, or tried to make them balls in a game, were always far faster than he was. Even if he could overcome them, where would he go? He had no idea where he was and no idea on how to get to where he was from. His accommodations might have been comfortable but he was stuck and a stuck Gunny was a no-fun Gunny. His strategy was to be such a completely belligerent guest they would be begging him to leave in the end.

Fairies, it must be remembered, are refined. They're beautiful and they like things that are beautiful. They follow rules – provided they agree with the rules. They surround themselves with the best of things. They're conscientious of hierarchy. They appreciate beautiful music and being in nature. They bathe, primp, smell divine, and disdain anything dirty.

Gunny defied and violated all of these fairy preferences. On purpose, every day. He was as loud as he could be. He refused to bathe. He burped after every meal and sometimes even during a meal. Before they took away his TV set he played every shoot-em-up he could find, real loud and acted out all the parts. He had taken to not changing his clothes, not combing his hair and, a couple of times, when some top fairies came by to check in on him, he was able to let loose with a couple of big ol super loud and super stinky farts. That had even pushed him past his own sense of decorum but hey, the fairies had chosen the wrong guy to mess with.

Under different circumstances, as a visitor, not a captive, he might have enjoyed his time there. But as a "detainee", as the fairies put it, he hated it. Every minute was sheer agony. They were polite to him, the few Shanelle fairies he met were downright kind, but he was a cowboy from the open ranges of Texas and they had him pent-up like one of the wild mustangs who roamed on his ranch back home. It wasn't a good fit and he wasn't looking to be tamed. He was looking to get out.

He wondered what everyone back home had been told. He wondered how Christmas had been without him there. He wondered if his ma had made his favorite pies for dessert. Most of all though, he wondered what Sandra knew and if she would forgive him for disappearing on her so quickly again just as it seemed they were finally going to get close.

That whole thought got him to pacing again. Sandra had finally seemed ready to move past that heartbreaker Jason and was coming his way. At last. He had cared about her from the minute he first saw her sitting in the stands at a Pole Pong game. He wondered if there was any way in the world he could stop caring about her if she wanted nothing to do with him once he got out of there. The fairies had arrested him because they believed he had Santanapped Santa. He hadn't, but what if Sandra believed them? He had taken her and maybe even worse, even though he knew who had taken Santa, he could never tell her. All of that went round and round and round in his mind and he couldn't sort out how it would all be okay again. That's why he wasn't behaving even worse actually. He wasn't completely sure he even dared to go home. Home to what? His own breaking heart?

Where was home anyways now? he thought again. Was it the ranch? He knew it always could be. The ranch was big enough, and demanding enough, that there would always be room for him there. But home now felt more like North Pole Village or, to be more specific, St. Annalise, or the South Pole Village barge, or anywhere else that Sandra Clausmonetsiamlydelaterra "dot dot dot", he said the last part out loud, wanted to live. Sandra was home to him. The agony was not knowing what he was to her. And, if he was anything at all to her, why in the Texas tarheels didn't she get him out of there?

It had been more than two months and no one would tell him anything. He had told his story to any fairy that would listen and to the rude ones who didn't want to listen as well. He didn't care if he bored them. He was bored too. He had felt certain he was getting out right before Christmas. Even Santa had visited and assured him that he'd be released. But then something changed. Santa wasn't allowed any more visits. Gunny was no longer questioned by anyone about the Santanapping and he was given no updates on his supposed "case." Fairies being fairies, none of them had any problem at all not giving him any answers. "When Reesa wants you to know she will tell you," was the answer he was given every day when he asked. He lived for the day he didn't need to ask again.

He wondered almost torturously so if Jason had returned from his visit to the fairies and if he might be the reason Gunny was still here. Had Jason's first act as king of the fairies been to have Gunny locked away to keep him from Sandra? Gunny wouldn't put it past him. He was no fan of Jason Annalise - for several reasons, not the least of which was that the girl he was crazy about had been crazy about Jason. It was more than that, though. The guy was a jerk most of the time. Even Sandra finally had to have known it when he broke her heart. On the flip side, Gunny never particularly felt one way or another about fairies. He actually liked a few. But being the king of this bunch of flighty, high maintenance prima donnas was not a job he would ever want. He doubted Jason wanted it either, which almost made him feel a little bit sorry for the guy. Almost. He kept having this gnawing feeling that while he was locked away week after week, Jason was back at the Pole and on St. Annalise, wherever Sandra was, trying to get into her heart again. He knew it was what he would do if he were Jason.

"Hey," he yelled loudly to the fairy right in front of him. "Am I getting out of here today?"

"When Reesa wants you to know she will tell you," the fairy orb said tartly.

He let out a really long burp as his response.

CHAPTER 4

Ghost

Location: St. Annalise

Gunny would never break their agreement to not tell Sandra, or anyone else, who had taken Santa, but Ghost was thinking hard about whether he should or not. It hadn't been Gunny, it had been him. He knew from Santa that his big brother was being held by the fairies because of what Ghost had done. They had arrested Gunny because they believed he had taken Santa. Now he was being held in exchange for Santa and Sandra handing over Jason and, despite what the fairies believed, they had no idea where Jason was. What a mess. It had become complicated but Gunny wouldn't have been taken away in the first place if the Esteemed High Council of Magical Beings hadn't believed he was the Santanapper. If Ghost confessed, however, the Council would hold him accountable and the punishment would be extreme. Right now they couldn't prove anything against him or Gunny. Santa had been very clear with him that he wanted Ghost to stay silent. "This will be a crime that goes unsolved," Santa said. "Let us move on and put this behind us."

That was a bigger punishment to a guy like Ghost than if he could have just confessed to it all and had it purged from inside him. If the High Council would order a reasonable punishment he would have preferred to come clean and take the punishment but Santa said that if he told, others, like Gunny, would also be punished, so Ghost agreed to stay quiet. He wished he felt more like Santa did, that, in time, the Santanapping incident would just fade away.

Making it all even worse was having Gunny gone so long. The whole Holiday family had missed him at Christmas. It had been a subdued holiday compared to a normal family get together on the ranch. Gunny was gone and Ghost was way too quiet. Everyone could sense that something was wrong and none of them could figure out what. With his broken arm healed up, Ghost just wanted to help get Gunny back. So when Santa came calling with a way he could help out, he was all in. That's how he had landed on St. Annalise with Sandra walking toward him with a happy smile on her face.

"Ghost! I'm so happy to see you!" Sandra came running up to him. He looked so much like his older brother it had taken a minute for her to realize it was Ghost there and not Gunny. She had kept her disappointment in check. It really was good to see this handsome Holiday brother.

Sandra hugging him was agony. He wanted to blurt out everything. Apologize, beg her forgiveness, and then he wanted to kiss her. Sandra was his dream girl from the minute he met her in a dark hall at the ranch. He was crazy about her in a completely unexpected way, even knowing his big brother was interested in her. He dreamt that it wouldn't matter once she fell for him and Gunny understood that was her choice. Now though, she was completely off limits to him. He knew his dream of her falling for him was over. Couples couldn't have secrets between them and he had a big one. He pushed away from her while he still could and got right to business.

"You should have called me, Sandra," he said, trying to sound as annoyed with her as he could.

His tone surprised her but lots of things about Ghost tended to catch her off guard.

"Well, you kind of disappeared on us there in the middle of the Christmas rush so you weren't the first person I thought to call," she said, not knowing how much her words hurt. He hadn't wanted to be away but when you Santanapped Santa and he says stay away, you do. "Besides, I kind of figured Crow would keep you up on everything."

Crow was Ghost's twin brother. He was dating Birdie and the two were inseparable these days.

Crow had stayed at St. Annalise with Birdie to help out while his brother was missing.

"We haven't talked that much," was Ghost's clipped response. They had talked at Christmas but even Crow, the brother Ghost was closest to, hadn't been able to coax Ghost out of the mood he had rooted himself in. Ghost had asked Crow to give him some space, so Crow had. They were brothers and best friend. He knew they'd be okay and he was busy with Birdie anyway.

"So what brings you to St. Annalise?" Sandra asked. "Did you come to visit your brother?"

"Santa said Rio found the cave you've been looking for so you have a lead on Gunny." Ghost said, trying to look straight ahead and not right at Sandra. He felt like she'd know he was hiding something. This was tougher than he had imagined.

Sandra stopped. "Not Gunny, Ghost. It's Jason. We have a lead on Jason."

"Jason!" Ghost exclaimed. Like his big brother, he never liked the guy. Liked him even less then Gunny did. Maybe because they were the same age. Maybe because they were actually a lot alike. "Why would Santa tell me it was a lead on Gunny?"

Why indeed? Sandra thought, but she knew the answer. Santa was a clever one. "Probably because the fairies are holding Gunny hostage until we release Jason." As they walked to the *Mistletoe*, she shared the whole story with him. By the time they got there, he knew exactly what he was going to do. What he had to do. He could see there was a crowd on the *Mistletoe*, including his twin giving him a shout, so he stopped Sandra before they got to the dock.

"Sandra, I'm going after Jason. Just me. No argument. If he's alive, I'll find him. Santa knew I was the guy and I do, too."

CHAPTER 5

Party Talk

Location: St. Annalise

The group on the *Mistletoe* that evening had a truly good time. There had been so much worry over their friends that laughter had been in short supply some days and it was good to set aside their worries. There was nothing that could be done that evening. Ghost had given them a reason to pause and gather, and they overfilled the big tug.

Of course, there was Sandra and Squawk and Cappie with Rio swimming about getting in her greetings and sweet-talking the group for some of their fish tacos – well the fish part. Thomas was there making googly eyes at Cappie (at least Sandra thought so) and Crow was there making googly eyes at Birdie. Spence was there with Network Naters talking on the latest and greatest technology they were planning to install on the South Pole Village barge. All the elves that were presently working at St. Annalise came by, of course, because no elf ever misses a party. Sandra was especially happy to see that Dear Lovey was down from the North Pole as well and doing just fine getting around in her wheelchair, despite all the sandy beaches on St. Annalise. Happily, with one of the best research and development departments in the world at the North Pole, and elves that adored her, Dear Lovey was outfitted with the very latest all-terrain wheelchair on the market. This was her second visit to St. Annalise and Rio was especially excited to see her. The two loved swimming together.

Maybe, best of all, was having Christina Annalise at the get-together. Since they had found out Jason was missing she was rarely seen smiling. She was gaunt from weight loss and her brow was furrowed. No matter how much people tried to assure her that they would find him, her worry could not be soothed.

Also joining the happy group that evening were many of their fairy friends. At least the non-fairy group considered them friends. Fairies rarely had friends outside of their own kind. They all politely attended the gathering at full-size rather than in their orbed state. Jason was their king so the current state of affairs was of high concern to them as well. Wistle had even joined them and Sandra welcomed her on-board. They had their differences but the evening was about inclusion not differences.

Cappie had made enough food to feed all of the island which was a good thing since, by the end of the evening, it seemed like most of the island had come by to visit. In fact, it seemed like happy old times. Sandra reveled in the smiles, the laughter, the silly elf jokes and watching Squawk help himself to several rounds of dessert. She caught herself missing Em.

Santa had asked Em to stay back at the North Pole to help with some moving projects. He needed assistance moving whole buildings about the Pole for some reorganizing they were doing and Em had, very reluctantly, agreed she was the right delgin to do the work. In the past, she had always been proud to be of such service, but now that she was Sandra's delgin, serving in the very important role of transportation for South Pole Santa, she was not as interested in helping in other ways around the Pole. She liked to be with Sandra and had to work not to pout about staying behind. Sandra had kept Squawk from teasing Em about it and making her feel even worse. She was due to check in at the North Pole in three days and she could hardly wait to see her little delgin companion. Nearly two months had gone by since the two were together. That was the longest time they'd been apart since they had realized they were the perfect team for serving children.

Amongst all the laughter and talk, Sandra realized Ghost and Crow were having a not-so-happychat on the dock next to the big tug.

"That is ridiculous talk," Crow was saying. "For starters, you have no idea where he is, you have no idea what has happened to him and you have no idea how to get there. That's just for starters. You can't just show up here wanting to be the hero and find Jason. Heck, you don't even like the guy!"

Ghost was clearly annoyed with all he was hearing but successfully managed to contain his temper. "I get it Crow, I do. It even scares me a little bit but whether you like it, or I like it, or any of these people here like it," he paused and swept his arm to take in the boat of party attenders, "I am going after him."

"Yeah, no, you're not." Crow said, not to annoy his brother but because he loved him. He had one brother already missing he couldn't lose another. Ghost gave him a look that said he was going. "Fine, then I'm going too." They were twins; Crow could be just as stubborn.

"Yeah, that is for sure not happening. I love you brother, but we cannot risk ma losing both of us and you know that, too."

Crow looked distraught beyond words. "You don't even have any magical powers!"

"He doesn't, but I do. I'm going too." It was the last person on the whole boat Sandra ever would have guessed who had said those words. In fact, all of the boat seemed to have heard the words spoken and were staring now at the fairy they knew to be many things but none of them would have described her as brave or generous.

Nonetheless, proving again that everyone is more complicated than they may sometimes seem, it was Wistle who had spoken. *She's the female equivalent in a lot of ways to Ghost,* Sandra found herself thinking. A little defiant. A little stubborn. Heavy on misplaced loyalties. Good deep down. Very good looking.

"No one's going with me," Ghost replied. "Least of all a fairy ball." He dismissed her to continue his conversation with

Crow but Wistle was not a "fairy ball" that you could just dismiss.

"Think what you like. You can either agree to take me along or I can simply orb around you constantly to make sure you don't leave without me." Before Ghost could continue to protest she plunged on.

"Jason is my king. *My* king. The King of the Fairies. All fairies greatly care about, or should greatly care about, where he is and how we can get him back. And I, as a fairy, have magical powers you have no access to and may need. I am going. You need not agree to others accompanying you but I will be going."

Ghost considered all that she had said and surprisingly did not protest further. "Agreed," he said simply. "You can come along on one condition. You will do as I say. An expedition has to have a leader and for this one, I'm the guy. Do you accept this term?"

Wistle hated being bossed with a passion but she hated her king missing even more. "Agreed.

But I will not wait on you like a common servant in any way. Otherwise, I accept your terms.

When do we go?"

"As soon as we figure out where we're going."

Sandra joined them now on the deck pleased to have Wistle going too. Two together was far better than one alone. "That, we will know tomorrow when Rio leads us to the cave opening."

CHAPTER 6

A Path In

Location: Cassandra Cay

The *Mistletoe* set out, following Rio to Cassandra Cay at dawn, to explore the cave Rio had found earlier in the week. While the bright green dolphin only "spoke" dolphin, the group had a way of understanding her intent in the same sort of way she did with them. That was the reason why Thomas had been certain Rio had spotted a way in and on this bright, early, morning she led the way to the cay.

Since he had left Sandra had suspected Jason had gone back out to Cassandra Cay, to start his journey to the fairy realm. She didn't have a good reason to necessarily think so, except she knew he had found a large cave when he'd been stranded on the cay during a rare storm. Jason had shown her a set of drawings he had copied that were on the wall of the cave and told her about how a "dragon-like" bird had emerged and spoke his name telling him never to come back. She begged him to promise he never would go back but he had hedged that promise. She and Birdie and Spence had been out to the cay many times since Jason went missing and never found any sign of a cave. Rio, though, observant dolphin that she was, had found it and she was right.

Mango had been right too, Sandra realized, as they came upon it. Mango had been with Jason in the cave during the storm. The devoted dog came back with them to the cay each time they visited and always led them to where they now saw the cave. For whatever reason, magic or something else, they had never been able to find it before. Now it seemed plain as day.

"How did we miss this?" Sandra asked aloud, looking at an obvious cave in the side of the cay. Birdie and Spencer stood there too, shaking their heads. They had been with Sandra at each search and had seen nothing. Mango was barking loudly as Christina stared too at the opening with hope in her heart.

"Well, let's go see what we can find out here. Come on brother," Ghost said to Crow as he dove off the boat and headed for the beach. Crow dove behind him along with Birdie, Spence and Sandra. Cappie called out that she would stay on the boat with Thomas and Christina. Mango jumped in the water with the rest and headed straight to the cave. Not knowing how to swim, Wistle quickly orbed to the cay, not wanting to be over water any longer than she had to be.

The party pulled themselves up on the small sandy cay. Wistle went to full-size and they waited for Thomas to row in the dinghy with their supply bags filled with cameras, flashlights, matches, plus some food and water since they didn't exactly know what they would be walking in to. Thomas had been a boy scout and always strived to be prepared. In fact, over prepared with over stuffed back packs brought him peace of mind.

Thomas couldn't restrain himself. "Careful now going in," he cautioned for at least the eleventh time. "We have no idea what might be in there. And remember our agreement. One hour and then out you all come with a report. All of you. Then we can make our plan." The group all nodded their understanding. It was the only thing that made sense as a next step.

As Thomas rowed back to the *Mistletoe* to wait with Cappie, the group on shore headed straight to the entrance of the cave. It seemed obvious it had always been there and Sandra was getting a sense about it as they got closer.

"Feels like there's some magic here," Wistle said at that moment. Sandra nodded her head. That would explain why they couldn't see it before but not really why they could see it now. Mango led the way in, barking the whole time.

The six explorers and brave dog found themselves inside a small cave that was just out of the sun and wind. They could see where a small fire pit had been set up and other signs that someone had been there. "This must be where Jason was talking about," Sandra said. As small and kind of spooky as it felt, she was glad he and Mango had found it and were able to stay out of the worst of the storm.

"It looks like the bigger cavern entrance that Jason talked about must be over there." Sandra pointed to a dark spot at the back of a small cave. They all pointed their flashlights in that direction and as they did, something moved.

"What was that!" Birdie cried out more as an exclamation than a question. Wistle popped back into her orb size and instead of retreating, she boldly went forward, with Ghost and Mango right beside her.

They reached the cavern entrance and shined their bright flashlights all around. Ghost stepped in motioning for the others, who followed more hesitantly behind him. "I'm not sure what it was,"

Ghost said, "but there's nothing that seems to be here now. It probably was some kind of sea rat."

The group heard a horrible cackle in response to Ghost's words and whirled their flashlights over to the shallow part of the cavern where it seemed to be coming from. Mango went mad with barking as their flashlights suddenly went dark and Wistle's orb light dimmed very low.

"A sea rat?" a voice cackled from above them. "I am far more dangerous than a sea rat."

"Show yourself," Ghost demanded with far more self-assurance than he actually felt.

"Show myself, young human? You have insulted me with your talk of a sea rat. Why should I show myself?"

"We meant you no disrespect," Sandra now spoke up. "We are simply on a search for our friend and came upon you quite unexpectedly."

"Ah, you are the one this cay is named after are you not Miss Claus dot dot dot.?" The voice seemed to bounce around the cavern. He added each dot slowly and drawn out.

"I am," Sandra managed to stammer, wondering how he knew. "And you are?"

"Someone you don't really want to know. I assume you have come for your friend then? This Jason Annalise? I warned him, you know, not to come again, when he came before. He paid me no never mind so I decided to let him pass. Shall I decide the same for all of you?"

"Please sir, do you know where Jason is? We would just like to collect him and be on our way never to bother you here again, of course," Sandra said.

"Oh, of course." The voice dripped back with sarcasm and then said nothing for a long pause with just Mango barking. "I am tired of that being's noise." Just like that, Mango continued to bark but she was making no noise. He had "turned off" Mango just as he had turned off the flashlights and dimmed Wistle's fairy light.

"Now let's talk further, shall we, about your options? You are where you do not belong and are not welcome. I have not invited you but you are here. Still, it is partially my own fault for preferring to enjoy some fresh air on occasion and showing the way in. I did not anticipate this discovery and wonder at your resourcefulness. These are the things I must consider."

"We have only come for our friend," Sandra said, apparently interrupting his thoughts. "We heard there was a message on the wall here and - "

"Silence Miss Claus with the dots nonsense, if you wish your party to be safe. The message essentially says 'All who enter here shall ne'er return.' Too bad your friend decided to ignore that. The question is - shall I save you, kill you, or allow you to be lost forever too?"

That not only silenced her but made her shudder. But not Wistle. It only made her mad.

"Oh for heaven's sake, you big, bad meanie," she said darting around in her orb state looking for him. "We're a bunch of kids, these are *human* kids, they don't even have any powers and you're trying to -"

Without any warning she dropped to the floor of the cavern.

"You will be silent."

"Wistle!" The group all exclaimed at once dropping to where she lie.

"How dare you mister meanie! How dare you!" Sandra exclaimed as she knelt by Wistle. "We are sorry we wandered into your special cave and that our friend did before us but, hello, there was no sign outside saying 'do not enter' or 'private cave for one.' Yes, you are clearly powerful and mean and do well in the dark but so what? We may not have any particular magical powers but we know manners. We know respect and we know how to be kind to one another. We also know not to leave one of our own behind. So turn us into a puff of dust or step aside."

She got no response. A long, silent moment continued.

"Hello? Hello? Mister horrible guy? Hello?" With her last "hello" their flashlights came back on.

There in front of them was a large arrow in the sandy floor pointing to the back of the cavern. "I am the dragoon, gate keeper for the drags, the keeper of this entry to inner earth," said the voice from somewhere hidden in the cavern again. "Yes, your friend passed here, and no he has not returned. Nor will he, as he is held by my kind. Nonetheless, you may decide the same. I will allow you to pass but you will decide now or never return. Choose."

Without hesitation, Ghost and the now full-size Wistle stepped forward. They hadn't planned to leave right away but they scarcely turned round to wave goodbye. They stepped through the opening where the arrow pointed and Mango ran behind them. Just as they stepped through, it closed.

"Be gone with the rest of you," said the dragoon. "Your friends' fate is now their own."

CHAPTER 7

A Good Cry and A Good Photo

Location: Cassandra Cay

Six had gone in. Four had come out. And gone was Mango, too.

Even those four hadn't really wanted to come out of the cave. They wanted to stay and protest, bargain with the dragoon, and most of all, run after their friends but the path was closed and the way was sealed. They had backed out slowly, almost holding their breath, until they were safely back out on the beach.

"*eeeeeeeeeee eeee eeeeeee*" Rio chattered from the water, relieved to see them.

"Yes Rio, you were completely right," Sandra said, dropping on the sand with the others. "It was the cave."

"*EEEEEEEEEE!*" she was now vocalizing particularly loudly, and with some urgency, pointing her nose and splashing toward the cave. They turned, expecting to see the dragoon by the urgency Rio was showing. Instead, they saw nothing. Rio was shouting because the cave was no longer there! The four-some ran back but could find no sign of it at all.

"The dragoon has used magic to close it again!" said Crow. He was beside himself on what had just happened. He realized there was a very good chance that was the last time he would ever see his brother. He turned to Birdie with tears in his eyes and complete frustration in his heart. There were no words any of them could think to say at the moment. Birdie reached over and squeezed his hand in support.

"Where's Ghost and Wistle?" Thomas said as he pulled up in the dinghy to bring them back out to the *Mistletoe*. "And Mango? Mango, here girl. C'mon, girl, let's go." He called out to the loved dog as if for assurance that his worst suspicions weren't true.

"They're gone, Thomas," Spencer said. At the moment, he was the only one of them who seemed able to speak.

"Gone? Gone how? We agreed that no one would be left behind and we would plan together." Thomas said stunned.

No one said anything in response until Spencer finally spoke up, reluctantly saying the words no one wanted to speak out loud. "It didn't go that way," he said as he and the others gathered their things and got in the dinghy.

On board the *Mistletoe,* the foursome found enough ener-gy to tell the story before the pent-up emotions of what had just happened caught up with them and they all cried. All of them, including Cappie, Thomas, and especially Christina. It was as if she hadn't allowed herself to grieve since getting the news of Jason and the sobs came in great waves. Even Squawk was upset, dashing to and fro, squawking in distress. Finally, it seemed they all were cried out and pulled themselves together to talk on what needed to be done. Sandra had a little bit of hope to share.

"That horrible dragoon, whether he meant to or not, did give us two important pieces of information," she said to the attentive group. "First, like we suspected, we know Jason came this way to wherever he thought he was going. And second, he told us that Jason was being held by the drags. That may not be good but it does mean he's alive, which is more than we knew before we went in. Now we need to learn everything we can about these drags." She shivered as she said the last word.

"I think I can help with that part," Christina said, shaking off her sorrow and feeling some hope for the first time in weeks. "We have reference books in the St. Annalise library about every kind of magical being. I'm sure I can get information in the *A to Z on Magical Species* reference set. It will have some details on the drags that will help us know what we're up against."

"Perfect," Sandra said. "I have to be back at the North Pole tomorrow and I'll talk with Santa about all of this. The fairies are going to want to know too, since now we know for certain who has their king."

"Think they'll believe you?" Crow asked doubtfully.

"I think this photo on my camera may help," Sandra said. As they were backing out of the cave with their flashlights still on, she had clicked off two pictures of the wall with the writing on it. It looked just like the writing Jason had so carefully copied into his notebook and shared with her months ago. Two things were different, however. One, for whatever reason, she could read what it said now. And two, in the far upper corner, she had managed to capture in the photo, the head of the dragoon who had terrorized them. It was as if he had photo bombed the shot. More likely, it had been where he had been hanging out just outside their flashlight range but within photo range. He looked evil and surprised all at the same time. Now she had some proof of what they had been saying about where Jason was to take to the Supreme Fairy Council. Maybe they couldn't instantly get Jason back but she had a shot now at getting Gunny set free!

CHAPTER 8

A Message of Hope

Location: North Pole

"Saaaaaandra!!!"

There were few things more wonderful in the world than having a delgin who loved you, Sandra thought, hearing her name called as she stepped out of the North Pole Express coach. She was barely out of the coach when Em flung her elf-sized arms around her. Sandra enveloped her in her own hug and swung Em about as she knew she loved.

"I've been waiting all day," Em said in her impatient way. "The coach was so much slower than me."

Sandra smiled, with a very big grin, at her little friend. She had missed Em and her little sassy ways.

"Em, I have to see Santa first thing. Would you like to go with me and hear my report?" She already knew the answer but liked to give Em options.

"Yes, thank you," said the little green delgin.

"Breezy, I'd love it if you would join us too. I know Santa has important updates for me but I've got some emergency information for him that you will be interested in knowing, too," Sandra said to the elf who was always there to assist her and counsel her.

"Of course, Sandra, but first, please enjoy your official welcome back." Breezy pointed down the street just as Sandra heard the music start up. She had only been gone a month but elves never let a chance to celebrate pass by! Coming up the way was the North Pole band with Ellen at the front, dancing away, and Buddy directing them all. They were wearing new uniforms, including red and green striped boots. Somehow the new look suited them all. Maybe because they all looked so happy to be wearing them and smiles always make everyone look their very best.

Whatever it was, it was definitely a spectacular welcome back.

"Thank you, one and all," Sandra shouted out as Ellen and the band finished up (three rousing Christmas carols, of course) and gathered around her for an elf pile hug. Her favorite greeting!

"Ho Ho Ho! What is all of this?" A voice beloved around the world boomed over the elf hubbub, and the pile quickly shifted from greeting Sandra to greeting the big man himself. Like Sandra,

Santa loved it all. He had had this elf pile greeting for hundreds of years and he never tired of it.

Sandra and Em joined right in. Hugs and elf piles were part of being at the Pole. Sandra hoped they would happen just like this on the South Pole Village barge too. She'd insist on it if necessary.

"It's wonderful to be back, Santa. I have important things to talk with you about so I wonder if we could get some time together in your office." Sandra selected her words and tone carefully so she didn't set off any worry amongst the general elf population. That always led to lamenting, which led to full-on worry, which then often led to full-on crying when they didn't even know what they were crying about! Santa was very skilled at this art of careful word selection and could tell by Sandra's request that it was a matter of some urgency.

"Of course, of course," he said. "Let's head there now."

The elves all followed along right to his office door, chatting away at the two Santa's and each other. Santa and Sandra loved all of it.

Once behind the closed office door, however, Sandra wasted no time giving the update to Santa on what had happened in the cave and who had Jason. Zinga, Santa's assistance, had joined them. She and Breezy both cried, and even Em, an elf with a lot of pride, reached for a tissue to "blow my nose." They all cared about Jason and Ghost and Wistle and Mango.

"Let's go get them back, Sandra!" Em said with vigor. "I am bigger and meaner than any of those drags."

"Thank you, Em," Santa said, meaning it. "You are very brave but you are certainly not mean. We need to study what we do next with these drags, however, before we send anyone else in to get our friends back. This is a real predicament."

Santa looked over the photos again that Sandra had managed to click on her way out of the cave. "I think you are right, Sandra. The one positive part to all of this is maybe we can get Gunny released now."

"Santa, I realized I could read most of what the writing says. It's written in ancient elfin and I think because I am a Leezle perhaps, it's become clear to me." She really wasn't sure of why she could read it now but hadn't been able to before but she did suspect it had something to do with her being of royal elfin heritage.

"Em understood this part first." Sandra nodded toward Em, who beamed a smile back. "She was right. Ancient elfins wrote in a box so this main part here," she paused and circled the middle of the photo, "does indeed read just as what she said and what the dragoon said, 'BEWARE!'"

"However, there is this second box right over here." She pointed to the corner right below where the dragoon had been hiding and the elves leaned in to see it. "That box of script is not as easy to understand and the dragoon is covering one corner

"I think I know what it says, nonetheless." She paused, looking at it again to be sure, but took too long and Em burst.

"C'mon Sandra!" Em said, voicing how they all felt, even Santa.

"I think it says, 'Safe passage to all who seek refuge or travel only to pass through.'"

Em and the others thought that was boring but Santa understood its importance immediately.

"This is ancient elfin script?" He asked Sandra to be sure that was the case. "And elfins have always been the rulers of the magical realm. That means this is a magical order, an edict, if you will. It was meant to scare and keep bad types out and away from Middle Earth. The drags were put there to do that. But it also allowed for those who had a need or purpose to advance through safely. Sandra, this is good news and magnificent work on your part!"

"Why Santa?" Zinga asked, not completely following why he seemed so much happier already.

"Because the drags, while doing their part in guarding the entry, are keeping away the bad, they have forgotten that they cannot intercept those who wish to just pass through, which is definitely Jason. It gives us something to provide the Esteemed High Council of Magical Beings so they can insist on his release and assist with the return of all our friends. Zinga, let's get word off to the Council of this news."

In her typical organized style, Zinga was already out the door as Santa spoke the words. Sandra smiled with relief. She had worked on the puzzle the whole way to the Pole and was hoping Santa would feel the same way.

Now they just needed to convince the Magical Council.

CHAPTER 9

Acts of Kindness by the Thousands

***

Location: North Pole Village

Sandra had spilled all of her news as soon as she arrived but Santa had things of his own he wanted to talk to Sandra about. Specifically, some logistics on where to store the thousands upon thousands of kindness lists that were pouring in from children everywhere.

"It's unprecedented, Sandra, simply unprecedented," Santa said, shaking his head as they walked along to the storage room where they were being kept. "We certainly get letters to Santa all year long but this time of year they are generally a steady, small, trickle. Not this year, though. It's only March and, well, see for yourself." With that, he opened the door to the room where Sandra saw the hundreds of stuffed bags already starting to fill the room.

"These are all addressed to you and all about the kind acts children are doing every day," Santa said. He added kindly, "It really was one of the best ideas coming out of this Pole in a very long time. I'm very proud you thought of it. You're helping to change the world, Sandra."

Sandra stood there staring at all the bags. It was going to take hours and hours and hours to catch up, and stay up, but the lists were so important she wanted to make sure either she or Santa or one of the elves read every single one of them.

"This is stupendous, Santa!" she said with joy in her heart. "Thank you so much for your kind words but I never, ever, could have thought of this without you and my St. Annalise family and the elves support. This is about all of us, but mostly, this fantastic room full of kindness, is about the children and that is beyond exciting!" She couldn't believe how happy she felt at that moment. It had been weeks since such happiness surged through her and she loved feeling normal for a few minutes, because normal for her was feeling happy.

Santa smiled at her happy face and got back to business. "Seriously though, Sandra, these are your idea and your new feature for children. And since we are getting close to getting the barge done, as the first official act of establishing the South Pole Village, I'd like to start redirecting the delivery of these letters directly to St. Annalise and, soon, to your own village."

"To your own village." Sandra wasn't sure she had ever heard sweeter words in any language. Her village. She had a village. She really did. It was getting closer and closer to being done and as her first official act of business she was going to need to determine how to handle the letters as they came in. Truthfully, when she had asked children to send in their acts of kindness, she had never envisioned such enthusiasm for the topic. She knew kindness was important, dreamt it could be embraced by them all, but never, in her wildest dreams, did she dare to imagine a yearround response like this. What a great problem to have!

"Santa!" An elf named Hiccup came running in breathlessly, waving a piece of paper and, well, hiccupping. "Come right away! *hiccup*! The Esteemed High Council of Magical Beings members are, *hiccup*, arriving through the, hiccup, portal in ten minutes! *hiccup*!"

"I see," Santa said, quickly scanning the notice they had just sent. "Well, I didn't expect them quite so fast and it's never ideal when they just drop by, but, in this case, it might be absolutely perfect timing." He headed down the corridor with everyone following close behind.

Sandra had already met the Esteemed High Council members before. She wasn't as convinced as Santa about the perfect timing. To her way of thinking, no time was ever a good time for these stuffy folks to just drop in.

CHAPTER 10

Calling in a Favor

Location: North Pole Village

It turned out to be a visit from just three of the Council members instead of the whole group.

Coming through the magical portal was Calivon, Grosson, and Reesa.

Santa greeted them each warmly. He had been Santanapped and missing the last time they had visited the North Pole but he had heard all about it from Sandra and Mrs. Claus. And the elves had all been sure to tell him, over and over, about how the whole Council had gotten accidentally glitter bombed. The elves all thought it was the funniest thing that had ever happened at the Pole but knowing all the Council members, Santa was actually glad he hadn't been there to witness it.

"There is a rumor that Jason, the purported king of fairies, has been found," Calivon began talking as he stepped out of the portal carrier, wasting no time getting to the point of their visit. Santa noted to himself again how fast word traveled in the magic realm. Secrets were very hard to keep.

"What a coincidence," Santa said. "I just sent Zinga to send you word. It is not as positive as you have heard. We have confirmation on who likely has him but he has not been found. A brave rescue party has gone in search of him including one of his own kind. A fairy named Wistle."

Reesa reacted to that news with surprise. "Wistle has gone on this journey without seeking prior consent? This I find surprising and troubling."

Sandra spoke up. "She did not plan it ahead. We were tricked by a drag and she ended up on the closed side of Middle Earth with Gunny's brother, Ghost." Sandra chose not to share more, as she did not want to risk having Wistle subjected to any repercussions from the fairy council for her bravery.

For the next hour, never moving to a more comfortable space, perhaps to avoid the chance of another run in with glitter, but standing right there outside the magic portal, Santa and Sandra updated the Magical Council members on what they knew. They showed them the photos and Sandra described several times what had occurred that day until they seemed satisfied and prepared to depart. They also asked them to appeal to the Supreme High Council of Fairies.

"We know little of these drags except that they are not as dangerous as they are unpleasant," Calivon said after conferring with the other two regarding their request. "We shall allow the search party to bring back their report before we take any action. If they find Jason is there and safe, we will have something to report to the Fairy Council that can get you the release of your friend. This is now probably just weeks or maybe months away."

Well, thought Sandra, *at least they felt the search party would be successful*. Even if they were right, months, even weeks of time of more waiting, was too long as far as she was concerned.

"So, you believe they will be safe in inner earth with these drags?" She couldn't stop herself from asking.

Calivon's face held a look of amusement. "Well, yes," he said at last, his eyes never leaving Sandra's. "I really hadn't considered their safety when I spoke but, yes, I do believe they will not be killed. That is all we will speak to on this matter." He turned with the others to leave.

"Excuse me, Council members, but I require a moment with Reesa before you depart," said Sandra politely but firmly. She had played by the rules and been patient but she was tired of the games. She hadn't hid Jason and Gunny hadn't taken Santa. She wanted Gunny back now, not months from now as Calivon had just indicated.

Calivon and Reesa both now stared at her for a moment as was their tendency. Never taking her eyes off Sandra, Reesa gave a slight nod of agreement. The two powerful young women stepped into a nearby room and Sandra firmly shut the door.

"You wished a conversation with me," said Reesa. "A conversation that I expect is about a favor."

Sandra wasn't surprised Reesa knew what she wanted to discuss. Sandra had found the royal fairy to be as smart as she was stunningly beautiful – and stunningly haughty as well at times.

Now did not seem to be one of those times, however.

"Yes," Sandra said, getting right to the point. "I have no wish to continue these games we are being forced to play. We do not have Jason. You now know where he is. We all want him back, not just you. To get him back, to get them all back safely – including Wistle as well, who is a Shan fairy – we are going to have to work together. It is enough to have all of them missing but to force us to work without Gunny too, for no reason, is simply too much. Not to mention being grossly unfair to him. He doesn't even like Jason!"

Reesa said nothing. She had a way of intimidating Sandra. She actually intimidated almost anyone she came in contact with, except Jason when he met her, which irritated her completely.

This time, however, Sandra felt strong, and sure, and equal, to Reesa. She had saved the fairy's life once and Reesa had promised her a favor in return. Sandra was ready to collect.

"I'd like to cash in my favor for the return of Gunny. Tomorrow," Sandra said directly.

"Tomorrow? Ha!" Reesa said, seeming truly surprised. She had expected Gunny's return was the favor that would be requested but she was taken aback by the demanded release date. "That is impossible."

"Impossible? For you?" Sandra said slyly. Reesa was the appointed ruler of the Shan fairy line.

In her world, that meant nothing was impossible. "I honestly doubt it would take more than five minutes for you to arrange if you simply insisted on it. I need you to do that."

Reesa was impressed. Sandra could be shrewd, she was learning, and not just the little orphan from an island far away who somehow became Santa Claus two. Like Calivon, Reesa had heard the rumors that Sandra was the long lost Leezle. She had her own suspicions about the red-haired beauty but no hard evidence that Sandra was anyone, or anything, but what she presented. Whether Sandra was exactly who she said she was, or exactly who the whispered rumors said she was, she had proved to be a close equal to Reesa, which impressed the royal fairy.

Reesa smiled. That actually scared Sandra. For a brief moment she thought about running. The crazy thought left her as she saw in Reesa's eyes that the smile seemed sincere.

"Alright, Sandra of St. Annalise, I shall choose to believe your story of where Jason is and that it is a mutual problem for us both. Frankly, I am personally not opposed to just letting your Jason stay there, wherever it is that he is, but, before you protest, I know my people will insist on working for his release once they hear of this news.

"I suppose you have provided us with enough evidence to prove that you did not hide him away and, therefore, I will have the vulgar man released." Sandra went to interrupt but Reesa continued. "by tomorrow. It really makes no never mind anyway since we could simply re-pick him up if we wanted. Are you sure you want him back, though? He's become quite unkempt and terribly smelly." She actually shuddered thinking about Gunny. Sandra smiled, knowing that making himself repulsive around the pristine fairies was exactly something Gunny would think to do.

"His release will also release me from the favor I owed you," Reesa said coolly as she walked to the door. "Are we agreed?"

"We are," Sandra said.

"Such a ghastly man to waste the favor on," Reesa shuddered again. "I may never understand you humans." They had rejoined the rest now and she addressed the Council members next. "I have changed my mind and this Gunny man that we are holding in exchange for Jason shall be released tomorrow." She offered them no explanation and neither did Sandra. The group lined up to go.

"One final thing Santa before we go," said Calivon. Santa tried to show no concern but casual "last minute" orders from the Council were not to be taken lightly. "There has been an increase in unfortunate incidents of human and magical being altercations around the world in recent months that have created some discord. It has brought us concern. Additionally, your popularity seems to be waning." Calivon took another long look at Sandra to make his point that he clearly blamed the situation on her. Sandra refused to look at him. Santa reached out and held her hand in comfort and solidarity for them both. Calivon gave the gesture a glance and smirked before continuing. Santa was important to both humans and the magical world but Calivon frankly had never really seen his appeal.

"The Council feels, after the greatly reduced number of personal appearances you were able to make last year that it would be of the greatest service to all – yourself, children and the magical realm – if the two of you could plan an increased number of appearances around the world this year. Get out and mingle with the children. Take some of the elves with you. Show the children how wonderful this connection to the magical realm is. The magical realm needs some good public relations and you are just the two to do it."

With that, the Council members said nothing else but simply turned to the portal, entered and left before Santa and Sandra could even wave goodbye. As soon as they were out of sight the two Santa's grinned and gave each other a Santa-sized hug. They were getting back Gunny, the magical realm was supporting the hunt for Jason and the two Santa's had an assignment to tour the world and visit with the children that they loved. Santa had been right. It was a pretty darn good visit by the Esteemed High Council of Magical Beings.

CHAPTER 11

Nowhere to Go but Forward

Location: Middle Earth

Mango had barely dashed through and cleared her tail when the space was filled behind them. There was nowhere to go but forward. The space around them was dark and filled with an eerie kind of hum but Ghost's flashlight worked. Wistle had switched to her orb state in full beam and Mango could bark again, though she was largely staying quiet. As their eyes adjusted, Wistle could see with her excellent fairy vision, very far off in the distance, what looked like just a spec of some kind of light. They chose that direction from what seemed like several possible trail choices.

In the beginning, as they walked along, they talked very little. Ghost almost never talked much, even when he was comfortable and with people he knew well, but now even the normally chatty Wistle was quiet. Mango would go out ahead of them for a few yards and then wait, never going too far away. The trio knew instinctively that they needed to stick together.

Ghost was quickly thankful that Thomas had insisted their backpacks be packed with water and food supplies. Still, the rations for three of them were slim. Finding water sources along the way was one of his chief concerns. His other concern: Where were they going? As usual, he had acted first and then thought about it. The folly of them stepping through a closing gateway had hit him full force. They had no idea at all where they were, where they were going, where they would find Jason, if they would find him, who lived down there, what danger they were in, and if they would ever see the people they cared about again. As they trudged, mile after mile, he berated himself that he never seemed to learn. Plunging through that entry so impulsively was a ridiculous move, he thought, over and over, and sadly not his first.

No, his first really absolutely insane move had been Santanapping Santa Claus. He could hardly stand to think about it because it just made him so angry at himself. How could that have ever felt like it made sense? It had created havoc and sadness all around, alienated him from his own brother and ended any chance of any kind of relationship, even just a friendship, with Sandra. He punched the air thinking about it and, Wistle, who was orbing alongside, gave a shout.

"Hey! What's that about? I'm walking here," she said as a retort.

"I wouldn't exactly call orbing walking," Ghost said. "Seems a lot easier."

"It is," Wistle said honestly. She popped to full-size then, realizing how far they had come and how far that meant Ghost and Mango had walked that day. The light was still just a speck in the distance but the cavern wasn't completely dark. It was like darkness at dusk – gray enough still to see. "Would you mind if we stopped here for the night? There's a grassy area over there we could use to try for some sleep and then start out again early."

Ghost was ready to rest. His watch said they had been walking for nine hours straight and he knew Mango too needed the break. "Good suggestion," he said. "Mango, come on, girl, we're done for this day."

The three of them exhaustedly dropped on to the soft, mossy, welcoming, patch of grass. As soon as they did it began to move! Ghost felt something snap at his fingers and pull on his clothes. Whatever it was rippled under them like a wave! They leapt up, and jumped away from the small green field trying to see what it was from the safety of the trail. Mango was now barking at the snapping grass. They realized the "grass" blades all had mouths and when they had sat down on it the mouths had come alive, reaching out, snapping, grabbing at them, ready for their next meal. "They look like a whole patch of Venus flytraps at home," Ghost said referring to the plants that eat flies. "We're not going to be your dinner," he said angrily, sounding braver than he felt at that moment.

The group had been exhausted but now adrenaline from the close call of being eaten by something as innocent-looking as grass pushed them forward farther until they simply couldn't go more. This time they found a large, flat rock. It would be a hard surface to sleep on but they knew, as tired as they were, it wouldn't matter. Ghost and Wistle climbed up and sat on a rocky ledge where they could see around them. Mango made her way up with them, curled up, and instantly fell asleep.

"Do you think we're safe up here?" Ghost asked Wistle. They had thoroughly looked around before sitting down this time.

Wistle nodded. "I'm so tired that I don't think I care," she said as she leaned back.

Ghost knew one of them should stay awake and be on watch but they were all too tired. He closed his eyes hoping when he woke up the next morning it would all be a dream.

Instead he woke up in the middle of the night to the havoc of Mango barking and when he turned to see what it was, a large, black something flew by with a cackle. A cackle that sounded a lot like the one from the gate keeper. They knew this was the land of the drags. They just didn't care to see another so close.

They felt like they were becoming drags as they dragged themselves off their perch and moved on down the trail. Five hours of sleep was going to have to be enough. They needed to find their friend and get out. Thankfully, they could still see the light ahead. It was clearly a long way off but they knew they were getting closer with each step. Closer to what, they didn't know, but closer was really the only way to go.

CHAPTER 12

Homeward Bound

Location: Somewhere Unknown to Humans

"Ah, hot fairy Reesa," Gunny said, totally to irritate her as she walked up. She was definitely beautiful but normally he wouldn't say so in such a rude way. Rude was his only real weapon, though, to get himself out of there.

"Ah, horrible, revolting, human man," Reesa said in return, standing far away from him to reduce his highly offending odor and prevent him from touching her in any way. Such an awful thought. She had just met with the Supreme Fairy Council and had come straight from there to him. She had shared with the Council her belief that Sandra did not have Jason as they had believed without having to share that she might know who did have him and where he was. She found that bit of information to be incidental and of little matter.

"You are being released," she stated to Gunny now, matter-of-factly.

"Really?" Gunny said, staring at her to be sure she wasn't just playing some kind of cruel fairy trick. She seemed to be dead serious and simply nodded her confirmation.

"WOOOO HOOOO!" he screamed out, dancing around with his cowboy hat in hand. He grabbed the two fairies closest to him and did an impulsive dosey do. It was Reesa's worst fear come true and she went into her orb state to be sure he couldn't grab her too.

"Humans," she said to herself as she orbed away without looking back but she added a little smile. Truth be told they did add unexpected comedy to life.

# # #

"Sandra! Santa! Hello? Anybody?" Gunny was shouting down the hall. As soon as he had been given the go to be released he had followed his fairy escort to the portal express. He had nothing he cared about in his room there that he cared enough to take time to collect or bring with him.

He didn't have the fairies call ahead. He didn't even shower. He just got in the express and headed for home.

While the Holiday Ranch in Texas was his home, so was North Pole Village at this point and he couldn't wait to get there. He couldn't wait to be busy again. He couldn't wait to be free again. He couldn't wait to be fairy-free again. He couldn't wait to see Santa and the elves and his family again. Most especially of all, he couldn't wait to see her.

"Sandra? Santa? Can't a guy get a greeting around here?"

"Gunny!" Three elves shouted at once as they saw him coming down the hall and threw themselves in his arms as a welcome. *Thank goodness someone was glad to see him*, he thought.

Well, for a minute they were.

Then they all started coughing.

"P.U. Gunny!" said one. "Gunny, you smell!"

"Yeah, really bad," said another.

"Worse than the barn!" said the other. "P.U!" They all were holding their noses.

"Alright, alright, I hear you," he said, knowing it was way too true. He could barely stand himself and desperately wanted a shower.

"Is my room still mine?" he asked the bunch, who nodded while they kept holding their noses. "Good. I'm going to take a shower and clean up so you can give me a real hug. Please go tell everyone I'm back. Make sure you tell Sandra! All three of you, tell her! Off with you now." He waved them away as he headed to his room. "Oh, and please bring me a double tall cocoa with extra whip cream and the biggest plate of cookies you can find."

He was back. He really was back. "Everything now can return to normal," he said to himself as he got to his room. He said it out loud to convince himself. He feared a new normal was what awaited him.

# # #

"Gunny! Gunny? GUNNY? Where in the North Pole are you?" Sandra had literally run the whole way from her office to the hotel when she heard the news he was back and now she wanted to see him. With her own eyes. Reesa had kept her promise.

She had checked his room, the hotel lobby and the *Eat Drink and Be Merry* diner. She had run to the village cocoa stalls and gone across the street to the factory loudly calling out for him with no response at any of them. She was getting completely frustrated and stopped to change her shoes before she went racing around some more and there he was. In her room.

"Gunny?" she said quietly, now that he was actually standing in front of her in the most unexpected place. A range of emotions flashed across his face. The biggest one looked like relief at seeing her again, at last. He took two giant steps to the door and swept her up in his arms for a huge hug. He didn't try to kiss her, though he would have loved to, but just took in the sheer joy of holding her in his arms. She held him tight back.

"I can't believe you're here," she whispered to him emotionally.

"I can't either," was all he said in return. They just held each other saying nothing else till she finally broke the moment.

"And I can't believe you're in my room."

He laughed. They both did. "I know, I know, it's weird isn't it?"

"Sort of," she said with a shrug.

In one breath he blurted out the reason. "I just had been everywhere and I finally came back here and decided you'd find me here eventually and then it was just overwhelming to be around all your stuff and I knew I couldn't wait and needed to find you and I was just going to leave and you walked in and …"

"Okay, okay, I totally get it and it's totally okay. You just surprised me. I love seeing you here.

Truly. I just love seeing you." She stepped back and took a good look at him. He was gaunt and tired-looking but there was happiness in his eyes and nothing there that couldn't be fixed with some time at the Pole.

"Come on," she said, taking his hand. "We have so much to catch up on, but first we need to feed you and the elves and Santa need to welcome you back. And then we'll fill you in on everything that's been happening since you've been gone."

She dreaded telling him about Ghost but it would have to be done. Not until after a proper North Pole welcome home, though. Bad news could wait a little longer until after some fun.

"Wait till Em hears you're back!" she said to him as he laughed thinking about it. "I'm not sure you are going to be strong enough to withstand her big hug!"

CHAPTER 13

A Special Occasion

Location: St. Annalise

It went about as bad as Sandra had expected when Gunny heard Ghost had gone after Jason.

"How could you let him do that?" he kept asking of her even though Santa is the one that had encouraged him and Ghost was the one who had insisted. "How could you let him go, Santa? Or Crow? Didn't he care? Why didn't he go with him? What good is Wistle going to be of all people? She's a fairy not a fighter."

"Well now," Santa said. "Let's not be discounting Wistle. There's plenty of fight in that fairy."

Truth be told, Santa wasn't happy with how it all happened either. None of them were. Just like with Jason, there hadn't been a single word on their whereabouts and it seemed the whole of the magical realm was now aware of the situation.

Gunny had insisted on hearing everything about how it had gone. Three times. And three times they had to tell him there was nothing he could do. Because there wasn't. There was nothing any of them could do but wait until there was something they could do.

"Gunny, I-" Sandra started again to try and explain and console him but the happy-to-see-her cowboy was gone and he cut her off.

"I don't want to hear anymore, Sandra," he said. "I'm almost sorry I'm back. At least there, in fairyville, I still had all my brothers and you hadn't tossed Ghost under the bus to get back your island boy."

She hadn't even objected to what he was saying. She had wondered it sometimes herself. Had she sacrificed Ghost and Wistle because she was blind to things when it came to Jason? She felt like she would have done the same for whoever had been taken in such a way. Heck, she had used her only favor with Reesa to secure Gunny's release though she hadn't shared that with him. Still, she understood why he thought what he thought.

Without saying goodbye to Gunny, she left the next morning for St. Annalise. Santa wanted them to follow the orders of the Esteemed High Council of Magical Beings and get in a tour of some European countries. Before she could go touring, Sandra needed to get home for a few days to oversee some things there and help Cappie with the big birthday party she was throwing for Thomas that weekend. His birthday was the first day of spring and Cappie wanted to go all out to make it fun. With so many missing, these were tough times they were all going through and chances to celebrate mattered.

"I sure hope this wasn't supposed to be a surprise party, Cappie," Sandra laughed as they hung balloons and streamers around the *Mistletoe* deck that could easily be seen from Thomas's boat the *Lullaby,* just a few docks down.

"Not a surprise at all. In fact, Thomas says he is very excited about it. He can't even remember the last time someone threw him a birthday party," Cappie said protectively.

"Really?" said Birdie, who was sprinkling confetti all around while Squawk followed her. "Well that means we need to make this one truly spectacular to make up for a whole lot of years."

". . . *squawk* . . . I want a party! . . . *squawk*!"

"You get one every year," Sandra admonished. "Let's not be selfish about it."

"I want one too," said Em, who had come along from the Pole with Sandra this time.

"Good news for you both," Sandra said. "You are both invited to this one."

"That works," Em said and hung up more streamers.

". . . *squawk*! . . . can't wait for the cake . . . *squawk*!"

"Hello, beauties," a flattering voice called out from the dock. "Might I be of service?"

"Thomas!" Cappie exclaimed looking pleased. "Absolutely not. This is your party and you are early."

"Well, I figure it's my birthday so I should get what I want and what I want is to spend the time with you all. And what I also want is to do this." He leaned over the side of the tug and gave Cappie a big kiss which made her blush.

"Thomas!" she said.

"It's my birthday," he smiled back mischievously.

"Okay then, well come on board. Your official job can be tasting the appetizers. They're in the galley so go on in and check them out. Our guests should be arriving in an hour."

True to elves and island style, almost none of the guests waited till the start time. Like Thomas, they all started wandering down to the big tug early. Sandra and Birdie, with Em in the middle, welcomed each one on the dock as Cappie did the same as they came on board the tug. By the actual start time, all the guests were there plus a few. And one of those few turned out to be Gunny who came wandering down with his brother, Crow.

Crow grabbed on to Birdie and the two caught up with Spence who had just arrived as well. The three got busy talking on some of the changes they were making at the barge. That left Gunny and Sandra standing there awkwardly with Em in the middle.

"Em, could you give us a minute?" Gunny asked. Em looked to check with Sandra before leaving her side.

"There's all sorts of good food inside, Em," Sandra said. "Don't let Squawk eat it all." That set Em running.

The little delgin had barely left when Gunny blurted out, "I'm sorry, Sandra. I never should have blamed you. Never. I was just so surprised about the news about my brother. That still was no excuse at all for what I said." He reached out for her hands and she let him take them.

"It's all right. It really is," she said graciously in return. "I'd be mad too. I'm mad at myself.

They're on my mind constantly. More than Jason even."

He might have been the one holding her hands at that moment but Gunny didn't find the last part of what she said comforting. He preferred to have her not thinking about the fairy king at all.

Before he could say anything more, Christina Annalise came walking up the dock and gave him a giant size hug. "I am so glad to see you here, Gunny!" she said. "I know you must be distraught about the news of your brother and I'm so sorry. Please give my love to your wonderful parents and tell them how often I think of them."

She squeezed Sandra's hand and then stepped on to the boat. "Geez," said Gunny. "She looks worse than I do."

"We're all worried about her," Sandra said agreeing.

"Everyone! Everyone! Hello! Could I get your attention for a moment, please?" Thomas was banging a spoon against a glass to get the noisy island partygoers' attention. It took a few minutes and Sandra and Gunny managed to squeeze onto the boat with the rest.

"Thank you all for coming tonight. I want to give a giant-size thank you especially to my wonderful, special, lady, for throwing me this party," Thomas said, smiling at Cappie.

"She asked me what I wanted for my birthday and I really couldn't think of anything grander than spending the day with her and celebrating with all of you - our very dear friends and family." He looked over at Sandra who smiled along with everyone else. She had come to love Thomas and loved especially how much he cared for Cappie, the most important person in her world.

"But when I got to thinking about it," Thomas continued. "I realized that wasn't true. There actually was something grander that I wanted for my birthday." He turned now to just face Cappie and took both her hands. *Oh, my goodness*, Sandra thought. *Is he about to do what I think he is about to do?* She held her breath. In fact, it seemed now, everyone on the boat was holding their breath.

"Margaret Thirza Richmond," Thomas started and tears of joy began to roll down Sandra's face. She was beyond happy about this. Gunny squeezed her hand in support, holding it tight. "I fear I am too old to get down on one knee," Thomas said directly to Cappie. "But I am hoping nonetheless, that you would do me the extreme honor of agreeing to be my wife, for I love you like no other and cannot imagine a more blessed way to spend the rest of my life."

Cappie smiled as she burst into her own joy-filled tears. Before she answered, though, she turned to Sandra, almost as if it was in slow motion Sandra would think later, and looked for an answer there. So tight was their bond they would always be a part of each other and every big decision. Sandra smiled brightly through her tears and nodded her head firmly. Cappie smiled at her in return and put her full attention back to the hopeful guy standing in front of her, waiting for an answer to the biggest question he had ever asked.

"Thomas Jackson you are a scoundrel for this big surprise but there is nothing I would like better than to make you *my* scoundrel," Cappie said. "Yes! I say an absolute, unequivocal, yes I will marry you!" With that she leaned in and kissed him big.

Huge cheers of joy burst from the big boat. So loud, Sandra was sure they could be heard at least one island over. Glittering fairy dust filled the air as the fairy guests generously shared their special occasion magic. *Two wonderful things had happened in one week*, Sandra thought as she made her way to the engaged couple she loved. Gunny was home and Cappie and Thomas were engaged. Things were getting better!

CHAPTER 14

Trudging Along

Location: Middle Earth

The trio had been walking for three full weeks by their estimate. Their supplies were low and they had gotten very little sleep. Since the unsettling experience of the first night, they had traded off watch each night. Even Mango had seemed to understand and take her turn. The result was a little more sleep for each of them but not enough for any of them. They were sore, exhausted, hungry, thirsty and very, very, grumpy.

"Quit buzzing around me all the time, Wistle," Ghost said, unprovoked by the fairy but annoyed that she could orb all the time. While Wistle did walk at times and had to be full-size for sleeping (a little known fact about fairies), most of the time she orbed along their path.

"I'm not hurting you," she snapped back and darted off to be away from his snarkiness. She knew she would never be described as particularly nice but she had met her match with Ghost.

He had nice moments but he didn't serve them up very often.

Very little joy had been part of their journey. Mostly there was just a lot of quiet and a lot of hunger. They had found water two or three times but all three were sick of eating the protein bars in their packs and longed for something different. They had met no one or nothing on their path. Once in a while they could hear rustling about so they knew there were other life forms nearby but they had no idea if they were friendly or not.

After weeks of walking up and around the rock-filled terrain, sometimes wasting days going in circles, they had moved into a new sort of topography. The light that they had used as their guide always seemed not far away but they never seemed to get closer. Now, finally, it actually seemed brighter and close. The air had become humid and had a more tropical feeling to it. There were plants now around them that were large and dense, unlike any they had seen before. They tried to avoid coming in contact with them, not knowing if they were poisonous or not – or had mouths like the innocent-looking grass had earlier. The greenery, however, gave them hope that they would soon find a strong water source with colder and fresher-tasting water than what they had been drinking.

They walked to the top of a big hill and there, at last, they found the source of the light they had been traveling toward for so long. It was daylight coming from a hole above! The opening didn't seem that big for all the sunlight it was letting in but neither of them questioned it. There was daylight ahead! There was even a way to access it by climbing on a giant-size rock pile. Wistle dropped down next to Ghost in her full size and they held back Mango. They wanted to view the situation first to see if it was any kind of trap or trick.

After waiting and watching for more than an hour, they decided to move forward - as much out of desperation as anything else. They needed water and Wistle was sure she could hear the flow of some kind of water source just out of view. It made sense to them considering the variety of plants that were all around them. Wistle reverted to her orb size and the three cautiously moved ahead. When they got right below the hole, which was roughly twelve feet around in size, Ghost estimated, Wistle went ahead to check it out while Ghost and Mango started climbing the rock pile.

"HELP! HELP!"

Ghost could hear Wistle screaming in her small orb voice but could not see her and panic gripped him. He scrambled as fast as he could over the big boulder blocking his view, looking in all directions until he spotted Wistle fighting for her life! She was trapped by a bullfrog! A giantsized, neon-green colored bull frog, about the size of a large house cat, had Wistle stuck on its very, very, long, bright purple, tongue and was trying hard to roll it up and swallow her! Wistle was pushing and hitting and screaming at the frog but it was not afraid or giving up.

"Use some of your magic against it!" Ghost yelled. He was afraid for her and still too many rocks away to pull her away. "Blast him!" He wasn't altogether sure the assortment of magic fairies had but he assumed she had a few tricks she could use.

"I can't! It doesn't work here, remember? Besides, he'll swallow me if I stop pushing on him!" she screamed, sounding terrified.

"Go full size! Go full size!" Ghost was screaming now too as it seemed the purple-tongued reptile was winning the battle, bringing Wistle closer and closer to his mouth.

Ghost was right, Wistle realized. That was the answer. As soon as he said it, she thought it, dared to quit pushing so she could swing her arms about and reverted to full size. Now the toad was the surprised one and the one who needed to watch out. Its eyes bugged out with shock at the change and before Wistle could do a single thing, it unwound its horrible, slimy, awful tongue, jumped at least fifty feet and was out of sight in two leaps.

"I'm going after him," Wistle said, wiping slimy purple slobber off herself. This was the worst kind of adventure ever for a fairy. Fairies hated being a mess and she had been a mess for weeks. "Oh no you're not!" Ghost called over, still scrambling to get to her. "You're going to stay full size and stick with me and Mango and the three of us are climbing up there together to get water and decide what we do next." He pointed to the opening.

To his surprise, Wistle actually nodded her head yes, sat down on the rock she was on and burst into tears.

Oh great. Handling girls who were crying was not one of Ghosts specialties. He found he usually made it worse, not better. A fairy girl crying couldn't be any easier. Still, at his core he understood and, to his surprise, he felt compassion for her and not exasperation. She was a high handed pain like he felt all fairies were, but the two of them were on this journey together. He respected her for coming. She had barely complained through any of it and it was all pretty awful so far, even for him, a human guy. And now she had almost been eaten by a really ugly toad. He probably would have cried too. The thought of it all suddenly made him laugh. Exactly the worst reaction, but he was so relieved she was okay that if he didn't laugh he might cry, too, and that wouldn't help anything.

She gave him a glaring look, that he deserved, but he looked at her with such appreciation and care at that moment that she had to start laughing too. Laughter was infectious and it echoed around the big cavern.

"Take that you, big, bad drags and toads and creepy crawlers and whatever else!" Ghost yelled at the cavern. "We're still here! We're coming for our friend and we can still laugh." Mango barked. "And bark!" Ghost added and the two laughed some more as his words echoed around the big cavern.

When Ghost and Mango finally made it to where Wistle rested he offered her his hand and pulled her in for a hug. He held her there just for a minute so she would know he did understand how scary that had been – for both of them.

"It looks like we're almost in some real daylight and out of the cavern for a change," he said pointing. "See? Just those rocks over there and we will be able to see where we can get water." He didn't know for sure that was true but, like Wistle, he could hear running water.

The three started back up the pile of rocks and finally pulled themselves into the light . . . and out onto an island on top earth again!

"This must be another opening like the cave we came through!" Wistle exclaimed, so glad to breathe the fresh air and feel the sunlight.

"It looks like it," Ghost said a little more reluctantly. *If it was, why wasn't it being guarded?*

Where was the dragoon?

Mango ran straight over to a small running waterfall, and pool of water, where she didn't stand and drink but jumped right in. Wistle and Ghost took one look at each other, grinned, and did the exact same thing! "Cannonball!" Ghost shouted as he made the biggest splash he could, landing in the water. Typically, fairies did not seek to be in water, but there was nothing that could have kept Wistle from this sparkling pool. She didn't swim but simply kept to the shallow area where she could stand. It was heaven. Pure complete heaven after so many weeks of constant walking and climbing without cleaning up or drinking nearly enough to fully quench their thirst and clean off. They spent almost an hour in the water before they realized the sun was getting low again and it was time to reenter the cavernous space. The water time had revived and refreshed them. The search was not fun but the quest for their friend outweighed any hesitation. They headed back to the opening . . .

. . . as it was closing!

"What?" Ghost and Wistle both exclaimed as Mango began pawing frantically at the earth.

When the space was no more than four inches around they could see an eyeball staring at them.

"Fools," said a voice that sounded similar to the dragoon in the original cavern on the cay.

"Fools to come and fools to leave. Be gone now, you fools. This gate is closed!"

"NOOOOO!" Ghost yelled, kicking the ground out of sheer frustration. He hated magical beings. They had manipulated him with his Santanapping and now they had ended his best hope of getting Jason rescued. He didn't know that Gunny was free so he felt he had also blown his chance to get Gunny released too. Now, it was Ghost's turn to feel like crying.

CHAPTER 15

First Stop: Iceland!

Location: A jet plane to Iceland

Sandra and Santa were ready to get touring and do some mixing and mingling with children. They were flying chartered jet because, this time, they were taking the elves with them. None of them had quit talking about it since they had heard the news! Besides the recent trips to St. Annalise that some of them now made to help build the South Pole Village barge, most elves almost never left the North Pole. They were elves, simple little folk who didn't need a lot of variety in their lives. It had taken a lot of coaxing to get them to St. Annalise the first time and they never envied Santa going round the world.

What made this trip different was that the first stop was Iceland. The elves knew what a lot of people didn't and that was that, besides those elves that lived at the North Pole, lots of elves lived in Iceland. The North Pole elves could hardly wait to visit and meet the Icelandic elves for the first time ever!

The plane Sandra and Santa had secured for the trip could take about one hundred average size people, but the elves were able to sit two to a seat and they filled every seat from front to back.

Laughter rang out everywhere, right up until the time of take-off when they all got very quiet. The quietest Sandra had ever heard them. A quiet elf, she knew, was a nervous elf. As the plane leveled out, though, and the flight attendant announced there would be food the noise level picked up again. Santa had arranged for the elves favorites to be served, so the trolleys going down the aisle contained cookies, thermoses of hot cocoa and big bowls of hard candies.

"Ho Ho Ho!" Santa's big voice rang out and could be heard above the crazy din of the elves patter. "The pilot is informing us that we will be landing in Reykjavik in forty-five minutes so please return to your seats and put your seatbelts on." For normal people, forty five minutes is plenty of time, but for a plane full of giggly elves, it was cutting it close. Somehow, they all managed to get back to a seat, though not necessarily the seat they were in when they took off. Sandra saw one seat with three elves squished in instead of two which made her smile. They worked together to get their seat belts on and were ready for touchdown just in time. As the plane landed, they all cheered.

Traveling with elves actually was a lot like what I imagine traveling with a plane full of monkeys would be like, Sandra found herself thinking as the plane came to its stop at the gate. *Madcap chaos at every turn!*

True to form, all of the elves wanted to disembark at the same time and, once off, none of them had patience for standing around waiting to be processed through customs. Santa and Sandra could have gone through easily but a plane full of elves, even for a country well acquainted with elves, was almost more than could be controlled. Finally, everyone cleared customs and, nicely, in single file, each got on the buses Zinga had pre-arranged to have take them out to a beautiful place in the Icelandic countryside where elves loved to congregate.

There was a little tussling on the buses as each elf scrambled for a window seat. Sandra and Santa both had to point out that the windows were big enough for them to see out no matter whether they sat by the window or the aisle. Not to mention, there would be things to see on both sides. If possible, the noise level on the buses seemed even louder than the plane, as the elves pointed out all there was to see along the way, moving from one side of the bus to the other for the closest look they could get.

They all quieted as the buses pulled up to where they would be staying for the next two nights. There, by the road as they got close, were the Icelandic elves jumping up and down with elfish glee. No elves had ever come to visit them from anywhere and they could hardly wait to meet two buses full!

Icelandic elves, like Icelanders themselves, were friendly but they kept largely to themselves. For centuries, that was primarily due to them being a remote island country that was not easy to get to or leave from. The world didn't really know much about Iceland. It was a mysterious country, far away from most, where the people ate a lot of fish and spoke a language with a lot of long words. It wasn't easy to get there and that was okay with the people who were there. They were used to being solitary, including the large elf population, who rarely mingled with the human locals but had found acceptance from them. For the most part, the Icelandic elves, like the North Pole elves, liked living simple lives full of routine and service. They preferred to stay home versus traveling. In fact, that they could recall, no Icelandic elf had ever traveled away from their island country. Consequently, while some of the North Pole and Icelandic elves were cousins, and had exchanged greeting cards at Christmas and occasionally received family news, none of them had ever actually met in person.

The buses pulled up, and as the elves filed off they stayed in a clump, shyly clustered to one side with the hosting elves clumped together across from them. While the North Pole elves were dressed in their usual happy clothes made up of reds and greens largely, the Icelandic elves looked equally cheery in pretty tones of natural colors. They had warm clothes of pretty shades of blues, browns and deep greens with bursts of yellows and oranges. Each side was full of elves smiling at the other but unsure what to do next and looking for Santa and Sandra to come direct them. The two Santa's, though, had deliberately hung back on the buses to let the elves sort it out for themselves.

Before long, one of the Icelandic elves stepped up. "Welcome to you all," she said. "I'm Nuka, mayor of our fair elf city. We are humbled to have you all here for this time of visiting. We would like to offer you our homemade butter mints as a welcome." She turned to her group and out came elves carrying trays piled high, not with cookies, but with delectable butter mints in all sorts of bright colors. The North Pole elves had never heard of a butter mint before, but they were pretty, sweet, and had the word mint in them. Plus the treats from the flight were long gone and they were hungry once again. They dug into the plates with glee.

"Mmmmmmm"

"These are delicious!"

"I'd like another please."

"I'd like five more!"

"Me too!"

"And me!"

Just like that, the shyness was gone as elves from both sides piled around the big trays of mints, laughing and talking as if they had always known each other, until there wasn't a single mint left.

"Ho Ho Ho!" said the booming voice of Santa.

"SANTA!" Every elf from Iceland screamed his name out of excitement along with all of the North Pole elves. They didn't care that they had just seen him. They were always willing to get caught up in the excitement of meeting Santa for the first time.

"Oh Oh Oh!" called out the happy voice of Sandra as she too stepped down from the bus to greet them all. She had deliberately hung back to let Santa and the elves have their special moment.

Meeting Santa for the first time was important for most children – and elves.

"SANDRA CLAUS!! Look everyone its SANDRA CLAUS!" The shouts were even louder for Sandra than they had been for Santa and the Icelandic elves came running past him to hug her. She welcomed them in with a giant-size hug of her own but both she and Santa looked at each other quizzically. *What was this about?*

"Sandra, you're back! You came to Iceland last year and we missed you. We wanted to see you but the line with the children waiting to meet you was too long."

Ah, Sandra thought. Now she was beginning to understand. As part of her European tour last year she had stopped in Iceland for a day and got a fantastic welcome. That was part of why she had wanted to bring the elves with her this year. The locals had told her all about their elf neighbors and how wonderful they were which was already proving to be completely true.

"We're so glad you're here and just for us this time!"

"Well now, not quite. You know that Santa and I will be meeting with the children starting tomorrow morning but tonight is just with all of you. And the North Pole elves will be here with you our whole visit," Sandra clarified to be sure they understood what the Santas' schedule looked like.

Their faces fell for a minute before a group "okay" seemed to come all at once as elf answers often did.

"Now, how about a big welcome for me too," Santa said, feeling perplexed and left out. He wasn't used to coming in second.

"OKAY!" the group hollered again with half of them heading over to elf pile on Santa. The other half, though, stayed right where they were, squeezing still on Sandra, until the North Pole elves asked about more mints.

"We have lots more," Nuka shared. "Creamy, sweet butter is one of our specialties here in Iceland. You all make toys but we make butter that people, from all over the world, clamor to order from us.

"We have butter cookies and Butter Baby suckers ready for you too," she finished saying, as the elves all gathered around to follow her.

"Hooray!" shouted the North Pole elves. "We'll trade you toys for some butter, when we leave," Rollo suggested.

"Hooray!" shouted the Icelandic elves in return. "We love toys!"

It was going to be a better visit than she had dared dream, Sandra thought, smiling after them as they all scurried off for their buttery treats. A very loud, and very joyous visit, just liked she had hoped.

"C'mon Santa," she said reaching out for her mentors hand. "If we don't hurry, all the treats will be gone!"

CHAPTER 16

Danger! Danger!

Location: Drag prison

Day after day, nothing ever happened.

That's what Jason was thinking, over and over. He had been there so long, without any word, without a single visitor, without even a moment of hope that it would ever be different. Just the drags, every day, reminding him of his dire circumstances.

"What's the matter, Mr. Royalty?" his drag keeper said as he took away his still full dinner plate.

"Not hungry again today? Drag food too good for you?"

"Leave him alone," Thogo said. The monuments were naturally protective beings and he came to the aid of both Jason and Danger whenever any of the drags were picking on them. "Bring it on over here and I'll eat what he didn't."

Thogo was the opposite of Jason. He greedily ate everything put in front of him and was always ready for more. He was a giant-sized guy who needed a lot to keep going. If Jason could have, he would have shared his crappy food with Thogo every day but they were at the mercy of the drags who seemed to possess no sense of kindness in them. Jason had gotten thin because he didn't want to eat. Thogo had gotten thinner because he didn't get enough to eat. Danger had just come in thin. The drags liked to badger him the most.

"What you got to say today, Daaanger?" The drag keeper drug out Danger's name in a mocking sort of way. As was his way every day, Danger said nothing. "Still don't want to make a full confession and get outta here? One confession and you can go."

The weary-looking drag said nothing.

"Heard your mother was planning to make a plea to Darshion," the drag keeper said casually as he picked up Danger's tray. The mention of this Darshion got Danger's attention for a change.

"Right, and you have a mother," said Danger, trying to sound like he didn't care but not fooling any of them.

"Well I do, and you do too and, yours, not mine, has requested a meeting with Darshion."

Jason had no idea who this Darshion was, though, he was getting the idea it might be the top drag. Whoever he was, the idea of his mother visiting him, had gotten Danger disturbed. "Tell her not to bother. Tell her I don't want any help," Danger said sullenly but with some urgency behind it.

"I ain't tellin' her nothin'," the drag keeper said. "I'm tellin' you what I heard but I don't really care about you or your mama. As far as I'm concerned, it ain't no worry to me if we have one less drag in our dogo."

His words got a strong reaction from Danger who leapt to his feet. He spread his dragon-like wings and bared his drag teeth.

"Oh, yeah, that used to scare people out here," said the keeper laughing. "But you ain't out here no more." He went to leave the room.

"Your mama won't be for long either." He flashed what must pass for a smile from a drag and slammed the door behind him with a cackle.

Danger flapped around, making angry hissing noises that even two cages away kind of freaked Jason out. He finally sat down against the cages of the bar, wings folded in, facing Jason and Thogo's cages.

"It is time we got out of here," he said calmly. "I am sure you both feel the same."

Okay, thought Jason. *Nothing ever happened just changed to something might. Hallelujah.* He was ready to go home or die trying.

CHAPTER 17

Where Are We?

Location: A Deserted Island

The first thing Ghost and Wistle did when they fully realized that the gateway to Middle Earth had closed, and got over the shock of being stranded, was to mark the spot where it had been by dragging over some big stones. They wanted to be sure they checked the spot daily as they suspected it would have to open sooner or later. The plants below would need the water and light and the creatures in that part of the cavern, like the big bullfrog, depended on the plants to live.

The drags would have to reopen it sometime.

"Maybe these rocks will fall on the drags head when it does reopen and we'll be able to score one for our team," Ghost said when they got the last of them in place. Once that was done, they spent time trying to figure out where they might be.

They were definitely on an island. A small one but one with a water source and some shady plants and trees. There were no other people or animals on it aside from some tropical birds, which surprised them a little, considering how pretty the island was and that it did have a water source. They assumed they were still somewhere in the Caribbean Sea because they hadn't walked far enough to be out of it. They also decided that the island was under the same kind of spell as Middle Earth since Wistle's magic still was limited to being able to orb and see long distances – both elementary powers for fairies.

Wistle had orbed right away to take a quick look at the whole island but it didn't take Ghost long to follow suit by walking around it. There just wasn't much to see.

They scanned the horizon constantly for ships sailing by and schemed on how they could signal any when they did see one. Despite Wistle's extraordinary fairy sight, day after day, there were no boats to be seen.

As island days turned into weeks on the small island, they established a routine. They kept busy fishing, gathering fruit from the trees, building three-sided shelters - mostly to use to get out of the sun - and collecting a mishmash of odd items that had washed ashore. Their best found item was part of a mirror. Wistle felt she was such a mess she had no desire to look in it but they had it ready to use to signal any boats.

Every day they scanned the horizon and every day they checked the entry. Only once did they see any action around it.

A small hole had remained open and they spied an eyeball looking through it. In response, they moved a rock over and covered it. If they couldn't get back in or know what was happening there, then the gatekeeper couldn't see out or know what they were doing either.

Their time together on the small island was challenging even on their best days. There was the daily need to get food and scan for help but mostly there just wasn't much to do. They swam, they exercised and tried to think of new things to talk about. Sometimes they made up challenges or played things like Twenty Questions or tic tac toe in the sand. Ghost had taken to whittling all the pieces in a chess set which helped him to stay busy. They were starting to get to know each other better, and despite their many differences, were slowly growing closer. As stubborn as they were, neither of them would actually call the other a friend but they would say, begrudgingly, that they had come to respect each other. It was a small but positive change. While they had their differences of opinion about most topics, one thing they both completely agreed on, was that they wanted OFF THAT ISLAND!

They worried they would never be found until the day when, finally, there was a tiny glint of bright light reflecting off a boat on the horizon and hope at last returned. They shouted and barked and jumped about waving their arms madly at the horizon. They scrambled to light the fires they had set up for just this minute and used the mirror to reflect sunlight so the boat could spot them.

But it didn't. The only boat they had seen in the two months they had been there and it didn't even slow down. They each individually stormed and mourned and then, wordlessly, began to rebuild their fire pit to get ready for the next one.

CHAPTER 18

Blue Times

Location: Iceland

The elves had stayed up visiting and partying long into the night getting to know each other and celebrating but it didn't keep them from waking up early the next day. The Icelandic elves had planned out a day-long field trip for them all starting with a morning spent at the world-famous Blue Lagoon. People came from all over the world to visit this naturally-heated hot spring pool and, on this morning, the elves would have it all for themselves. It was one of the Icelandic elves favorite activities and they could hardly wait to share it with their North Pole visitors.

Santa and Sandra had their own things to do for the day. They were scheduled for personal appearances all around the island country. They were spending the entire morning in Reykjavik since it was the largest city where most of Iceland's children lived. They waited to help get the elves reloaded on the bus before they headed by private car back to Reykjavik.

The elves spent their time on the buses singing Christmas carols and old Icelandic elf songs. The North Pole elves weren't familiar with the folk songs but that didn't stop them from humming along.

They all had their swimsuits on under their heavy clothes and big coats. It was spring time in Iceland but it still felt like winter in most of the world. None of the elves noticed at all since cold was their natural and preferred temperature.

Inside the lagoon locker areas, they excitedly got down to their swimsuits and headed to the big, natural, pool. Nuka had them all line up along one edge so they could jump in together. They stood, their knees knocking and teeth chattering, but loving the suspense.

"Okay, are you ready?" Nuka called out as the last of them came out from the locker rooms and lined up. "One . . . two . . . THREE!" She yelled out the last number and they all jumped in at once with glee . . .

. . . and the North Pole elves all scrambled out nearly as fast as they had jumped in! The Icelandic elves were still in the lagoon trying to figure out what was going on.

"It's HOT!" the North Polers said in unison.

"Really hot!"

"Boiling hot!"

Nuka scrambled to get out and check on their guests. "I'm sorry," she said. "You don't have hot tubs at the North Pole?"

"No, but we have a swimming pool. Dear Lovey, who isn't here on this trip, gives us lessons so we all know how to swim but our pool isn't hot. It's nice and perfect," said Barney.

Truth be told, the pool at the Pole was kept on the cool side because that was what the elves preferred. Most people would have liked it heated a little more but for the elves barely warm was just right.

"Well then we'll all get out with you," Nuka said as the others headed to the edge of the lagoon to get out too.

"Nonsense!" said Zinga. "We can sit right here on the edge and dangle our feet in while we watch and talk with all of you in this beautiful place." She looked at the others who all nodded and scrambled for a spot on the edge where they tentatively dangled their feet in the hot water.

Some made faces but most seemed like they it wasn't too bad.

"See? We'll be fine here," Zinga said. Nuka chose to agree. She could see how much fun the elves in the lagoon were having and hated to spoil the treat.

"I'm just so glad I didn't jump in like the rest of you and ruin my hair," Diva said, while the others rolled their eyes.

"Diva, if you keep talking about it, I'm going to get up and push you in," said Goldie. The others laughed as Diva looked indignant. She sat down on the edge too.

"This is fun," Barney said, kicking his feet around in the water. "I don't think it's as hot as it seemed at first and they're all having fun. I'm going to try again."

Barney bravely slipped into the pool and gritted his teeth for a few minutes until his elf body got used to the heat. "It's sure not perfect," he said. "But its water and water is fun. See ya guys!" He swam off to play with his new elf friends.

"Hey, wait a minute," Dervish called after him. "C'mon Peri, we can do it too." Perriwinkle looked a little skeptical but if her boyfriend was going in, so was she. Pretty soon, every elf but Diva and Hiccup had hopped into the lagoon.

"Well, I'm glad to have someone to talk to while they all swim," Diva said. "I just saw a report on some of newest fashions this season out of Paris and-"

"*hiccup*! Sorry Diva, *hiccup*, I'm going in too," Hiccup said. He wasn't usually very excited about swimming – he tended to suck water in when he hiccupped -- but he decided he liked swimming better then listening to Diva talk fashion for an hour or more. *That* would be way worse than a hot lagoon!

"See ya! *hiccup*!" He took a big breath and jumped in like the others.

In the end it was only Diva who never went in. Even she ended up having fun talking with the others as they swam over for a chat or to ask her to take a picture with Clickers camera that he had brought along to capture the fun of the day.

When they all scrambled out and headed for the locker rooms to get changed, the North Pole elves understood better why people came from all around the world for time in the lagoon. They felt renewed and relaxed. As they left, there was a long line of people waiting to get in who exclaimed with delight when the elves came walking out. People there that day felt they had got two world-class tourist treats – the beautiful Blue Lagoon and the biggest sightings of elves all at once anyone in the world could recall seeing!

As the camera's clicked, Diva thought again how glad she was that she hadn't gone in the pool.

CHAPTER 19

The Team Back Home

Location: St. Annalise

Things were busier than ever on St. Annalise. School was in full session so Christina Annalise was kept busy with all the work that entailed. With her son missing, and now Ghost and Wistle as well, she had to fight the desire to just go through the motions of her everyday life and instead she worked to be fully present for each of the students. They needed her as much as each student that had ever attended St. Annalise Academy. More than ever, she needed them in return.

In her spare time, she had been learning all she could about the drags from studying the library reference books. Just as they appeared to be, drags were a dragon bird species, known for their preference of not mixing with other beings of any kind. They were dark by color and by nature. Sullen and sour, they rarely were kind, hardly cordial, but also not known for being violent. They were not very bright in comparison to many kinds of beings but stubborn, uncaring and, nonethe-less, believed themselves to be superior to others. Christina shuddered reading the descriptions but was grateful to find they were not known for outright violence.

Also, very notably, which helped explain in Christina's mind how Jason might have been captured without much struggle, she learned that most magic did not work in most of Middle Earth. Those from Middle Earth had magic, but those who were not from there were subject to a magic-blocking system believed to have been built by wizards thousands of years ago for use in their jails and stolen by the drags. The drags had put it in place in Middle Earth. It allowed for small kinds of magic, like fairies orbing, but almost all other magic was blocked and it was all controlled by the drags.

Christina and Birdie were also working, at Sandra's direction, on a "top secret" project that they weren't talking with anyone about. The two women would huddle together for a couple hours every day, in deep conversation, writing things down, and sometimes even walking around the island as though they were looking it over for the first time. No one else was allowed at their meetings. Most especially, Em and Squawk were banned.

". . .*squawk*! . . . not fair . . . want to know . . . *squawk*!"

"Squawk is right," Em said in a huff. "You shouldn't keep secrets from us."

"If we didn't keep it a secret from you then the whole island would know about it," Birdie said.

"Not the *whole* island," Em protested. Birdie just rolled her eyes.

Gunny, too, had stayed on the island. Em and Squawk had both spent a lot of time with him pouting something fierce about being left behind and not allowed to go on Santa and Sandra's mini world tour.

"I got to go last year," Em said with her hands crossed. "Now only Santa gets to go. It's not fair."

". . . *squawk!* . . . I know her best . . . *squawk!* . . . not Santa . . ."

"You just have known her the longest," Em fumed at the parrot. "That doesn't mean you know her best."

Gunny just smiled at them. They had this constant patter going on and on but he understood how they felt. He would have liked to have gone on the trip too. He'd spent too much time away from Sandra as it was. Even though Squawk and Em were arguing, Gunny didn't mind. He liked that they both cared about Sandra as much as he did.

Even if he could have accompanied the two Santa's, though, he probably would have passed. Birdie and Crow had been doing their best to oversee the building of the South Pole Village barge but it was his project and he wanted to get back to it. He had come up with the idea, designed it, and been the project manager for most of it. He wanted to be there. He cared about every single detail and making it all perfect. This wasn't just a big barge, this was a labor of love to him.

Besides, he needed the massive project to keep his mind off thinking of where his brother and Wistle were, and even Jason. He wasn't wild about the guy but he knew Sandra could never be happy as long as Jason was missing. It was complicated but his own happiness was tied to the fairy boy. Like Christina, he had to work hard at not going through the motions of his life at the moment, and the barge was the perfect project for that because he cared so much about it.

To the casual observer, the barge actually looked like it might be completed. It had all the decks in place now, the exterior sidings were set, and the paint job was better than Gunny had dared to hope. The elves had developed a new paint that changed to match whatever setting the barge was in. It was kind of mind-blowing to look at it sometimes, Gunny thought. You could always make the barge out, of course, but from the land side, it looked mostly like sand and palm trees and from the sea side it was an aqua blue, like the water. He hoped that feature would mask it if Sandra ever came up against someone, or something, dangerous while out sailing the seas.

The decks for mechanical systems and toy storage deep down in the barge were already done.

There hadn't been much they had to do for the storage except make it huge. It was one of Gunny's favorite areas, though, because he knew it would be full of toys once the barge got operating and he had made sure there was enough room to store toys for a growing world. Large bins along the walls would allow for easy organization, as well as some practical new innovations they had installed like putting moving bins on a track. The system was for moving toys in bulk easily but Gunny had taken the time to make each bin look like a colorful car or truck. He knew the elves were going to love "driving" them.

The rest of the decks had lot of work still to be done. Eventually, there would be a gym, a large cafeteria, some hobby rooms and many rooms for elves. They were close to finishing the top decks where Happiness Hall would be; offices and meeting rooms; a mini hotel for guests; a "downtown" shopping area with cocoa stands, diners and gift shops; and Sandra's living quarters. All of those areas were especially important to Gunny and he was putting his focus on special touches on each of them now.

He made sure he took time off each week and every day off, he headed to Cassandra Cay. He took Crow with him the first couple of times so his brother could show him exactly where the cave was but neither time could they locate any sign of it. The next two times, he had Rio and Squawk go out with him, but there was still no sign of the cave from the air or the sea. It was as if the small cay had always been whole. As if it hadn't swallowed up his brother, the fairy and the island's favorite dog.

Still, even with no sign of any entry into middle earth, Gunny sat out there on the cay for hours each weekend. Just as Jason had for years before him. Just because he found it beautiful and haunting, just like they both found Sandra.

Two men, two different times on the planet, sitting on one aptly named cay.

CHAPTER 20

Digging Deep for Answers

Location: Tropical Island Somewhere

Ghost, Wistle and Mango had been trapped on their island for so long that they were starting to run out of things to talk about. Ghost had even let down his guard and confided his story about how he was the one that had Santanapped Santa Claus and how Santa and Gunny had made him promise not to ever tell anyone, including Sandra. He figured there was a good chance they were never making it back home, so telling Wistle wasn't that big of a deal. And, honestly, he needed to talk about it to someone. Since she was the only one, she was the one.

"That's part of why I volunteered for this," Ghost explained, digging in the sand and not looking at Wistle directly. "I owe Santa and Sandra. Really the whole world. I can never make it up to them but I thought this would help."

"I don't really get what the big deal is," Wistle had said in response. "I mean you didn't plan to keep him and it ended up fine. What's the big deal?"

"The 'big deal' is that I had no right to do it in the first place and now my brother hates me. Even worse, he's been paying the price."

"He'll get released and cleared of the crime," Wistle said. "Santa will never let him take the rap and you just need to get over it."

"Get over it?" Ghost snapped at her incredulously. "It was the stupidest thing I've ever done in my whole life. I lost my brother. I lost Santa's trust, and I lost any chance I had with Sandra."

"Oh, so that's really it," Wistle snickered. "What is it with that girl that every guy is crazy about her? Well, get over it. You would never have a chance with her anyway. She only has eyes for his highness, who she totally has no chance with. He's the king of fairies. He is never going to go for some human even if she is the new Santa Claus. You humans are a mess."

"You don't know anything," Ghost retorted, wishing he had never brought it up. "Look, I'm sorry I brought it up. Just forget it. Please. Truly, just forget it. I shouldn't have told you or anyone."

"We're friends, human," Wistle said. "We're weird friends but being stranded together on an island surely means we've become friends. As your friend, I am telling you this. Don't live your life with this regret hanging over it. Yes, fairies don't usually struggle with regret but humans shouldn't either. Learn from it and let it go. You're not going to take Santa again, are you?"

Ghost grimaced at her with a "duh" kind of look and she smiled at him. "Well, so you see, you already learned something from it," she grinned trying to lighten up the always serious cowboy. "And we have recently learned not to go in deep caves or climb out of big holes on to small islands. It seems we are both learning a lot lately."

He grinned at her, appreciating her efforts to make him feel better. To his own surprise, he had actually grown to like her, despite her often superior fairy ways.

"When we leave here human, leave those regrets you hold here on the island. It will lighten your burden and allow us to move faster. You're already not that person," she said, sitting down next to him where he sat in the shade.

"I'll think about it," he said to her sincerely. It was a heavy burden and he would like to leave it behind but it was his burden to bear. "I do promise you one thing. I will not regret getting off this island!"

Wistle had also shared her own secret of sorts. "As you have shared a secret, I shall tell you something private in return," she said carefully. "We fairies rarely talk of things that matter so take this and honor it.

"I do not feel as capable a fairy as most Shan fairies. Most are more beautiful, more talented, more intelligent. Most would not find themselves in this situation we are in today. I have often been eclipsed by other students at St. Annalise whether they were wizards, sprites, moonrakers, or even just humans."

Ghost couldn't help but smile at that. Fairies found humans so completely lacking. He overlooked that however, and focused on what mattered most to him in what she had said. He felt compelled to change her mind on her self-assessment.

"Wistle, you are the *only* fairy I admire and one of the bravest people I have ever met. You are more than all of the other students put together and any doubt you have on that needs to be left behind here with my regrets."

The two sat together in silence then, taking in the bonding that sharing doubts and secrets can create toward healing regrets and doubts deep in the soul. Perhaps they could leave the worst behind and go back lighter and brighter.

Most days, when they were not working on staying alive and scanning for boats, their new routine had shifted to digging a hole near where they had come out onto the island before the way was closed. Neither of them wanted to go back into Middle Earth but it at least represented a way to get back to St. Annalise. They strategized if they could just get back in, they would work to retrace their path back the way they had come instead of going forward. The pair hoped that by moving back the drags might let them pass. Hopefully, they'd also avoid everything else under there that could kill them too like the giant-sized purple-tongued frog that got Wistle. They couldn't just keep waiting around hoping to be found. It was time for action so they had rigged up digging tools out of coconut shells and now spent their time digging a hole big enough to break through to the inside. They had set up a makeshift cover over their dig site to keep the worst of the sun off of them. Despite that, it was hard work and too hot most the hours of the day to spend digging without risking the danger of overheating. Every night they slept well, completely exhausted from the hard work.

They woke up every morning with stiff muscles but renewed enthusiasm for the project. After they're big talk on secrets they were more at ease now and laughed more often despite the toil and worries they carried. Every day, they felt like they were just feet from breaking through to the cavern and that it could be the day they had some hope for going home.

Mango spent much of her time barking. Barking at birds. Barking at the occasional turtle. Barking at dolphins. Some days Ghost felt like the noisy dog would never quit barking. On the small island it was often nerve-wracking.

"Mango, for the tenth time already today, please be quiet!" Ghost yelled over at her. The big dog came over with a wagging tail and Ghost stopped to lean down and give her a squeeze and a scratch behind her ears. She started barking right in his ear.

"Mango! Mango! Geez, easy on my ear drums!" said Ghost pushing back as the dog pushed forward into the hole. Ghost and Wistle looked to where she was barking just in time to see the eyeball again showing through a small hole within the hole.

"Quit digging," hissed the voice of the gatekeeper. "We will not allow you to breakthrough in this way."

Ghost jumped down and put his own eyeball close to the hole. "I hardly think you can stop us," he said, sounding braver then he felt. "We can't stay here forever and going back the way we came is the only way we know how to leave. We wish to go home."

"You wish to return to where you came from and not go forward?" the gatekeeper asked, seeming surprised at this news.

"We want to know what has happened to our friend, but most of all now, we wish to return home. Safely. All three of us." He stressed the safety angle since he didn't trust the drag at all.

There was a long silence until Ghost finally called out. "Helloooo. Are you there still?" They heard nothing. Ghost stood up. "Well, back to digging then, Wistle," he said, picking up his coconut shell and filling it with dirt. He felt nothing but frustration to be both tormented and teased by the gatekeeper who, truth be told, really held all the advantages. As Wistle joined him back in the hole for another long day of digging, they heard the drag hissing again.

"I will discuss this with my superiors and, while I do, you will quit digging. This must stop," said the drag.

"When will you give us the answer?" Ghost asked.

"It will take time," was the drag's drab response.

"We will give you two days," said Ghost firmly. "Then we start digging again."

"Impossible! You will give me six days. I will tell you by then. Until that time, no more digging."

They could tell he had really left this time because Mango finally quit barking.

"Six days, Wistle. Six more days before we head back to St. Annalise."

"You humans are funny," Wistle said. "You believe that guy? Like the drags are going to go for that. If we're done digging for now, let's go back to looking for boats."

CHAPTER 21

Loving up the Children

Location: Iceland

"Sandra Claus!"

"Hi Sandra!"

"Welcome back Sandra Claus!"

Everywhere Sandra and Santa went around Iceland, the children all lined up to meet Sandra. Sure there were some who wanted to visit with Santa and all of them were happy to see him, but not as happy as they were to see Sandra. She and Santa couldn't figure it out.

"It is extraordinarily nice of them to be so welcoming to me," Sandra said, not knowing exactly what to say. The situation had become rather awkward for her, though Santa seemed more amused about it all then distressed. "I truly can't think of any way I was particularly special to them last year that would create such a loyal welcome this year."

"Ho Ho Ho Sandra, this is a wonderful problem, really," Santa said. "Children are starting to know and love you."

What they seemed to know and like about her the most, was her kindness initiative. Everywhere the two went, children brought their lists of kind things they were doing. They didn't just want to leave them with her, they wanted to read their lists to her. They would sit for a quick minute and tell Santa what they wanted for Christmas and then they would sit for several minutes with Sandra telling her all about the ways they were being kind and the kind things people had done for them in return.

"Sandra, my brother isn't always nice," one little girl said as she sat on Sandra's lap talking about her kindness list. "He just doesn't always know how to be. Somebody needs to teach him how to be kind."

"What a good idea, Emalyn," Sandra said, knowing the little girl's name without even asking, as any good Santa does. "Shall I tell you a secret?" the little girl nodded her head excitedly. "I've been thinking of starting a school all about kindness and when I get it going, I'll be sure to invite you and your brother."

"Especially my brother," said the little girl with earnest. "I'll come too, though, since I love you."

"Oh Emalyn, how kind you are to say that!" Sandra said, squeezing on the sincere five-year-old.

"I love you back."

"I know," she said sincerely. "You're Sandra Claus dot dot dot. You love all children."

It was one of those moments when Sandra wouldn't have chosen to be anyone else in the whole world, no matter what. No other job, no other person, was living a better life.

Wherever they went, whether in the main city of Reykjavik or any of the smaller cities, they were greeted with love and smiles and lists and lists and lists of ways the children had been kind and good. Even Santa was in awe of how that one request by Sandra had started to change everything about how they met with children.

While the two Santa's met with the Icelandic children, the elves were out on more adventures. The local elves had planned a whole day of touring so after the fun at the lagoon, the buses had headed out to a national park on the island that featured the world famous Gullfoss Falls, a spectacular waterfall. The Pole elves had never been to a waterfall before so they were all sitting on the edge of their seats hoping to spot it first (though the falls couldn't be seen from the road.) Pretty soon, something else caught their attention in the countryside along the way.

"Look!" Waldorf shouted out. "Elf sized ponies!"

All the elves rushed to his side of the bus at once.

"They have sweaters on!" said Clicker, grabbing his camera.

"Stop the bus please!" called out Perriwinkle. "We want to ride one."

Icelandic horses have been in Iceland for centuries. While they can grow to be a full-size horse many of them remain the size of small ponies. Tourists loved to click pictures of the ponies wearing warm sweaters the locals knitted for them. It was a herd of small, sweater-wearing, Icelandic horses that Barney had spotted. Nuka moved to talk with the bus driver and the bus slowed down along with the one behind them.

"We can stop and take pictures, and you may pet them, but no riding on them, please. They aren't ours, after all. We would need permission."

The elves were hardly listening to a word she was saying, wanting to be off the bus and over to the ponies as fast as their little legs would move them - and elves can go fast for their size!

"Go slow! Go slow! You'll scare them off," Nuka called out but her worries were for nothing.

As fast as the elves were running toward them, the little horses were running to the elves as well.

They were kicking up their heels along the way seeming happy to see the little visitors.

The elves were beyond delighted with finding horses their size. Not a one of them tried to ride one. Instead, they all just enjoyed spending time with the little ponies that looked as festive as the Icelandic elves did in their folkloric style sweaters. It took Nuka more than an hour to get the elves organized and reloaded back on the buses to head out to the falls.

"Okay, next stop Gullfoss Falls!" Nuka hollered out to her bus when everyone was back on.

Except that it wasn't the next stop. This time it was Brainy who looked out the window and started pointing. "Look!" he shouted. "There's water shooting way up high in the air! Stop the bus please!"

Once again, all the elves in both buses rushed to see out the windows as the buses came to a stop and the elves hopped off. There were plenty of steam vents in Iceland and even geysers that send water far into the air. They had stopped at one of the especially tall geysers.

"Look! There it goes again!" said Brainy.

"Ooooohhhhh," exclaimed the elves in unison. "Aaaaaaahhhhh."

"Stay back, everyone," Nuka said nervously. "The geyser water is hot."

"Yeah, and it smells a little, too," Xylo said holding his nose as all the others nodded and copied him.

The group all stood there a minute, holding their noses and quickly getting restless waiting for the geyser to go off again. When nothing happened immediately, elves being elves, became bored and headed back to the buses, running and giggling.

Again, the buses headed out. This time there were no extra stops before they arrived at Gullfoss Falls. "Before you get off the bus let me be sure to tell you to stay on the marked trails and do not go near the edge of the waterfall. Oh and also, wear your coats. It's cold here at the falls," Nuka said seriously.

They all nodded their heads and slipped into their coats. The local elves had been here many times but never got tired of seeing the beautiful attraction.

"Also, this is a great place to purchase post cards if you'd like to send one home," Nuka finished.

"Tee hee Nuka," Diva said. "Who would we send one to? Almost all of us from the North Pole are here!"

"Let's send one to Dear Lovey and to Rollo!" Breezy said. All the elves loved the idea, so the two elves who had volunteered to help on St. Annalise would now receive lots of postcards from Iceland.

"Hey, let's send one to ourselves!" said Dervish. All the elves applauded that idea. They would love getting their own mail.

"You're so smart, Dervish," Perriwinkle said, as she planned out what she would write on her postcard.

Gulfoss Falls are a world-renowned, natural, attraction so it shouldn't have been any surprise that the park was full of tourists from all over the world. Seeing so many elves, all together in one place, made many people ignore the falls. Instead they focused their cameras on the elves as they got off the bus and as they moved around the falls area.

This was part of the reason humans rarely get to see elves – most elves hate attention. They like being in the background. Even though they're funny and rambunctious with each other, they are actually quite shy in public. Diva was one of the few exceptions. She actually enjoyed the attention and never made it up the trail to see the falls as she smiled and posed with anyone who asked. She was joined by a few of the local Icelandic elves who enjoyed getting out for a visit and mingling. The rest of the elves, whether North Pole or Ielandic, did what they do. They clumped together and tried to ignore the attention while they oooohed and ahhhhhed over the majestic falls. Then they hit the gift shop for their post cards. And store-bought butter mints to eat on the bus ride back.

"Well, that was marvelous," Diva declared as they settled back on the bus.

"Yes, these are delicious," said Breezy, enjoying her bag of mints. "But not quite as good as the homemade ones we had last night!"

"Oh I don't mean the mints, silly," said Diva.

"Well you sure don't mean the falls," said Breezy. "You never even saw them."

"Oh no, I mean all the lovely tourists. I felt like a celebrity. Almost as popular as Santa Claus," Diva tucked at her hair while she smiled at the thought.

"Ha!" Barney chuckled. "That's a good one Diva." The little fashionista was miffed that he didn't believe her. She was about to correct him when Nuka interceded.

"Anyone ready to go home and have Iceland pastries with sweet butter and big cups of cocoa?" Nuka asked.

"YESSSSSS!" screamed out the bus and Buddy started them up with another round of Christmas carols.

After a long day of meeting with children at towns all around Iceland, Santa and Sandra were waiting there tiredly to greet the buses as they pulled up. It had been big days for them all. As the elves got off the bus, one of the tallest and gangliest of the Icelandic elves hung back after the others had gone in for cocoa and treats.

"Come on, Redwood," Nuka called to him, making sure no one was left behind. "Santas, I hope you're joining us?"

"We would never miss it," Sandra called back as she hurried to catch up with Nuka. Santa felt Redwood's hesitation.

"Just give the two of us here a minute, Nuka. We'll be right there. Save me the tallest cup of cocoa please." He turned to the gangly, reddish-colored elf. "Is there something you wanted to talk with me about, Redwood?"

"Yes, sir," the elf burst out without any hesitation. "I want to go back with you all. I want to be a North Pole elf. I know it's a wonderful thing to live here in Iceland but I have never quite felt like I fit in and I long to help make toys."

"You were born an Icelandic elf," Santa said a little surprised and wanting to be sure Redwood had thought through his idea completely. "The elves' lives at the North Pole are truly ones of service while that is less so here in Iceland. Have you thought about that? Are you sure that is a change you would like to make? As you know, we don't visit here very often."

"I'm ready, sir," Redwood said. "I've never completely fit in. I'm always carving things from wood, making wooden toys, and building our homes out of wood instead of rock like is the tradition here. I'm a wooden toy maker deep inside, Santa and would be so honored if you would let me join you."

He looked at Santa with his large, beseeching eyes and Santa couldn't possibly turn him down. Any elf who wanted to build toys for children was welcome at the North Pole as far as Santa was concerned. Redwood was a little different in his height and color and long, branch-like arms and legs but every elf at the North Pole was different in their own way, from the others. Redwood would fit right in.

"Well then, let's go tell the others that we'll have one more on board tomorrow and give your Icelandic tribe a warm good-bye," Santa said reaching to pat Redwood on the back but the elf had already scurried away to share his news. Santa scrambled after him, ready for a whole plate of those mints they had tried the day before.

CHAPTER 22

Time to Head Back

Location: A Lonely Tropical Island

The six days had gone by without a peep from the dragoon. Mango had gone back to barking at birds and crabs and waves. Ghost and Wistle were getting out their digging tools again since the dragoons order changed nothing as far as they were concerned. They had waited the six days he had insisted on and they weren't going to wait a minute more.

Then, just as quickly as it had closed on them months ago, the gateway reopened. It was what they had been hoping for and they were ready for it. Their backpacks were packed complete with bottles full of water. They ran for their supplies, scared to go back in to the big cavern full of drags and other dangers, but more frightened of the inaction of staying where they were for even one more day.

"C'mon Mango!" Ghost called out. "We're going home."

CHAPTER 23

Bye-Bye Iceland!

Location: Iceland

There was wailing and tears all around the next afternoon when it was time for the elves to say goodbye and head for the plane back to the North Pole. Both Santa's tried their best to keep them all happy but even those they could usually count on for help, like Zinga and Breezy, were sad to go.

"Come back!" called out the Iceland elves as they lined up waving at the buses. "Redwood, we will miss you! Come visit us, everyone!"

"We will!" the North Polers called back, knowing it was true. They now had new members in their elf family and they would come again. Except for the sadness the elves were feeling about leaving, Sandra and Santa were pleased with how the visit had gone. Fortunately they also had the magic cure for brightening up any elves' day: candy canes!

The two Santa's had filled a very large, oversized suitcase with the sweet treat to share with the island's children and now they shared the leftovers. The crying changed to happy sounds as the waving elves faded out of view. Elves were fickle little folk. Sad could change to happy in the span of just a few good licks of a North Pole made candy cane.

At the airport, the elves and Santa's were parting ways, so Sandra handed out another round in hopes of avoiding more tears. The elves were heading home to the North Pole and the two Santa's were continuing on their European publicity tour. As they rode along, Sandra found herself lonesome to talk to Cappie. They had so much to do to plan the wedding and Sandra had been so busy. Neither Cappie nor Thomas had been married before, so they were both hoping to have it be an extra special occasion. Sandra didn't want to miss a minute of any of the planning for it.

Having grown up on an island where phones simply weren't needed, Sandra, like Santa, still didn't have a cell phone. None of her friends or elves did either. They were all a little oldfashioned that way. She was hoping to locate a phone at the airport to call home before they hopped on the plane heading for Ireland and Scotland next. After that, they had plans for quick stops in some countries Sandra hadn't personally visited yet. They were going to stop in Poland,

Hungary, the Ukraine, and then pop over to Germany for a quick hello with Nicholas Tannenbaum, one of Sandra's favorite contestants from the South Pole Santa tryouts. (Truth be told, she loved them all.) Finally, on the way home, they would stop in London, England, for an interview with Beatrice Carol, the intrepid World Wide News reporter that covered everything Santa related.

At the airport, Sandra zeroed in on a phone to use but her calls to locate Cappie and Birdie went unanswered. She didn't even try Spence because she knew he was back down at the South Pole outpost finishing up the last of the needed upgrades to the remote location. She dialed Gunny, who picked up on the first ring.

"Sandra? Is that you?" The big cowboy didn't even bother with a hello.

"Gunny! It's so good to hear your voice!" Sandra realized, as she said it, how much she meant it.

"How are you? How's everything going?"

"Fine and fine and never mind about anything here, tell me all about Iceland," he said, so relieved to hear her voice that he wanted to hear her talking about anything at all, just to hear her speaking. The months away had been harder for him than he had let on to anyone.

"Well, it was a big hit with the elves," Sandra said with lightness in her voice. "They all had so much fun together just like we had hoped.

"And the people of Iceland are exceptional," she continued. "You would not believe how kind the children are. Gunny, they had long lists of all the kind things they had done just in the first four months of this year! It was so impressive. One little girl I talked to really liked my idea for a kindness school that Birdie, Christina, and I have been scheming on."

She was talking fast now and Gunny loved hearing her excitement.

"Seriously though, how's everything going there? Anything new on Ghost and Wistle or Jason?" She was almost positive there wasn't, since she and Santa would surely hear first but she was compelled to ask anyway.

He hated not having anything to tell her. "Nothing," he said miserably. "But on the positive side of things, I'm sure you'll be pleased to hear that Squawk and Em are down to arguing less than ten times a day."

She laughed out loud, thinking of them and feeling blessed to have Gunny who didn't mind their squabbles.

"Tell them again how much I love them," Sandra said.

Gunny found himself wanting her to add, "and you." He waited just a beat, just in case, before he shared another update with her. "I actually saw Christina smiling this week talking with Cappie about possible places on the island to hold the wedding. She's starting to feel a little better I think.

"Hey and when you get back, you are going to have to pick out the colors for your new Happiness Hall. We're just about ready for it to get some paint."

"I am so excited!" Sandra said, her voice going up. "Now I just have to come up with a special name for it. I love Happiness Hall but we can't have two of those. I'm thinking maybe

Happier Hall." She was joking with him now and pleased with her joke.

"Yeah, where the smiles are bigger and the laughs last longer," Gunny said, going along.

"Ha! I'll be lucky just getting the paint color picked out and calling it the Big Room," she said, still laughing. "Gunny, our planes being called so I've got to go. I'll check-in soon from one of the countries okay? And please tell Cappie and Birdie I tried to get hold of them and I'm dying to talk to them. Okay, gotta go. Byeeee."

The phone clicked before she heard his response. "Bye Santa girl. Love you."

CHAPTER 24

Making a Run for It

Location: Drag Prison

The three prisoners had conferred for many hours on how they could get away from their captors. Talking had brought them all closer – even Danger who Jason hadn't thought was possible to like when he first came in. But sharing tough times often has the hard-won benefit of getting to know someone and, more often than not, when you really get to know someone, it's hard not to find some things to like.

One thing the three captives definitely had in common was that they had all been imprisoned unfairly and without cause. It seemed the only "crime" that Jason and Thogo had committed was the unfortunate choice to have wandered off the main path in the part of Middle Earth the drags considered their own.

The other beings in Middle Earth scoffed at the notion that the drags owned any of the area they all lived in and the drags would never dare to "arrest" one of them. Visitors from out of the area, like Jason and Thogo, however, were on their own and subject to being harassed by the drags.

Most beings of Middle Earth had no cares as to what the outcome was for visitors. Living in Middle Earth was hard even on a good day. Every being needed to take care of themselves.

The drags had their own rules of governing and as long as Jason had stayed on the main routes clearly designated for common travel, they had chosen to let him proceed. When he had strayed from that path, "looking for a way out", he had insisted, the drags felt justified to pick him up. He was just going to be trouble. They had no interest in letting the purported fairy king roam around Middle Earth. It would only invite trouble.

It had been the same for Thogo. He was a wanderer by nature, he explained, and actually from a far-off part of Middle Earth. He had just been wandering when he came into that fairly unknown part of the inner planet. He had been lumbering along without a care to anything but the journey, when out of the blue, a drag had picked him up from behind and brought him there to be locked up with the others.

Danger, on the other hand, was reluctant to say anything about why he was there. What Jason had deduced, by the very little the drag had said, was that he was actually more of a "political" prisoner than a crime prisoner. It sounded to Jason, like Danger had been overthrown from a position of power and stored away there without most anyone else of his kind knowing where he was being kept.

After scheming and planning, the three were ready to try for a prison break. They all, separately, got a short amount of time out of their cages each day. When the guards arrived and released Danger for his break, Jason and Thogo began coughing and choking as if something was terribly wrong. Their role was to distract the guards and give Danger enough time to overcome them with his strength and cunning and grab the keys.

The part they all - including Danger - miscalculated on in their planning, however, was thinking the drag guards would care that either Jason or Thogo were choking. They enjoyed harassing Danger so much every day that they barely gave a look to the two chokers.

It didn't take any of the trio very long to realize that their plan, which they all knew was a stretch from the beginning, was impossible on that day. They would come to know it was impossible on any day as they tried it day after day.

It didn't matter that they were innocent and being held unfairly. It didn't matter that they all dreamed every minute of being let go. There was no getting out.

CHAPTER 25

Oh No!

Location: Middle Earth

The island entry dragoon had agreed to the trio's terms. They would be able to travel safely back to Cassandra Cay but only under drag escort, and frankly, every day since, that had turned out to be, well, a total drag. The drag that had been assigned to escorting them, had no real interest in hurrying, was taking them on a zig-zag path that was adding days – maybe even a full week – on to their already too long trip out of Middle Earth. When they tried to move along at their own pace then the drag would come flying at them, wings out, teeth showing, claws out and hiss until they slowed. Worse than all of that as far as Ghost and Wistle were concerned, was that Mango barked constantly. Constantly. From the minute she woke up, to the minute she finally got some sleep out of exhaustion, Mango barked.

She disliked the drag intensely, and unlike Ghost and Wistle who felt the same way, she refused to keep quiet about it.

There was one positive thing to their drag escort: he loved to talk. Ghost and Wistle were trying to use that to their advantage.

"So it seems like no one is in this whole giant cavern traveling about except us. What's the deal with that? Have you ever seen anyone else down here besides your normal basic underground stuff like other drags, those giant toads, and a bunch of oversized insects?" Ghost asked. Wistle shuddered. She had stayed full-size, this time through the cavern to avoid being bug bait or dinner for some big frog or even a snack for the very gross drag who seemed to eat anything that moved.

"Except the three of us, has anyone else been crazy enough to come here?" Ghost pressed the drag for an answer.

"You humans only care about you humans," the drag hissed.

"No I don't," Ghost protested. "For starters, I care about Mango and she's not human and I care about Wistle and she's not human." He realized how much he meant that as he said it. Caring about Mango was easy. He had always loved animals. The surprise was how much the totally annoying fairy mattered to him now. They had gone through so much together and succeeded because they had learned to work together. Getting her home safe was more important to Ghost now than finding Jason or even his own safety.

"We drags are so good at guarding the portals that few of anything passes through and if they pass without permission, we catch them. Yes we do. We catch them and we lock them up and we keep them locked up and they know who the boss is and it's definitely not them."

"Yeah, sure you lock em up," Ghost baited him. "You guys don't even have a place to put anyone down here."

"Oh, dumb, stupid, human you would never find it even if I told you. This fairy might. Fairies can be smart. We caught a dumb one, though."

That made Wistle too angry to stay full-size. Before Ghost could so much as protest, she had orbed over to the big bully drag with such ire that even he stepped back with a quick thought of fear. "You insult our king with your hissing drag ways! You should never have taken him and someday you shall pay!"

She had come too close to the drag for her own safety and he had recovered from his surprise. He was also much bigger and meaner and didn't care about fairy balls. With one swoop of his wing he sent Wistle flying through the air, spinning and tumbling, completely out of control, until she finally smashed into one of the large boulders around them. She immediately went to full size and Ghost could see, at once, that she had been hurt.

"YOU BEAST!" he shouted at the horrible drag escorting them. "How dare you! She wasn't hurting you! She was small and you are large. You say things about humans, but you are the nasty species."

Ghost turned his attention away from the drag and completely to Wistle. He was scrambling to get over to her through the many rocks and boulders between them.

"Wistle! Wistle talk to me!" he called out to his fairy friend who hadn't moved since she had gone to full size.

As he scrambled over one of the tallest rocks he saw that a nasty-looking, large, beetle type of bug was heading her way as well. It was about a foot long and where other beetles might have had simple antenna, this bug had antenna out in front with pinchers on the end! It might not be lethal for Wistle but it appeared able to easily harm her. Ghost looked at it, looked back at Wistle and realized the bug's pinchers were big enough to snap off one of Wistle's slender arms.

He scrambled even faster, shouting at Wistle to wake up, but the fairy didn't so much as moan. The drag sat where he was on a boulder near her chewing on some kind of ugly bug he had snapped at and showed no concern at all for the fairy he had injured or the massive sized bug heading her way. "Wistle! Wistle! Wake up!" Ghost kept shouting, nearly breathless, trying to climb and shout at the same time.

It was Mango who was the hero. Barking the whole way, she made a heroic leap from one boulder to the next to protect Wistle, at great personal peril, as the giant-size beetle snapped at her with its huge pinchers. Wistle was just out of its reach so the bug scrambled to come at her from a different angle, and as it did, Mango managed to catch its back leg and fling it to the hard ground below where it landed upside down. It whirled and kicked and made a high-pitched keening kind of hiss but no matter what it did it couldn't get itself turned up. Right then, Ghost made it to Wistle's side.

"Watch that bug for us, Mango," Ghost said to the brave dog, as he reached out gently to carefully see what injuries Wistle had sustained. He could tell without even touching her that her left forearm was broken but it seemed that was the only thing. Her head had a large bump on it from when she hit the rock. That was probably what had knocked her out and what worried him the most.

"Wistle," he said to her softly as he gently worked to get his arms underneath her. He needed to move her over to the trail and away from the darker area of the cavern where she had landed. The whirling bug looked like it was getting closer to getting itself righted again and Ghost had no idea if there were more of those around.

Moving her, though, presented more than just the need to be gentle with her. The rocks and boulders were challenging to go up and over with one person, let alone one person carrying another. Plus, he had just recovered from a broken arm himself. He knew how much pain there was from a broken bone and didn't want to hurt her any more. Unfortunately, they didn't have many alternatives.

The drag sort of cackle laughed, watching Ghost move the two of them. A shot of real hate moved through Ghost.

"You're lucky I'm only human and don't have any magic" he said menacingly to the drag. "If I had so much as the smallest spark of magic in me, I would use it this minute to change you into some kind of squishy blob of gelatin that would be dinner for that bug."

"Ha!" said the drag leisurely, not the least bit concerned by Ghost's empty threats. "Your magic would not work here even if you did have some. And as for the basker," he paused as he reached out for the now turned back up and snapping beetle. "They are quite good raw." He picked it up with one of his talons as the bug snapped and hissed. The drag popped it in his mouth, crunched on it once and then swallowed it whole.

Ghost gasped, held Wistle tighter in his arms, and took a rather risky jump between rocks. He had to get them somewhere safe. Wistle cried out. As much as Ghost hated the sound he was so glad to hear the cry. She was waking up!

"Ghost?" she managed to say weakly, clearly confused.

"I got you, Wistle," he said back to her as reassuringly as he could. "I'm not going to lie to you, we've got a couple more big leaps and it's going to hurt. Probably, really bad. Can you hold on to my shoulder with your good arm?"

She did her best but her grip felt weak. He tightened his arms around her. "Here we go," he said as he leapt and she screamed in pain.

"Ah, Wistle, I'm so sorry, babe, so sorry," he said, feeling almost as much pain as she was with each jump. He was making leaps he normally never would have tried by himself, let alone with Wistle in his arms, but the adrenaline running through him drove him forward.

"One more and then we reach a flat spot, with more light, where I can set you down. Here we go." He leapt and stumbled on his landing but managed to keep them both upright. Mango was right behind him. Wistle was crying out with each move and he worried that between the broken arm and the bumped head she was in danger of going into shock. He propped her head up by putting her backpack behind it.

"Darn, you and the little sassy fairy made it. So boring," said the drag.

Ghost ignored him. It didn't matter what the hideously mean beast said or thought, he decided.

Saving Wistle was on him and Mango and the three of them hadn't gone through all they had to leave without one of them. Not an option.

"Mango, come lay over here next to Wistle. We need to keep her as warm as we can." The smart dog seemed to know exactly what to do and laid down with her head placed gently on Wistle's stomach, eyes open watching her. The fingers on Wistles non-injured hand lightly petted the caring dog.

"Thank you, girl," she whispered and the dog whimpered back to her.

"Wistle, I'm not going anywhere. I'm right here," Ghost said, jumping down off the flat rock they were on. "I'm just looking for a stick of some kind so we can set your arm. Got one!" He picked up the "stick" and started screaming in pain himself. "OWWW! What in the Middle Earth?!" he screamed flailing his hand around as his "stick" scurried off to hide under a rock. "Ha! You tried to pick up a board beetle. What a dummy. Those sting. Not deadly but you will have a swollen hand and bad rash for days. Sometimes people cut their hand off actually after picking up a board beetle. Woo, what a pair you two are," said the drag, cackling and whooping it up like he'd never laughed before from his perch above them.

"Ghost, are you alright?" Wistle called out, trying to sit up and crying out in her pain when she pressed on her hand attached to the broken arm.

Ghost gave his throbbing hand a look and saw it was already swelling. He needed to forget the pain and work fast to get a real stick wrapped around Wistle's broken arm. He spied another one and kicked it with his foot first before trying to pick it up. It was a real stick this time and he moved to her side as quick as he could. He got gauze wrap from his first aid kit in his back pack.

"This is going to hurt bad, Wistle, and I'm so sorry about that." He dreaded the next minute. As a fairy it was unlikely Wistle had ever been in pain before. Fairies were known for their good health and well-being and any rare accident they might experience would normally be healed very quickly through their own magic. Here in Middle Earth though, she had no magic. Without the use of both arms she couldn't even orb since orbing involved being able to move both arms. As Ghost expected, Wistle screamed in agony as he put her arm on the wood board he had found and wrapped it tight together with the gauze wrap to try to keep it stable. Mango didn't move even once when Wistle's fingers painfully dug into her fur to buffer the pain.

"Okay, now you're going to have to help me for a minute. I've got an epi-pen right here but I can't get it open because my hand is too swollen." Wistle looked at his hand and arm with concern that she didn't even know how to fully express. The whole area was breaking out in blisters and his hand was twice its normal size already. It was alarming. Wistle could see the pain on his face and suspected his injury was actually worse than hers. He held out the pen with his now shaking good hand and she removed the top with her good hand. He shoved it in his thigh per the instructions on the pen for use. He took out another and they did the same thing again. He hoped that the poison from the board beetle would be counteracted by the epi-pen. They could only wait and see.

"Bravo, bravo!" said the drag after causing all the trouble and not helping, at all, with any of it.

"Now we need to be on our way."

"Yeah, right," said Ghost, completely exhausted and knowing they couldn't go another step on that day.

"I say we move forward so we will move forward," said the drag.

"We say we won't. What's your sudden hurry? You always want to go slow and now you want to go fast? Go ahead without us. We don't care. We sure don't need your help," said Ghost, not feeling afraid of him at all in that moment.

"So you say, so you say, but you don't really even know your way back," said the drag, tauntingly. Ghost and Wistle knew he was right. When you didn't even know where you were it was almost impossible to find where you wanted to be.

"Fine. Stay with us then. But we are done moving today no thanks to you. Tomorrow, we will make up the time," said Ghost.

For once, he won the argument with the drag.

"*I* have decided that will be fine," the drag said, after a moment, emphasizing the "I" so the two would hear again that he was the one in charge. "I have an acquaintance nearby that I shall visit this evening. Heed my warning, though, and do not try to move." With that he flapped off.

"Yeah, no moving," Ghost repeated after the drag. He lay back on the ground next to Wistle and Mango with a big sigh of relief and used his good hand to hold her good hand. They were in bad shape but they were alive and together and that would have to be enough for that night.

CHAPTER 26

A Spires Way

Location: Middle Earth

None of them slept. Maybe not even for five minutes.

Wistle and Ghost were in too much pain and Mango was the self-appointed sentry. Thankfully, she didn't bark through the night but she was turning her head one way or another listening to the scurrying that seemed to come every night in this part of Middle Earth though somehow they never really saw anything. Now they knew for sure, though, they weren't imagining it. Things – bad things – were out there. Ghost was glad they had always chose to sleep on top of tall boulders. It had probably helped keep them safe.

Like when they came through the first time, it was surprisingly easy to see in the giant-sized cavern. It was like being in a constant state of a gray-colored day at dusk on the topside of the planet. At night, it dimmed further making it almost black, but not completely dark.

Ghost and Wistle were fully awake and whispering low to each other about possible next steps for hours. No matter what option they could think of, their chances of making it out alive didn't seem very positive. They knew the drag would make it difficult and time wasn't on their side.

Ghost's hand seemed to have stopped swelling but the pain whenever it touched anything was excruciating. Wistle, on the other hand, had, not just a throbbing arm, but a throbbing headache and pain in her chest area that the two believed was a cracked rib. The normally sassy fairy found herself feeling so thankful for Ghost and Mango and that she was not there on her own. They were whispering about the limited options they had, yet again, when they realized a set of eyes were looking at them from the nearest boulder. Ghost released Wistle's hand getting ready to defend them somehow if needed. He went to scream in hopes of chasing whatever it was off. "Shhhhhhh," said the little being, putting his long fingers to his lips, warning him not to say anything. "Hello to you both," he whispered. "I heard the shouts earlier. I have no fondness for the drags so I came to see if I can help. I believe you need some assistance."

"Uh, hello," said Ghost, feeling hopeful and fearful at the same time. *Now what?* Mango leapt up and gave a low growl.

The little being made some clicking sounds and the brave and loud dog sat back down, quiet again.

"How can you help us?" Ghost asked.

"I already did but I am here to help you more."

"Why, you're a spire sprite aren't you?" Wistle said with some excitement. The little being nodded. Wistle continued. "This is an honor dear spire sprite. I know you get to show yourself only a few times in your life time so we deeply appreciate your help."

"What?" Ghost asked, not sure he understood. "These 'spire sprites' usually can't be seen?"

"Or even heard really. Well some beings can hear them. A fairy, for instance, could likely hear a spire sprite but we would have to know to be listening for him. It is the limits of their kind, but on the days they show themselves their power is far greater than their size," Wistle explained with true awe in her voice. She spoke again to the spire sprite. "Truly, I am honored, as I'm sure my human friend is as well, that you have come to our aid."

"Thank you, Wistle of the Woods," said the spire sprite. It didn't matter to Wistle or Ghost how he knew their names. "I am Grander a Middle Earth spire and today and tomorrow and the next day as well, I will be at your service and then I will be gone from you.

"I see that things are very dire for you," Grander said, continuing to talk as he hopped over to their boulder. He was about a foot tall, very gray and thin, with a pointed head, and large luminous eyes that held concern for them. He didn't share his concern with them, but without him, he doubted they could make it out of the cavern alive. Maybe not even through another day.

Even with him, he wasn't sure they could but, he, at least, could give them a chance. This was the way of a spire. His kind were limited on how many times they could be seen by others who were not his own kind – and there were not that many of them – so when they were seen they liked it to be for a noble cause. This was one of the noblest that he had ever come across.

He only had three days, no matter what, from the moment he had made contact with them. That's how many hours until he faded from their vision and their hearing. He would see them all – and what happened to them – but he would no longer be able to assist in any way. He shivered to think about what would happen to them from the drags if he did not succeed. He had seen their friend Jason go through the area months before and regretted that he hadn't assisted him out of the cavern before the drags found him and took him away. He could make it up to him now by helping his friends. But they needed to get moving.

"I believe I can help you," Grander said, still whispering. "I know you are both badly injured but, for you to be safe, we must move from here before the drag returns, which could be soon."

"But how will he not find us no matter where we go?" Ghost asked confused and wanting to be sure it was the right move to make. *How could this little guy help us?* he was thinking to himself.

"I can mask his sight," said the spire, zipping around to pick up all of their items. "We must leave no sign that you were here. That will confuse him immediately and waste his time looking for where he left you. As you know, in this area, most the boulders look the same. Though he thinks he knows where he left you, he will become confused when you are not here and there is no sign of you. This will enrage him and cause him fear since his assignment was to not lose you or allow you to escape and become a problem to them again."

"We are both badly injured," Wistle cried out as she moved to stand and swayed from her headache. "We will not be able to move fast. You should not risk yourself for us." Ghost rose to his feet quickly to help Wistle. The spire whisked up the rest of their things at a speed Ghost had never seen. *Even the elves don't move that quickly*, he thought.

"It is the way of a spire to be of service in this way. It is my great honor." He turned then and with those words he bowed at them in sincerity. They all nodded, Mango too, in return, deeply grateful for this meeting. "But to save you, we must get moving." He glanced about nervously.

"Lead the way," Ghost said, hopping down from the boulder and gently lifting Wistle down with his strong good arm as Mango jumped down and joined him. They hadn't considered this miraculous way of escape but it was his favorite, by far. In this option, they had a chance.

CHAPTER 27

Day One

Location: Middle Earth

They had a chance but it was still slow going. Each step, for both Wistle and Ghost, was incredibly painful. Wistle hurt pretty much everywhere from being slammed on the boulder in her small orb size. Because she was in her magical state when the drag struck her it had probably saved her life but it did not save her from being injured or the pain that came from those injuries. The normally condescending fairy was, just-like-that, now completely humbled by her circumstance and the kindness being shown her.

For Ghost, the pain from his hand radiated up his arm now, and while the swelling was in check the pain was not. It was almost impossible for him not to cry out constantly but somehow he managed. Mango walked slowly between the two allowing them to use her as a support when they needed.

They walked this slow and agonizing way for nearly two hours, not having gone very far but apparently far enough for the spire's satisfaction that he lead them to a quiet, hidden, spot where he allowed them, at last, to sit down.

He ran around as if to do a check of the area. When he seemed satisfied they were indeed in a "safe" place he came and sat with them now speaking in a louder tone then before.

"I believe we are safe here, for the moment, though we will have to keep moving," he cautioned.

"This is a good place to tell you of what is ahead.

"As a spire, I am able to come to your aid. I can keep you hidden from all things that would do you harm for three days' time. This means that while you will sometimes be in plain sight of the drag and perhaps other drags and other kinds that would like to aid the drags, none will be able to see you since you will be under my protection."

Ghost could hardly believe their good fortune. He wiped a tear from his eye. Geesch, the last thing he wanted to do was cry in front of Wistle. She reached out and held his hand as tears ran down her face. The hours of pain combined with the relief of this kindness was too much to hold back the tears of relief and gratitude. Looking at them, even the spire had tears threatening. His resolve to see them safely out became even stronger. Their fates and paths had converged. He cleared his throat and tried to sound confident.

"But that won't keep them from looking. Probably constantly," Grander continued ominously.

He had to be sure they knew that, despite his help, the trio was in a precarious position.

"Eventually, they will suspect you have received the help of a spire. The trick for you is that you must give them no clues to where you are or where you have been. While you are with me, you cannot be seen or unmasked by any that I protect you from, but anything left behind will not be masked. Also, we must be sure we are not walking or standing or sitting anywhere a drag might land." The two nodded with understanding but Ghost had a pressing question.

"Why can't he just let us go? The drags know we just want to be out of here."

"It is the way of drags. They are most pleased when they can create displeasure for others. This drag has been ordered to see you out but if something were to happen to you or you break his set of 'rules' as we have, then he is released of his orders and can have you jailed, just because. He knows you want out, which makes him want to keep you in. When you wanted in, they wanted to keep you out. They are contrary by their nature. What you want is never what they want. That is a key to understanding the drags."

"Seems a pretty miserable way to live," said Ghost.

"Perhaps to you and I. To a drag, miserable can equal happy. Who are we to say what way is right? Right for me is different for you. I dare say, however, I would rather be a spire." Grander smiled and Ghost realized Grander too found the drags troubling though he allowed them more room to be who they were rather than judging them for their choices.

"Now then, the drag will not want to alert others that you have been lost out of fear for himself so that will work in our favor." Grander continued. "Even the dragoon at the portal where you came in will probably not know. I am counting on that." He paused as if thinking about what they should and shouldn't know.

Ghost reached out to reassure him. "Grander, don't hold anything back," he said and Wistle nodded. "We know this is a bad situation and that we still may not make it out. We will be of the most help to you if we know what we need to do."

Grander appreciated his courage. "We must go as fast as we can," he said with urgency in his voice. "Each day is dangerous here, of course, but, most pressing, is that you only have my protection for seventy two hours and the portal you seek is nearly that far away. Normally, this would not be of that much concern but with your injuries it is of grave concern. You cannot move quickly and must have rest."

The two of them looked at him miserably. The damage was done and they could not right it on their own.

"This then is part of my quandary," Grander continued. "Do we just push on or do I risk four hours of our precious time to veer us off course and get you some relief from your pain from the healing spring? Perhaps the time could be made up then? You should know, however, that there is a good chance the drag will look for us there."

For Ghost and Wistle there was no question – the pain was so great that they would risk the time lost. Things were dire either way. They would prefer dire with a dose of pain relief.

"We're ready, Grander," Ghost said, getting to his feet with more ease then he felt and reaching to help Wistle. "Lead us to this spring and thank you for your caring service."

CHAPTER 28

Waning and Surging

Location: On Tour

Sandra and Santa had been gone for weeks and were finally getting ready to head home. They had visited eight countries before they landed in London to another crowd of enthusiastic children and their parents all there to see . . . Sandra.

In each country, it had been Sandra that everyone was turning out to see at every stop they made. Somehow, the protest of her being named South Pole Santa had shifted and now it was Santa whose popularity had waned. Santa was the old and Sandra was the new and after her solo tour last year and launch of the Kindness List, everyone wanted to meet the new girl wonder called South Pole Santa.

At first, the two were a little amused about it, thinking it was an anomaly to just the first countries they stopped at. But as the response continued and dominated, in each country and at every stop, it became awkward. Both Santa's were embarrassed by it. Sandra, because she was getting so much attention, and Santa because he wasn't. It was a new role for them both and neither were enjoying it.

"Ho Ho Ho!" Santa said as he stepped out of the plane first and greeted the English crowd. The sight of so many children always made his heart turn over with joy. Sandra liked him to step out first. He was Santa. The Santa of lore and love for centuries. He would always be her mentor and hero.

"Hi Santa!" You could have heard the happy greetings for miles as Santa smiled and waved at them all. After a few minutes of that, Sandra stepped out to join him and, like everywhere else, the noise went up to a sonic boom level.

"SANDRA!" The crowd shouted out as if on cue. It had happened like this at every stop but neither of them were used to it yet. Santa had found himself feeling conflicted. He wanted so much for Sandra to be accepted and successful but he had never even considered the chance that she would eclipse him in popularity. It had brought up a tinge of something he hadn't remembered feeling since the year when he was young and his brother got to go sledding while he stayed home with a cold: jealousy.

He fought back against the feeling hard since he knew the best way to move through something like that was to be glad for the other person's success. He knew the children loved him as dearly as he loved them and now they loved Sandra too. The best thing about love is there is always more than enough for everyone, he reminded himself. When he thought of that, he was better able to celebrate and enjoy the change. He turned to Sandra and applauded her with a big, sincere smile as the children surged forward to surround them both.

"Oh Oh Oh!" Sandra called out as she was whisked away and a smaller group stayed behind with Santa. One of those in the smaller group was Beatrice Carol.

"Santa, oh, Santa," the intrepid reporter called out. "Yoo hoo! Over here! It's Beatrice Carol with World Wide News."

Santa had seen the reporter and had amplified his attention on the children hoping the reporter might move on while he was busy but there she was as the last of the kids finished up talking to him.

"Beatrice, how nice of you to turn out to welcome us with the rest," Santa said. "Did you have a Christmas list to leave me?" He joked with her as the kids laughed with him.

"Why no," she said, seemingly surprised by his jest and taking it more seriously then he meant it for sure. "But I did bring my list of kind acts for Sandra."

Santa kept his smile as he said. "She will certainly love to get it. Why don't you head over her way to hand deliver it?" He reached down to pick up a little boy who had a Christmas list in his hand.

"Mommy says you're the only real Santa," the little boy said. "Is that true?"

"Well, I sure was the only Santa when your mommy was little," he said smiling over at the young woman he recognized as Graciela Ponze. "She was a very good girl." He added that with a wink and received a big smile from the mom.

"Santa," Beatrice Carol interrupted. "How do you feel about the new Santa getting all the attention?" She pointed to the large crowd gathered around Sandra, with a long line of children waiting with lists in their hands, to meet her.

"Honestly?" he said, looking over at his mentee with pride and love in his heart. "I think it is great! Ho Ho Ho! Now let your mommy's Santa look over your list Sebastian." He turned his full attention to the little boy in his arms and away from the reporter. She could make a story out of the change but he was going to do what he had always done: love up the children. It was something he was really, really, good at.

CHAPTER 29

A Soothing Spring

Location: Middle Earth

The idea of pain relief urged them on and Wistle and Ghost had managed to move a little faster than Grander had estimated. The group arrived at the spring in less than two hours and, best of all, it didn't appear the drag, or anyone else, was there at that time.

"This is excellent," Grander said, whispering again though he didn't have to since no one else could hear him. It just came natural in dangerous circumstances. "Wait here while I go and check." Like they had come to see, his perimeter check happened very quickly before he returned.

"Let's make haste," he said, helping to unload the backpacks from Ghost. He was carrying both of them and cried out when one caught as Grander tried to ease it over his swollen hand. "Slip into the water as silently as you can. Float gently about and ask the water wizard who graces the spring to work her healing ways on your injuries. You should need to spend no more than five or ten minutes total there. Mango, you too." The happy dog headed straight to the water without hesitation. She loved getting wet.

Ghost and Wistle didn't hesitate either. Again with this spring, Wistle held no fear of the water as she entered into it and dipped herself fully in its magic. The idea of cleaning off and drinking some fresh water was as appealing as the promise of healing and she had no reservations stepping fully forward. As they slipped into the welcoming, cool, sparkling, waters they smiled for the first time since they had left their deserted island. Immediately, the two could feel the magic of the waters working. They somehow knew to float on their backs. The splint on Wistle's arm floated off and down. It felt as if caring fingers were wrapping around the broken place in her arm and, being a fairy, she could hear a lyrical voice chanting over them. A soft touch of watery hands felt each spot on her that was in pain as the chanting continued. Ghost could not hear the chant but he felt the relief of pain from his hand and arm. The healing waters also mended a deep gouge on his leg he had not mentioned and aided in the healing of his own still healing arm that had been broken during the rescue of Santa months ago.

Both of them expressed their gratitude to the waters as they floated there, not wanting to ever leave. The calm time, however, was short lived.

"GET OUT!" screamed Grander. "GET OUT! The drag is on its way!" The three scrambled for shore but only Mango was able to make it and dash over to where Grander was hiding, without even shaking off, before the drag arrived. Ghost showed Wistle silently how to take a deep breath of air, dove under the water and pulled Wistle with him. He pulled her along to a quiet spot along the side where they had slid into the spring in hopes they could make a quick and silent escape at their first opportunity.

Which wasn't then as the drag swooped down on the sparkling spring scraping its long, sharp talons through the water, clearly hoping to find and injure them that way. As he came to where they were, Ghost and Wistle dove deep down. This time Wistle hadn't even needed Ghost to help. They held their breath as he passed again and they could come back up.

"I know you are here! I shall find you," the drag cackled. "This has all the markings of a spire sprite, disgusting little nobles that they are."

Grander stayed where he was. Truth be told, the drags scared even him. They were a nasty breed. He had kept Mango calm and quiet by his clicking that helped ease distress. While Mango was masked too, running about barking would have added nothing but chaos to the already dangerous situation. Grander knew he had to keep a clear head to get them all away from the spring. He just wasn't sure yet how.

It seemed he wasn't the only one, however, who disliked drags. Ghost and Wistle felt the water around them pulling away and wondered what was happening as they realized they were suddenly fully exposed, without any water to dive into if the drag dived at them again. The previously almost still water had formed into a whirling waterspout rising far above all into the shape of a beautiful mighty water wizard, showing herself in her full form. This drag had dragged his talons one too many times through the glistening, clean spring and the water wizard had tired of his antics.

"Drag," the lyrical voice Wistle had heard chanting quietly over them earlier now boomed in the cavern and it seemed everything, everywhere, silenced. Grander himself watched in awe. Seeing a water wizard in their full water form was more rare then seeing a spire sprite. He bowed in deference to her and she nodded slightly in acknowledgement before addressing the drag.

He, being a drag, showed no deference to her, at all. Instead, he actually looked as though he intended to fly through her! As he came forward boldly, she reached out a watery arm and slapped him back as easily as he had slapped Wistle back earlier.

"You dare to challenge the Lady of the Waters!" she called out with a hint of an unbelieving laughter in her voice. "What do you seek here? How dare you pollute my waters with your foul talons? Be gone with you. There is nothing for you here."

The slap had helped slap some sense into the drag and he came back to her with less hostility now. "Begging your pardon," he said, sniveling. "It's not like anyone *really* knew you lived there. No one ever see's you or anything."

It seemed the whole of the cavern was holding their breath listening to his insolence toward the Lady of the Waters. They all knew she lived there and was responsible for the healing ways of the spring that they all needed and used. There were few bright spots in that part of Middle Earth.

The healing springs provided by the service of this water wizard was probably the best of them. Right now, the drag was lucky that her mission was healing. A different water wizard would have simply drown him with her water.

"Drag," said the water wizard, with annoyance wrapped all around the edges of her voice, that the drag was not bright enough to hear. "I ask again. What is it that you seek in my waters?" She knew, of course, having healed what he was seeking but she had seen and felt the injuries he had forced on Wistle and indirectly on Ghost. They were now under, not just the spire sprites protection, but hers as well.

"There is a human and a fairy who hide from me," he said, flying up closely, and boldly, to look her in the eyes. "They are in my charge."

"If they are in your charge, as you say, why do they seek my waters?" She asked this as innocently as she could. Truth be told, she felt great anger at him for injuring them in the ways he obviously had.

"They are clumsy," the drag replied, flapping back out of reach from the wizard and not looking her in the eye. "They are clumsy and slipped away from me during the night. I believe with the help of a spire sprite."

"A spire sprite?" said the wizard, knowing this to be true. "Surely a spire would not step forward if you were without guilt in their injuries?" It was good the drag had moved from her reach.

The drag ignored her question. He didn't care what she thought. "Release them from your protection," he demanded before adding, "please."

The water wizard smiled and laughed. "Drag, I will allow you to depart far from me, never to return, even if you are injured, for you shall find no healing here," the Lady of the Water bubbled. "Mind my words. Do them no further harm for if they do show up here, it is you who will be well to hide." The whole of the cavern shivered with fear. The spire was pleased. Her words provided them with further needed protection. All others would hesitate to cross her command.

Except the drag, who scoffed. "You are nothing but water who must stay near your pool," he said. "I am much mightier." Giggling could be heard everywhere in the area at his ridiculous words. Nonetheless, he came up closer again but out of her reach still. "Freeze your waters and do not allow them in if they do come this way. Any who aid them will feel my wrath." He spoke it boldly, clearly oblivious to how ridiculous his boisterousness was to all who knew the difference in power between the lowly drags and the mighty water wizards. Drags were only mighty in their own minds.

Powerful water sprayed the drag and dropped him to the ground like a mosquito in a rain storm. He sputtered and spat and tried to fly up again. The whole of Middle Earth knew, however, including the blowhard drag, that until he was completely dry of the Lady of the Lake's water he would not be able to rise again. It was one of her special powers.

"And any who harm them will feel mine," said the stunning water wizard slowly returning into her own form. "Heed my words drag." With that, the beautiful pool was filled again and she was gone.

While she had addressed and splashed the drag, Ghost and Wistle had slipped from where they were and joined Grander and Mango. As the drag squawked and rolled about trying to dry off, they came out and dropped to their knees next to the beautiful, glistening springs.

"Thank you for your healing and protection, dear Lady of the Water," Wistle said for all of them.

"We are deeply indebted and will pay your kindness forward."

"Get safely to the portal so you can," sang out the lyrical voice. This time they all could hear her. "Grander, come back when it is done and tell me your tale so we can live the joy of your quest together. Now, go with haste, and know there are many, even here, that wish you well."

CHAPTER 30

Scooting Along

Location: Middle Earth

For hours, with every step, Ghost and Wistle gave thanks in their heads to the Lady of the Lake for her healing. Their wounds were not gone but they were healing and the pain was greatly reduced. Ghost's hand remained swollen but it could be touched now without him wanting to scream out from the agony of it. Even better, as far as he was concerned, Wistle's arm no longer was visibly broken and her headache was completely gone. The gash on her forehead had closed and she could breathe without pain in her chest. They had made a sling to protect her arm but they knew, with certainty, their injuries would not keep them from safety now. It was only the drag that they feared and that was for good reason. As their spire had predicted, he was searching everywhere for them.

Thanks to Grander, the big bad meanie was having no luck seeing or hearing them but he was remarkably good at swooping down directly toward them, at times. He would be gone, searching other places for hours, and then suddenly they would have to run to get out of his possible path as he swooped low over their area dragging his talons "looking" for what he couldn't see. Once in a while, he swooped so low he would catch on a dried up bush or living plant and pull it up with him, snarling about "plants growing wherever they wanted" as he landed to pluck them off his talons with his beak. The group would take advantage of him being occupied to surge ahead on their path.

Spire sprites, it turned out, needed little rest, but both Ghost and Wistle, and even Mango, felt like they could have slept for days. They were badly in need of some rest and slowing down as a result.

"We stop here for the night," announced the spire suddenly in what was indeed a perfect spot. "You must eat and have sleep." The three had no arguments. They had no interest in food. They were too tired to eat. "I will check the area." As fast as he was, the three were faster. By the time he returned, they were all fast asleep, leaning on each other as they had been the whole way.

None of them so much as stirred even once in the night being so far past the point of exhaustion.

The spire had to shout to wake them.

"We must be going again, my friends," he said, as they all struggled to wake. He had let them sleep six precious hours but they could not risk any more time. Getting out was more important than sleeping. They knew it, too, but hunger now had replaced sleep as their top problem. Grander had anticipated that as well and had a spread of dried fish, coconut, and bottled water out for them. They feasted on it like they had sat down to a banana split with extra chocolate sauce and whip cream.

"Today, we are going to try a shortcut to gain time," Grander said, as they finished up and gathered everything around them so nothing was left behind. "We should be able to save the hours we lost going to see the Lady of the Waters."

"What's the negative side?" Ghost asked, suspecting there was something iffy about the new route.

Grander minced no words. "There is nowhere for us to hide if the drag comes upon us in that stretch." He let the words sink in as Ghost and Wistle looked at each other for confirmation. After so much time together they had developed a way of knowing what the other was thinking without needing words. They nodded their understanding of the situation to Grander and their willingness to take the chance.

"Well, then we best get going so we can get it behind us," said Ghost, checking around them again. Two more days till they could put this all behind them. That kept him going forward. "C'mon girl," he called out to Mango. "Lead the way."

CHAPTER 31

A Tricky Shortcut

Location: Middle Earth

The intrepid group had stayed the course and made good time the whole morning. They were standing on a high ridge looking over the area that Grander had deemed a shortcut. It was a stretch they hadn't crossed when they came into the cavern. From their vantage point, they could see it was a long trail of flat land - a welcome change from the constant up and down of crossing over and around and back down and up again, of the boulders and rocks that were everywhere.

Flat land felt like a huge relief, and would be, as long as the drag didn't come upon them there. There had been no sign of him since the afternoon before but none of them believed he was gone for good. Sooner or later, they knew he would happen upon them. They just didn't want it to be sooner if sooner meant now while they were crossing this long, flat expanse free of any place to hide.

"Okay, here we are at the valley of the sand," said Grander. "As you can see, there is nowhere to hide along this stretch. Normally that should not be a problem since you still can simply continuously move out of his way, but we have an unusual situation where nowhere to hide is more of a problem than it appears. However, I estimate this should take us about an hour to cross as we walk and jog it but it will save us about five hours of time in return."

"That is fantastic, Grander!" Ghost said grinning. He was so ready to be done with this adventure.

"Before you decide to go forward, you need to know something else. You can't step off the path."

"We can't step off the path?" Wistle asked, puzzled. The whole expanse, as far as they could see in all directions, was flat with just a lightly worn path lined out from use over the ages.

"I know the land looks safe but sand snappers live in this valley and you don't want to deal with a sand snapper. They're a lot like the grass snappers you told me you ran into on your way in but much bigger and more voracious. They would like nothing better than to have one of you for dinner."

"So, abuse at the hands of a horrible drag or being dinner for a village of sand snappers?" Ghost considered this. "All to shave five hours off our time? Should we do this?" He didn't ask Grander. He was talking to Wistle and Mango.

"It's an hour Ghost. Surely we can dodge the terrible drag for an hour crossing." Wistle was trying to convince herself.

"Sorry," the tall young cowboy said quietly, making a tough decision for the group. He was willing to risk himself for the time saving, but he wasn't willing to risk Wistle or Mango. "I know its five hours of time we need to save, Grander, but we gotta go around. Better late than bait is how I see it."

Grander didn't argue. He had thought this course might be best for them but even he had to agree as he looked at it that it seemed longer than he remembered. As the group turned around to double back to the turn in the trail, the drag came sweeping by them, talons down. Worse, he had brought another drag with him!

The group watched from the safety of their rock as the two drags took turns scraping back and forth on the path not missing a foot of it.

"I know you're here, human and fairy girl," called out the drag sickeningly. "I won't hurt you. The sand snappers will, though, if you step off this path. I just want to get you safely out of here." As if to prove his point, he deliberately drug his talons into the sand and stirred up at least a dozen eel-like creatures with big eyes and snapping mouths.

"Ha! Sure you do," said the other.

"Silence!" said their drag escort as the group on the boulder shivered. Ghost had made the right call. They would have been in great danger if they had chosen to cross and save the time. The drags would be dragging the valley path for at least an hour. They turned to put that time to good use.

CHAPTER 32

Getting to the Gate

Location: Middle Earth

The rest of the day, hiking the long way around to the gate, passed surprisingly pleasantly. There had been no further sightings of the drag and they hadn't run into any other challenges, other than the hours and hours of circumventing the rocks and boulders all around them. They did so without complaint and shared stories with the spire sprite who seemed to be enjoying having their company. Finally, they got to a point where Grander said they could rest for the night. He checked around while they all plopped down, exhausted and relieved to get a break. Mango fell asleep immediately. Ghost felt awake. He and Wistle had something they wanted to talk to Grander about. When he finished his usual check of the area, the two sat him down.

"Grander, we will never be able to thank you enough for all you are doing for us," Ghost said.

"But we need to ask you another favor." He looked over at Wistle, who nodded her encouragement.

"We've been through a lot and we know we still have to get through the portal soon – probably the hardest thing of all," Ghost said. "Despite everything you're doing for us, we know there's a chance that it won't go well. Or something else could go badly before that even. The favor we need to ask you is that, if anything happens to the two of us, we, well, we would hope you would take care of Mango for us. We could never forgive ourselves if something happened to her, too.

For Wistle and me, we chose this, but Mango just bravely came along."

The spire sprite was too choked up over the sentiment to say anything. It was the most selfless favor anyone had ever asked of him. Spire sprites, being powerful beings, were often asked for favors but nine out of ten requests were for self-serving purposes.

"I will do my very best to keep her safe, no matter the circumstances," he said at last, with more confidence then he felt. They were getting closer to the portal location and he hadn't figured out how he'd get any of them out of Middle Earth but he felt more resolve than ever before to make it so. He had to. He cared now deeply for all three of them. Plus, he was a spire. Spires didn't keep dogs. His friends would laugh at the very notion. The trio needed to get home safely.

"Sleep, human and Wistle of the Woods," he said. "I will think on our plans for escape. Ye on the top side and we of Middle Earth will talk on this tale for all of time to come."

CHAPTER 33

Oh Beatrice Carol

Location: London, England

"Welcome everyone all around the world to our special program "Talking One on One with Two Santas!" Beatrice Carol was shouting her greeting. Not so she could be heard over the loud din of the audience in the stadium, but because she was so excited. "Today, World Wide News, your station that features North Pole news, brings you an exclusive interview with the two Santa's of our world and you are going to love them." The reporter emphasized every word. Sandra found it funny and broke out in a girlish giggle. She and Santa were standing off stage waiting to be introduced.

"She is so dramatic," Sandra said, laughing at the reporter with a measure of true affection. She and Santa had worked with Beatrice enough now that they both enjoyed the interviews and dreaded them all at the same time. The dread came because she usually managed to make their talks together quite dramatic and while the two didn't shrink from attention, they did try to avoid drama.

"Here comes our intro," Santa said to Sandra as Beatrice began the build-up they had become used to hearing from her.

"So children, parents, Christmas-lovers, let's give two of our favorite people in all of the world a giant English welcome! Come on out Santa Claus and Sandra Claus dot dot dot!" A thunderous applause broke out as the two Santa's came out waving at the crowd before they moved over to Beatrice and took their seats on the stage.

"So, Santa and Sandra, it is such a thrill again to sit with you and get caught up on everything that has happened since we met last year on your tour," Beatrice Carol said. "Tell us how this last year as South Pole Santa has gone?"

"Oh, Beatrice, you don't even need to ask!" Sandra said sincerely. "I have the best job in the whole of the world so, of course, this has been a fantastic year." The world didn't know – and didn't need to know - that Santa had been missing for most of the past year, her boyfriend had dumped her and was now missing, the barge building was behind, children seemed to be preferring her over Santa Claus, and she was homesick for St. Annalise. She had no plans to share those things or the angst those things had created within her. Despite having lost her parents at an early age, Sandra had retained her optimism about life. She believed that things generally came right in the end, as it had with Santa's return. Jason would be found, the barge would get done, children would always love Santa, and she would be home soon to St. Annalise. Not to mention that, despite those challenges, the past year had been full of a lot of wonderful things too. In fact, too many to even mention.

"What do you say, Santa?" Beatrice said, turning to the big guy. "How has Sandra done? Is she the perfect South Pole Santa?"

"Ho Ho Ho!" Santa boomed out. He knew how to work a crowd and he knew the devotion to Sandra would be wonderful for this moment. "I think there is no one more perfect in all of the world to be South Pole Santa but let's check with your audience. What do all of you think? Do you believe Sandra is the best South Pole Santa ever?"

The response was breathtaking. The noise level of support the crowd made was even more than Santa had anticipated when he asked.

"Do you need more proof?" he shouted over the crowd to Beatrice Carol, who had to wait a full minute before she could quiet them down and regain control of her interview.

"Okay, I believe that issue has been settled," she said, smiling as the two Santa's continued to smile and wave at the crowd, who went wild again.

The original Santa felt great about it. *Beatrice Carol wasn't the only one who had a flare for the dramatic,* he thought to himself, grinning.

"So the two of you have been on a six-week tour. Any favorite moments to share?" she asked.

The two looked at each other before Sandra answered. "I honestly think we both felt every country was even better than we expected and we had high expectations," she smiled at the reporter. "Everywhere we went was a blast but, for me, I have to admit that I am a little bias and there was one place where I had a little more fun than the other places."

"You did?" Beatrice Carol exclaimed, sure she was on to an unexpected scoop. One of the Santa's had a country she preferred. Surely that wasn't very "Santa like" to admit.

Santa thought he knew where she was going with her answer so he encouraged her. "Yes, yes, I agree, Sandra. One spot did stand out as a favorite," he added in.

"Well, please, don't keep us waiting. Where is this special place? Which country is the most fun? I hope it is my own home country of England, of course," said the reporter as the crowd cheered with agreement.

"Iceland!" the two Santa's burst out together, laughing.

"Iceland?" the reporter repeated, thinking she had heard wrong. She had been to Iceland. It was a nice place but a bit out of the way and too cold for her tastes much of the year. It certainly was no England

"Yes, it's a really wonderful country but, in truth, no more special than every other special place we visited this trip. Except in one way," Sandra said.

"What made it extra special for us this time was that the elves all came with us so we actually got to have a short vacation with our very favorite people," Santa said.

The elves at the North Pole were all watching the broadcast live in Happiness Hall and burst out in cheers. They loved their Santa's. So did the elves watching in Iceland.

"How did I miss that?" Beatrice Carol exclaimed with some exasperation. That would have been a great scoop for her station and she felt a bit like they had pulled a fast one over on her. Sandra could see that look on her face and hastened to alleviate her frustration.

"It was a last minute opportunity and a very quick weekend. But we all loved the special memories we made there."

"How special for the elves," Beatrice said, still a little icily. "So, Santa, moving on. Is there anything special or secret you'd like to announce here this year? Any top-secret toys we should know about early?" She leaned in conspiratorially, hoping to encourage some sharing.

"Well, yes, Beatrice, as a matter of fact, we've got a toy that makes toys that we are anticipating will have huge demand. I mean, what child doesn't dream of being able to make their own toys," Santa knew his crowd and was talking directly to his audience and the camera now. "This year many children will be finding a 3-D Printer for toys under their trees! It's going to be very exciting! That's part of why the elves had to get back – we have lots of these to get in production!"

The audience cheered with excitement over his news.

"What?" said Hiccup, too surprised to even hiccup. "They aren't going to need us anymore!"

"I just got here. I want to make toys," said Redwood with dismay.

"Santa didn't even tell us," Goldie said.

"Hey, now," said Tack loudly. As Toy Production manager he knew about the plans. "It's just a toy that will make other *little* toys. Nothing big. They'll still need us for all the big stuff that the children really want."

The elves were quiet for a minute wanting to believe Tack but very suspicious of this new toy they hadn't heard about.

Redwood summed up their feelings the best. "Well, please don't assign me to that toy-making line, Tack," he said. "I don't want to make any kind of toy that makes other toys. No way."

"Me neither!"

"Or me!"

Oh gingerbread snaps, thought Tack. "Shhhhhh!" he said. "Watch the show!"

"I hope some kids want something made out of wood," said Redwood wistfully. "That's my specialty."

"*hiccup*! Please pass the candy bowl. *hiccup*!"

"My, oh my," Beatrice Carol was saying. "A toy that makes toys. That does sound exciting indeed. Now Sandra, do you have something to add? Last year you asked children all over the world to be kind and send in their acts of kindness lists to you. As I recall, you wanted to encourage kindness and reward those efforts by drawing twelve children's names from those submitted to visit the Pole. Do you have an update on that?"

As a matter of fact, she did. She had spent hours and hours on the phone with Birdie and Christina to talk about her idea and flush it out. She was actually beyond excited about her news now, and only wished the two women were there with her to share in the announcement. Santa knew all about it and thought it was one of the best ideas he had heard in centuries. He wished he had thought of it and was glad he had shared his news about the 3-D printers first before she made her announcement.

"Yes I do have something special to share," Sandra said. "An announcement of something I'm really, really excited about." Like Santa, she, too, now turned to talk to the crowd and the camera instead of just facing Beatrice.

"Today, right here on your show, Beatrice, we, Santa and I," she emphasized the two of them. She wanted nothing that wasn't done in complete accord and approval of her mentor. "The two of us announce that we are going to be starting a new school called, 'The Academy of Kindness.'"

The crowd in the arena went crazy! So did Beatrice. So did the elves.

"The Academy of Kindness?" they pondered almost altogether. This was news to them too. Elves loved surprises, if they were sweet like candy or came in Christmas wrap, but surprises about fancy toys and new schools just made them concerned. Tack passed the candy bowl around.

"The Academy of Kindness," Beatrice Carol repeated. "How spectacular does that sound?"

"Oh, it really is going to be," said Sandra, exuding the enthusiasm for it that she felt. This was her new baby and she was looking forward to everything about getting it up and running. "It is going to led by me and one of my very best friends in the whole world, Ambyrdena Snow, Birdie to her friends. Christina Annalise, of the spectacular Annalise Academy where I attended school, has agreed to be our advisor on this project. We haven't got all the details worked out yet but it will be called The Academy of Kindness or AOK for short. And our slogan is 'Where everything is A-OK.'"

"Where everything is A-OK," the reporter repeated her words again as if stunned by the announcement. "I get it A is for academy, O is for of and K is for kindness! So clever! Makes me want to go back to school!" she said, surprising the Santa's. "How do I get in?"

Sandra laughed. "Well Beatrice, this school is strictly for children and, more specifically, for children selected from the kindness lists they send in. We don't know exactly, yet, how many, or for how long, and exactly what they'll study or what activities they'll do, but we do know that we are establishing the academy to help change the world."

"You are a strong supporter of the power of kindness, Sandra," the reporter said as if that was a strange thing to believe in.

"Oh, I am," said Sandra smiling. "And so are boys and girls all around the world! They are so amazing and changing the world with their devotion to making a difference through being kind. It is remarkable, Beatrice. Of course, I believe in kindness. I see and read about it in action every, single, day."

"Well, while I love the idea, I do have to say, it does seem simple to be kind," said Beatrice. "Do we really need a school for it?"

"That is an excellent point," Sandra said. "In truth, absolutely not. You're right that all of us can be kind simply by choosing that as our way of living. In reality, though, as a world, we still have a long ways to go on kindness being a priority. At this academy – which really will be more like a camp since time spent there will only be a few days – we will be emphasizing all sorts of ways children can help lead the way in changing our world. They will leave as certified 'advocates of kindness – AOK's' and we hope that certification will grow to mean something in this world of ours."

The audience broke into applause as Sandra and Santa grinned and Beatrice Carol waited again for a break.

"Well, Sandra, you have done it again," she exclaimed. "You've brought us big news."

"Oh I'm not done yet," Sandra said, so excited to share the next part of her surprise.

"Really?" Beatrice said, trying to contain her own excitement about this big scoop she was getting again for World Wide Network News. "Please continue."

"The biggest news is where this school is going to be held," Sandra said teasingly. The auditorium broke out in an overall buzz as they all considered this news. She waited. *I'm getting to be just like Santa,* she thought. *I like to be a little dramatic.*

"Where? Where?" the elves were all yelling at the TV screen. They were excited themselves since they loved children and kindness and were experts on both.

"Okay, okay," Sandra said grinning as people were shouting out "tell us! tell us!"

"Well, starting next year, which will be the first year, the Academy of Kindness will officially be held in a special part of the all-new, still-being-completed, South Pole Village barge!" She was grinning so hard about it her mouth hurt.

"Did you hear that, everyone?" Beatrice Carol shouted out to the room who obviously had heard it but the reporter always went for the dramatic. "We are at last going to get our first look at the South Pole Village barge!"

"Yes indeed," said Sandra. "The barge is scheduled to be completed - including with rooms for the academy members - by ths time next year and we will be giving a brief media tour then so all the world can have a quick look before the important work of Christmas preparation gets fully underway. That's all we want to say about it today," she glanced at Santa, who nodded his head in confirmation and as a strong sign to Beatrice not to ask more, "but I am beyond excited about my new home and how spectacular it is going to be."

"Sandra! We love you!" The audience burst out. "Sandra! Sandra!" they chanted. It was a wonderful end to her announcement. Unless you were Santa. No one was shouting his name.

CHAPTER 34

The Academy of Kindness

Location: North Pole Village

Sandra wasted no time at all when she got back from the tour to get together with her friends and get some solid planning started on her announced Academy of Kindness. It was the perfect something to take her mind off her friends missing in Middle Earth. Making a difference in the world would help make a difference in her own life. She smiled at the thought, thinking of the irony in it.

"Hey Bird, what you reading?" Sandra asked, as she joined her best friend in one of the meeting rooms in Happiness Hall. Birdie seemed deep in thought, with a rare frown on her face, reading over the paper she held in her hands. She hastily folded it and put it in the envelope she also held.

"A letter from my mom." Before she could say more, Spence came bounding into the room with an unusual level of exuberance for him.

"Hey Spence," Sandra said, still looking at Birdie, feeling like she wasn't telling her something.

"I have missed you two," Spence said coming over and giving Sandra and Birdie both a big hug. His hug seemed to shake Birdie out of her fog over the letter and she gave him a big hug and smile back.

"Thanks for coming to meet with me up north here, you two. I know it was a last minute change of location," Sandra said, happy to see both of her best friends smiling. "Now that I'm back from the tour, I'm just so excited to get started on the plans for the new Academy of Kindness program. I have so many ideas! I couldn't wait another day to talk about it!

"So, first of all on our agenda, thanks to you both for agreeing to be on the board of directors.

And Birdie, thanks for agreeing to be the official director of the academy!"

Birdie nodded and smiled at her best friend. She was very excited about the opportunity. She had spent hours with Christina walking around St. Annalise and talking about possibilities for the new endeavor. It all felt custom made for her talents. She and Spence had actually been taking college classes online now that St. Annalise was connected to the outside world thanks to Spencer's and Network Nater's work. The little elf had worked tirelessly with Spencer and the two had become close friends.

Spence, not surprisingly, was acing all his online classes in his double major of physics and cyber technology. Birdie was doing equally well in her customized world cultures major that combined her love of cultures – human and magic – with her love of languages. She and Sandra both were gifted with picking up languages easily. Birdie was especially lucky to understand bird languages. To Birdie, being the head of an academy that would welcome children from all over the world to share the power of kindness seemed to be a dream job made just for her from her best friend.

"I've asked Christina to also be on our board and would like to add one more," Sandra said. "Do either of you have any ideas for who could be our fifth member?"

"What about Santa?" Spencer asked.

"I thought about him too, Spence, but he turned me down. He didn't really give me a specific reason but I felt a little like he wanted this to be my thing," said Sandra still wondering about it a little.

"How about Crow?" Birdie asked. She loved doing things, of course, with her boyfriend but she also felt he was the perfect choice to be a board member for the Academy of Kindness. He loved kids and was always kind.

"I like that idea," Sandra said. "He's like Gunny – just a big goofy kid himself. Must be a Holiday brother's trait."

"Well, don't forget Ghost is a Holiday brother, too," Birdie said, thinking of her boyfriend's complicated and moody twin.

"Ha! Good point," Sandra said. "Maybe acting like a big kid isn't a Holiday trait, maybe its immaturity that is!" The two girls giggled while Spence rolled his eyes.

"Hey, no picking on the guys," he jumped in to defend his friends. "Ghost is just misunderstood."

Now it was the girls who rolled their eyes but neither said anything negative. He was their friend too and he was currently doing something very important for all of them. Plus, they had no idea if he was even safe. Just thinking about all that made their mood more somber.

"Moody or funny, he's a good guy," Sandra said to be sure they knew how she really felt. She was very thankful for all the members of the Holiday family.

"Yes, Crow would be a great addition," Sandra said. "If he agrees, we have a full board. I am so excited about this! Now can we talk some logistics? Like when we hold our first session?"

"How about the first week of August of next year? That's usually one of the slowest weeks of the year for production it seems like," Spence suggested.

"I think that is a great week too," Sandra said.

"Me too," added Birdie. "So it sounds like we have a date for our first ever AOK session but what about this year? Do the children selected for the tour of North Pole Village wait till next year and get in the first class? Or do we have to speed it up and hold a first session this August?

That's not that far away! Not to pressure you Sand, but I really don't think we can pull all of this together by then."

"I've been thinking a lot about that," Sandra said. "I would like them to be in it since they are obviously all kind but we're just not going to be ready and it's not really what they signed up for anyway. Instead, let's give them an overnight at the North Pole as we planned, and a full tour since there is nowhere like it in the whole of the world and you just know they will love it! I mean who doesn't love the North Pole? We all sure did the first time we came here."

"And every time since then." Spencer added sincerely.

"Exactly!" Sandra said. "I think we'll have every class come here for one night every session of AOK camp, if it's okay with Santa. The South Pole Village barge is going to be spectacular but there is nowhere anywhere like North Pole Village."

"Perfect," Birdie said. "How about, for this first group, since we don't exactly know what we're doing yet, we see how it goes and then maybe invite them back in the future to be part of the academy?" She looked at Sandra and Spence who nodded in agreement.

"Okay good. So now, what do we do with this year's group and what will we do with the future academy members?" Birdie asked.

"Oh, I have lots of ideas," Sandra said. She reached for her big book full of notes so she wouldn't forget to share any of them.

CHAPTER 35

Time to Go

Location: Middle Earth

The group in Middle Earth got a minimum amount of sleep wanting to push on to allow as much time as possible to get through the entryway. They knew that the drag would undoubtedly be waiting for them there. They also knew their time of being masked by Grander's magic was soon coming to an end. Somehow, they were going to have to convince the dragoon posted there to open the gateway and then get through without being caught by the drag that was relentlessly looking for them. It seemed almost hopeless, but Grander had a plan.

"You know that as a spire, I have the ability to mask perceptions for a short time," he said to the traveling duo, who were still setback by their injuries but getting stronger each day. "I believe that should allow me to be able to influence the dragoon to open the entry point just long enough for you to slip through." Ghost and Wistle were listening closely to every word, encouraged by what he was saying.

"To work, it will mean we will have to get you in a place close to the opening without the searching drag finding you. That may be our biggest challenge but it can be done. We have been fortunate and clever so far."

"I know we can," Ghost said, feeling both exhilarated and concerned about the day ahead. He reached over and held Wistle's hand. The fairy was surprised but pleased. They had come so far together and his reaching out said, without words, that they would see it through to the topside together. "We are under the protection of a wise and caring spire. No matter the outcome, you have given us your all."

Wistle nodded at the words and Mango barked.

"Then we must be off," said Grander wanting to waste not a minute of the day. "This is the day our paths will part but it will be a fond farewell for sure."

They spent the day as they had almost every other day in Middle Earth, going up and around the many boulders that made up this part of where they were. Rarely did their trail take them to flat places with nothing in their path. It was slow going but, at last, they arrived at their destination.

To no one's surprise, the opening was closed. It would have been too good to be true if it had been open. The guard dragoon appeared to be dozing on his perch next to the closed gate. The group stopped far back from the area where they could see the situation and decide their next step.

"This is good," said Grander. "We are here before the drag so the dragoon does not know of our situation. He has no need to feel particularly concerned. Typically, absolutely nothing interesting happens at these portals – few want to visit us here in Middle Earth. I doubt you two will be surprised to hear that." He broke out in an impish spire sprite grin.

"Here will be our plan," he continued. "We will take this same zig-zag path between and over the rocks until we get there." He stopped and pointed to a wide space just before the portal. The area right in front of the portal was bare for about a hundred yards. It had what looked like beach sand there that had probably blown in from the big cavern on the other side over hundreds of years.

"Then I will not speak with the dragoon but instead give him the idea that he must open the portal. As soon as he does, you three must rush through without turning back or slowing down.

Run until you are clearly on the top side. The cave on the other side is still dangerous for you so go through it quickly to the top of the cay. Only there will you be safe." He urged them knowing their injuries were repairing still. They had been able to remove Wistle's sling and Ghost's hand was smaller in size but still almost twice its normal size. Their injuries were better but still painful.

Neither Ghost nor Wistle thought moving fast would be a problem at all. They wanted to be far, far away from this adventure they had started months ago. Mango was always fast with her four strong legs. They nodded their understanding.

"Good," Grander said. "Then we must say our goodbyes now. I shall never forget your bravery and our time together. It has been my honor to serve you."

"Despite this difficult time," Ghost said. "I believe I would still choose this path, if I had it do over again, simply to have met you, Grander of the Spire. It has been *our* honor to know you." Wistle said nothing but reached down and pulled the spire to her for a great hug – a very rare action for a Shan fairy but words fell far short of the gratitude she felt for this mighty miracle worker. She reached out and pulled in Ghost and even Mango came over and got in on the group hug.

"I shall tell fairies everywhere of your kindness to us," Wistle vowed to him. "You will be known in lore for time to come as a hero to our kind." Then she stepped away from Grander, turned to Ghost, pulled him close, and kissed him. Ghost realized in that moment how right that was. They had become more than then mere friends. They each cared more about the other then they did themselves. A look of genuine affection passed between them followed by a big grin as the kiss ended, knowing it was the promise of more to come.

"We move on now, my friends," Grander said, catching the meaning in their sweet moment. Spires too appreciated the wonder of love. "Safe travels to you and please, never return, for this part of Middle Earth is really meant only for those of us from here. There is peril for all others.

Goodbye, girl." He reached out and pet Mango awkwardly. She licked him with gusto in return.

It helped lighten the mood as they all laughed at Grander's expression.

Despite their cautious, circuitous approach, it took them little time to get to the entry area and they scrambled to get in position. Grander zipped over to the dozing dragoon and whispered words that neither Ghost nor Wistle understood. Just as he did, he turned, waved their way with a smile and faded away. Their three days were up. There was no time for any of them to be nostalgic as Grander had been successful. The dragoon stirred, reached to his left and the gateway opened – just as the searching drag arrived!

"STOP!" he screamed to the dragoon. "STOP! You are being bewitched by a spire! Close the gate!"

"Go, Mango, go!" Ghost shouted as the dog surged through the opening. "C'mon Wistle! Hurry! It's closing! We must get through! We must –

"AAAAAHHHHH!" He screamed as the drag swooped low and caught him up in his claws.

"I GOT YOU!" the drag snarled. Their masking had worn off at the same time as Grander had disappeared. "And now you." He said looking at Wistle as he moved Ghost to being held in just one of his strong talons and swooped down again to collect Wistle.

"RUN, Wistle!" Ghost was shouting. Grander too, though none of them could hear him.

"Not without you!" she shouted back, furious at the drag that had ruined their return. "Drop him now!" the brave, bold fairy swung her backpack at the drag as he came at her, which kept him from snagging her and getting only the backpack, but now she had nothing to swing at him as he came around for his next dive.

Ghost was kicking and punching and swinging at the drag but to no travail. It was as if he was a toothpick to the strong creature.

Grander too was now powerless to help. The gate was all but closed and Wistle couldn't get through any longer either.

"Run, Wistle!" Ghost shouted again. "Take cover!" And then he had an inspired thought.

"Orb, Wistle, orb!" he screamed as though his life depended on it and perhaps it did now. "Orb and save us both by telling the others."

She knew he was right. The gate was nearly closed but she could still fit through in her orbed state and with her sling off she knew it was possible again but the agony of leaving him behind played across her face. She looked at the gate closing and back at Ghost, whose face reflected nothing but love and concern.

"ORB!" he shouted as the drag began his swoop down on the fairy he had grown to care deeply about.

And she did.

But she was Wistle, a mad Shan fairy now in love. She did not go direct to the closing but instead flew to Ghost. "I will bring help, my hero," she said as she darted to the closing entryway giving the nasty drag one last look of complete disdain.

"Never come back!" Ghost shouted. "Never, Wistle! Do you hear? Tell the others! Never!"

She heard him as she darted all the way out of the cavern in her orbed state, clear up to the top of Cassandra Cay next to Mango, where she returned to her full size and broke down sobbing.

From start to finish, the whole rescue attempt had been horrible. Now it was tragic.

CHAPTER 36

A New Inmate

Location: Drag Jail

The prisoners almost never heard anything happening outside their bleak, quiet room of cages but on this morning they heard the yelling far before they knew what was happening. To Jason, he thought it sounded like English being spoken, or yelled to be more accurate, but he couldn't quite make it out. In fact, it sounded like Gunny if his ears weren't deceiving him.

His heart raced and he dared for a minute to hope. He didn't much care for the big Texan cowboy but that was all about Sandra and, right now, he was thinking the runner-up to Sandra would easily move to the top of his favorite person list if he was here to get him out. They could call themselves "brothers from another mother." Any guy who came that far to set him free was family to him.

"I said, for at least the eighty-fifth time, keep your creepy beak, your creepy claw things, and your smelly feathers off me! Don't you birds ever take a shower?" The voice was yelling loud enough to hear parts of it now. *Probably coming on a little strong for the drags*, Jason thought.

Better tone it down Gunny. Stay calm.

"Quit touching me!"

"I'm walking here!"

As the door to the cage area opened, the captives could hear the drags just cackling in return.

"Why we're starting to get right crowded in here, boys," the drag guard entering first said to the three prisoners, who were all staring his way trying to figure out what was going on. Nothing ever happened there, including no new ways to break out, and this felt big.

Please let it be Gunny, Jason thought. *Please.*

It was! Jason actually smiled as he saw the lanky cowboy coming into the room. He hadn't smiled since the day he arrived.

"Jason!" the cowboy exclaimed, as he scanned the room he had entered and looked over at Jason and the others. Jason could now fully see who it was that was making all the noise.

"Ghost?" Jason stammered, the smile vanishing, as he saw the handcuffs Ghost was wearing. In all of the versions he had played out in his mind about how he would get out of there, or who would come and get him, not once had Ghost ever made the mix.

"Jason! I sure didn't want to find you this way but I've got to tell you that it sure is great to see you," Ghost said forgetting for a minute why he was there in his Texas-size excitement to finally see his quasi-friend that he had set off to rescue months ago.

"Oh, such a lovely reunion," cackled one of the drags. "That's exactly why we brought you here.

See? We're actually very thoughtful. We knew you would want to spend some quality time together." He reached for the keys to one of the remaining cages, the one furthest away from Jason, while the other held back a defiant Ghost who glared at his ghastly captors. The drag barely noticed. They ate defiance for lunch around there.

When the door swung open, the drag who had kept him from returning home shoved him into the cage. To Ghost, it actually felt great. For the first time in days, he wasn't being clawed at by that giant drag buffoon. His loud mouth returned.

"I demand to see a lawyer!" he yelled. "I know my rights! You can't keep me here without a reason. I've done nothing!"

The two drags stood back, looking amused, before they burst out laughing. "A lawyer?" one said. "Can you believe that? He wants himself a lawyer. Uh," he paused and got close to the cage. "I'm afraid we are fresh out of those down here."

"Fresh out?" the other drag repeated cackling loud and slapping his wing against his side in merriment. "Yeah, as in, we never had 'em in the first place." The two cackled loudly about their private joking that wasn't funny at all.

"Then I demand to send a letter to my family!" Ghost sputtered, taken aback by this news. *What were his rights down here?* He was beginning to wonder. And worry.

This time the two doubled over laughing and headed to the door. "That one there," one drag said, pointing over at Jason. "He ain't nothing but boring, but you, Mr. Cowboy, you are a funny human." He shut the door with a clang and Ghost hit his still oversized hand on one of the bars of his cage. It throbbed but he welcomed the pain. It felt real when nothing else really did.

CHAPTER 37

Cooking up a Plan

Location: Drag Jail

Jason and Ghost spent several hours catching up once Ghost settled down and could listen. He met Thogo who joined in the conversation and Danger who didn't. Jason struggled with the conflict he felt of knowing how badly things had gone for his rescue party and the feeling of relief having Ghost there with him. Another human. That he knew. Who cared if they hadn't really liked each other when they met at the North Pole last year? Now they had something in common. It was awful and fantastic at the same time.

Jason particularly had quizzed Ghost, over and over, on how Sandra was doing. The truth was, Ghost didn't know much. He had purposefully kept away from her most of the time before he had volunteered for this rescue mission. Ghost had left before the agreement for Gunny's release was worked out so he gave Jason a full report on what he knew. Jason was heart sick realizing that his selfish actions had such deep repercussions on so many others. Ghost could totally relate to those feelings since his action taking Santa last year had also had impacts on Gunny and others besides himself. He came clean with Jason on what he had done. Jason didn't care. Ghost had more than paid a price for it, having looked for him for months, and now landing there in drag jail.

Jason wanted to know, too, about how Christina Annalise was taking him missing for so long.

"Did you see my mom?"

Ghost hesitated. He wasn't sure what all to tell him but finally decided the truth was best. "I did," he said. "She didn't look too good. She's pale and she's lost weight. She's worried but everyone is keeping an eye on her and they're all leaning on each other."

Jason winced at the news. *I'm such a jerk*, he thought. *I should be king of the jerks, not king of the fairies.*

"Might be the same thing," Thogo noted, smiling. He couldn't help it if he could hear thoughts.

"Fairies aren't my favorite."

Jason just cocked an eyebrow at him. They weren't his favorite either and he was one.

"So is anyone else coming for us that you know of?" Jason asked Ghost, trying not to sound hopeful and trying to ignore any more comment about fairies by Thogo.

"I told Wistle, no matter what, no one was to try. No matter what," he said it again to emphasize his strong instructions and to believe they were heard. "No one should come look for us through that entry. I really don't believe they will. Wistle knows it's not the way."

"Even if they try, I really doubt they could get in. The dragoon there is likely to keep that gate locked shut. It may never be opened again," Jason said. He didn't feel as confident as Ghost. In fact, knowing she had already been trying to find him he suspected that now, with two of them missing, Sandra would be hard to stop from coming, if there was any way that she could. He could only imagine how tough it must be for her having the two of them, and Gunny, all gone.

Ghost didn't say so, but he was thinking the same thing about Wistle. There was no way she wouldn't keep trying to get them rescued. He had hope. Jason felt the same. He had pretty much decided that all hope was gone but now it came flooding back to him. He dared to day dream and he dared to hope. After more than a year there, however, he was also a realist.

"Danger," he nodded over to the sullen drag. "Let's talk again on ways to escape this place so Ghost can hear too. Maybe he'll have some new ideas."

Rescue attempts and negotiations take time. They had to find a way. More than ever, he wanted to go home.

CHAPTER 38

An Important Appeal

Location: The Supreme Council of Fairies

Wistle and Mango had not been on the cay long when Rio spotted them and brought help. Despite objections from everyone there, Wistle barely rested at St. Annalise before heading to the one place she felt could help – with her own kind. It had taken weeks to get a chance to be before them but now the Fairy Council had been meeting for hours.

Somehow, it seemed, Reesa had failed to mention to the other Fairy Council members that she had heard from Sandra about the cave entry and had information on where Jason, their returned King of Fairies was likely being held. She now insisted that it was simply because the information was just rumor and she did not address rumors. Not to mention, there was a rescue party, including one of their own, that had been sent and needed time to succeed. None present there on the Fairy Council could challenge her on whether that was why she hadn't mentioned it, or not, since she was the appointed ruler and therefore beyond reproach. They knew, however, rumor or not, that Reesa had no real interest in helping the supposed fairy king return.

The truth was that Reesa did indeed prefer to have Jason stay where he was. He was safe enough.

She didn't really care that the drags had no right to hold him. The drags were unpleasant but they were not a killing species. His return would be disruptive to her rule and, in true Shan fashion, she didn't want to be bothered with something so inconvenient.

Now, as she sat listening to the debate amongst the others on the Council about what to do, Reesa felt herself feeling nothing but complete annoyance with Wistle, the would-be rescue fairy who had insisted on time in front of the Council and caused all this stir. Reesa had managed to keep Wistle away from the Council meetings for several weeks and refused to give her time to plead her case before them, which was her right as the appointed ruler and Council chair. The very determined fairy had dared to violate Reesa's order to stay away and had boldly burst into their meeting that afternoon. Reesa had called for order, and to have her removed, but Wistle called out that she had news of their king and the others had insisted she be allowed to speak. They had peppered her with questions as she blurted out her story, not once looking at Reesa but only at the others. They all looked aghast when they learned that it wasn't Sandra who had been holding Jason, as they had been allowed to continue to believe, but the drags. This was devastating news. They knew that drags were notoriously hard to bargain with and even the most supreme fairy preferred to avoid any kind of encounter with them at all. To hear Jason was being held by them was grave news indeed.

"Reesa? Reesa? Do you have an answer to that question?" It was Juna, the outgoing chairperson, addressing her. Reesa had so little interest in this topic that her attention wandered in and out.

"What was the question?" she asked in her sullen, haughty, way. She actually felt like sticking her tongue out at Wistle despite how childish that was for a Shan fairy – or anyone else over the age of say, ten.

"Who shall we send to call on the drags and insist on our king's release? Really, Reesa, this is a matter of grave concern. You must give it your full attention," said Juna.

"I must?" Reesa said, amused. "I believe you forget yourself on who you are speaking to. Your ruler 'must' not do anything."

Boldly, Juna continued. "Forgive me, Reesa, but you are our appointed ruler only until our king has returned."

This only served to enrage the ruling fairy but she said nothing to give her anger away. Calmly, she inquired, "Who here than in this hall would care to call on the drags?"

No one raised their hand or called out that they would. Only Wistle. "I would," she said strongly.

"If no others will join me, I will still go."

"Even after everything you have been through?" asked one of the Fairy Council members just short of amazed. Few fairies were willing to be inconvenienced in such ways, especially when they understood it would be unpleasant.

"Even now. Jason Annalise is our King! You all should be volunteering." She said, despite knowing she could be addressed for insolence. None challenged her because each of them knew she was right. "And Ghost Holiday is my friend. He saved my life! Not once, but several times. I owe him my life and I will keep trying to secure his release until he too is free."

"Reesa, it is traditional that the ruler of our kingdom represent us at such times as this," said Juna. "Perhaps you should be the one to volunteer to go as our negotiator and representative."

Reesa looked at her as if she had grown another head.

"I do not wish to go," she said simply. "The drags are smelly and unpleasant and I do not believe that human-raised Jason is our king. He is not worth the bother and neither is the other. He is a human. There are already too many of those."

"A human who saved my life!" Wistle protested. "And you do know Jason is our king, I know you do. We all do. You may not like it - I admit I didn't like it either when he was uncovered - but we do not get to decide the ways of our world."

"Well, you cannot go on your own since you do not represent us officially, and no one else has agreed to go so, happily, this talk is over." Reesa said, still unmoved by Wistle's protest and moving to adjourn the meeting and put the matter behind them.

"I will go."

All the eyes at the table turned to the quietest fairy there and the only Shanelle allowed a place on the Supreme Fairy Council.

"You, Divina?" Reesa said, surprised. "You would go and represent this Council to argue for the return of a Shan fairy king?"

"A Shan *and* Shanelle fairy king, your reverence," Divina said, using the title given to Reesa as the acting ruler.

"All the more reason we should leave him there," Reesa sniffed. "So appalling."

"I will go with you, Wistle," Divina continued. "I am a representative of this Council and therefore can officially help bargain for his release." She turned to face the Supreme Council members. "Do I have your consent?"

There were "ays" of agreement from all but Reesa who had simply stood and left the room. This matter was of no interest to her.

# # #

Wistle left the meeting with the Supreme Council of Fairies trembling, but humbled by the Shanelle fairy's willingness to accompany her. She had likely made an enemy in Reesa and that caused her some discomfort to consider. "Thank you

Divina for your willingness to be my escort," she said to the quiet Shanelle fairy. "We must next visit the Esteemed High Council of Magical Beings and expand our numbers. You and I alone would have little impact on the difficult drags but if we are enough in number, they will have to see us and comply."

She said it with confidence. More confidence than she felt.

CHAPTER 39

Staying and Going

Location: North Pole Village

The appeal to the Esteemed High Council of Magical Beings had gone better than the appeal to her own kind, Wistle thought afterward. Sometimes even she found the Shans to be too much.

"Oh, fairy dust!" she exclaimed to no one but herself. "I have been hanging out with humans too much if I'm thinking thoughts like that about my own kind." *Or at least one human*, she thought.

One human who she was trying hard to get rescued right now.

The Council had respected Divina making the request on behalf of the Supreme Council of Fairies and therefore elevated the matter to take action. They didn't personally care about Jason or Ghost, but if the fairies did then they were obligated to visit the drags and secure their release.

The team had agreed they would leave in the morning using the magical realm portal system. The same system that allowed the Council, and other magical beings, to travel anywhere in the realm, including the North Pole, when they visited. The minute Sandra heard the news that Wistle and Divina had arrived through the North Pole portal, and had managed to get a rescue team in place, she went running to find them. She had been trying to locate the fairy for weeks as she wanted to hear everything about what had happened in Middle Earth. With Wistle in the fairy realm she had had no way to find her. As she walked up, Wistle began shaking her head.

"No Sandra, no," Wistle began firmly. "I have no time to talk and I know you are going to say you want to go on this rescue too. But only five of us can go and I managed to talk three of the Magical Council members into coming along. That means there is no extra room for you to come too."

"Wistle, I'm going," Sandra said obstinately, feeling determined. "It's not a choice. Surely you can understand that. I know how hard you have worked to put this rescue party together so I can only believe that it isn't just for Jason but that you've come to care about Ghost too." Sandra looked at Wistle and, by her expression, could see that she was more right than she realized. The fairy had never told anyone how she felt - not even Ghost directly yet - but her actions and words had said volumes to anyone paying attention. Sandra had been. Wistle started to object to what she had said and then thought better of it. She didn't care that Sandra, or anyone else really, knew how she felt. "And we both care about Jason," Sandra finished. "I have to go."

"Divina, would you mind going on this release mission orbed?" Wistle asked the kind fairy, giving in to Sandra's demand.

Divina didn't even hesitate. She felt relieved. She was kinder than she was brave, though both Wistle and Sandra, would forever call her brave, and forever feel in her debt for stepping up.

Without her, they would likely not have had this chance. But Divina had never met a drag and what she had heard of them frightened her. Staying orbed made it more likely she could stay out of their reach. "I am happy to attend this important meeting in my orb," she said.

"Okay, Sandra, you're in," Wistle said. Sandra nodded her head and ran off to tell the others.

It took no time at all for Sandra to regret telling anybody else anything about her plans. Between Gunny and Em, the decibel level at the Pole must have raised one hundred percent.

"HE'S *MY* BROTHER!" Gunny shouted at her again, as if yelling would make her understand his point better. He paced around the room, talking as much with his hands as his voice. Em only made it worse.

"I am going Sandra. These are drags, a kind of inferior dragon. Very inferior. I will go in my elf state and change into my mighty delgin state when we arrive," Em said as boldly and assuredly as Sandra had ever heard her. "They will have to bow to my size alone."

They both had powerful arguments, Sandra thought. She knew if it was her brother, probably nothing could keep her from going and both Em and Gunny had committed their own lives to saving and protecting her.

"Em, that would be fantastic. I know you would be the bravest one of all of us," Sandra said sincerely. "But I've learned from the studies Christina Annalise has done about the drags that part of the peril of visiting them is that no magic works in their part of Middle Earth so you wouldn't be able to go to your giant delgin size."

"If there is room to spin, there is no way to stop me," Em said defiantly.

"I wish that were true," Sandra said.

"Well Ghost is still my brother and I've never had a spec of magic in me to count on, so I'm going," Gunny was talking quieter now but in some ways Sandra was finding that more intimidating than when he was shouting at her because the answer was still the same. No.

Truth was, in her perfect world, she would take both of them. Having them by her side would feel safer and more powerful to her then the royal bunch she would be accompanying. But the choice wasn't hers and the time for talking was done.

"I can't take either one of you," she said quietly, suddenly overwhelmed with the emotion of the importance of the next day. "It isn't my choice to leave you here. It is the requirements of the situation and nothing else. Can you now just, please, help me think about my appeal to them?"

Santa was there with them as well. Zinga and Breezy, too, but now it was Santa who wanted to speak.

"Sandra, would you like me to go in your place?" he asked, catching Sandra a little off-guard.

She didn't want anyone to go in her place but Santa was her mentor and harder for her to turn down than Em and Gunny. She stood there thinking about it, until she realized they were all standing there waiting for her to answer.

"I appreciate it so much Santa, and perhaps that would be the best choice under the circumstances, but I feel in my heart that I must go." She didn't look at Gunny when she added, "I need to see Jason for myself. It's been too long and I need him to know, from me, how hard we've been looking for him. I think he would want me there."

"Ha!" said Gunny out loud. "Just another thing I don't like about the guy then. I have to hope the last person he would want to see there in this super dangerous situation is the girl he used to care about." He suspected Sandra was still the girl Jason cared about but he refused to say it out loud.

"I'm sorry, Gunny," Sandra said quietly, feeling a little bit of anger now at him and walking to the door. "I'm going." She said this to the whole room. "I will be back tomorrow with Jason and Ghost. Work on a celebration party if you'd like to help."

Her voice, and her hands, were both shaking as she closed the door behind her.

CHAPTER 40

The Rescue Delegation

Location: Drag Jail

They all were there the next morning with worried expressions on their faces, waiting at the portal to see Sandra and the two fairies off. They were there to show support and wish the rescue party all the best in the challenge they faced: bringing home their friends – a brother and a king.

They each hugged them all with Em clinging to Sandra's leg to where Sandra had to lean down and promise her little delgin that she would be back.

"It'll be okay," Sandra whispered to Em. "We'll all be back, with Jason and Ghost, very soon. I won't let them keep us too." She knew that was part of what they were all worried about. No one understood the drags well so they couldn't be sure this rescue party wouldn't be held against their will too.

"I don't care about Jason and Ghost," Em said in her stubborn way. "Please just stay."

"Em, you love everyone," Sandra reminded her. "You can't fool me." She knew the tough little delgin's true heart.

"Okay, brave, rescue girl, please be careful. Come back to us," Gunny said, before leaning in and whispering to her only. "Come back to me."

She leaned briefly against him in return and brushed his cheek with a kiss. "Come get us if we don't," she said, squeezing his hand, and looking at him so he would see she meant it. "Nothing, or nobody, could keep me from it. I'll bring Em," he said the last part with a smile, knowing it would help lighten up the mood. Sandra smiled too and a laugh escaped her lips.

"Ready, girls?" she asked of Wistle and Divina. They were joining the rest of their delegation at the Council headquarters along the way. Divina switched to her orb size and the three entered the portal. Wistle hit the go button before anyone even had a chance to wave.

At the Council headquarters, they picked up Laile, Grosson, and Calivon. Sandra was delighted to see them all. These were powerful members of the Magical Council. Laile hugged her with affection. Grosson simply nodded his head and gave her what passed for a smile on a granite.

"Sandra," Calivon said. "This is a surprise. Wistle failed to share you were accompanying us."

"She didn't know, your royalness," Sandra said, trying to be as proper as she could. She knew the royal elfin leader didn't altogether trust her for his own reasons. He was the one individual that actually could keep her from accompanying them.

"You will stay to the back and let us do the negotiating on this," Calivon stated to her directly but Wistle and Divina felt he was talking to them as well. They all nodded their head in agreement. "These drags are unpleasant but we do not anticipate this will take much time. They are a part of the magical world and therefore subject to our commandment. It is nothing more than an annoyance, really, that we must call on them, but it seems it is the only way they will respond. I anticipate they do not realize they hold the king of fairies, which is why he hasn't been released."

Sandra breathed a sigh of relief. She felt better already hearing the elfin ruler speak so assuredly.

"As you can imagine, we are not as concerned about the release of the human who is being held," he continued. He held his hand up to wave off Sandra's protests. "However, we do understand that he risked his own life in trying to secure the fairy king's release. For that reason, we will insist on the release of both."

Sandra said, simply, to all three of the Council members, "We are in your debt."

Despite the drags being located deep in Middle Earth, the trip in the portal mover took just a little over two minutes as Calivon knew where the drag headquarters were and could pound the coordinates into the locator. The Council members had chosen not to let the drags know they were coming, so they wouldn't do something rash like move the prisoners. As hoped, the element of surprise played to their advantage. As they stepped out of the portal, the drags on duty were completely taken aback. It was rare for the portal to be used for any travel since the drags preferred to stay below, and no one from above ever wanted to visit below.

"Your Royalness?" a drag said to Calivon as he stepped out first. The drag stared as the rest stepped out as well. Calivon spoke up. "Yes. As you see, you are hosting, this day, a group of representatives from the Esteemed High Council of Magical Beings and our guests. Are you the one in charge of this facility?"

"Ha ha ha! That's a good one, sir!" the drag cackled, finding the question to be very amusing.

"I'm so low on the food chain, I could be the food." He laughed and laughed at his own "joke" until Calivon had to speak up again.

"Then I suggest, Mr. Food, that you call for whoever is in charge," he said. That seemed to get the drag out of his mirth and back to business.

"That would be me," said a deep voice entering from a door behind them and surprising the group. They took a collective gasp as they caught full sight of him. He was a fearsome drag in appearance who consumed the empty space left in the room with his very size. Unlike the other drags, who had their wings tucked away, this drag had his wings partially spread. Scars ran down his neck and across his nose. A chain of keys hung around his neck. He showed no deference to the group through his actions or his tone of voice.

"Why have you come?" he asked directly to Calivon. The royal leader was more polished in return.

"Ah, Benigaar," Calivon said, apparently in recognition of the over-sized drag. "You are still the director here then?"

"I am," said the drag. "This should not be of any surprise to you, Calivon. Or I suppose I should call you 'your royalness.' Actually, that just doesn't feel right with someone I've known for so long. Far before you assumed your new title. If you even should have that title." For some reason, at that moment, the drag chose to look over directly at Sandra. He stared at her and then turned back to Calivon. The moment seemed to raise an ire in the magical ruler.

"The past is long gone, Benigaar, and the circumstances do now call for formality, so, please, address me accordingly," Calivon said.

Benigaar ignored him. "Who have you brought with you on this surprise social call?" he asked, moving closer to the delegation members.

"I am Grosson, leader of the mighty granites," Grosson said. He was large himself. No drag, even one as aggressive as Benigaar, could intimidate him.

"Yes, yes, I know the granites," Benigaar said. "We have held, er, met several of them here. And you, lovely madame?" He turned to Laile, trying, apparently, some charm. He sounded a lot like a talking giraffe – unbelievable.

"Laile of the Moonrakers," she stated. She was more polite than the others. "Thank you for seeing us."

"Ah, but I really have no choice now, do I?" was all Benigaar said in return. "And what of the rest of you? Fairies, are you?"

"Wistle of the Woods a representative of the Shan fairies," Wistle stated in her usual fearless way. "This is Divina of the Shanelles. Representative of the Supreme High Fairy Council."

"And this?" he said now, getting very close to Sandra. She worked not to flinch or show the fear she felt of him in her eyes.

"Sandra Claus," she stated, leaving off the dots for the sake of time.

"South Pole Santa is here in Middle Earth?" the drag asked loudly hearing her name. "I thought upon sight of you that was the case but then thought, surely, that could not be true. By our request, Santa has never delivered here. What an interesting day this is becoming."

What a strange race they are, Sandra thought. *Why would anyone ban Santa?* Her fear of him shifted to including some sadness for them all.

"Yes, well," Calivon now said, clearing his voice. "As you know by our numbers and representatives, we are here in an official capacity representing the Esteemed High Council of Magical Beings. We are here to retrieve two individuals you hold. Jason Annalise of St. Annalise Island and Ghost Holiday of Holiday, Texas. Please have your staff deliver these individuals to us so we can be on our way."

"Oh, Calivon, my long-time friend," Benigaar said as Calivon visually flinched at the words.

"Who says we have these individuals and why should we release them if we do?"

Sandra realized in that minute this was not going to be as easy as the Council members had anticipated. They were going to have to bargain for their friends' release.

"Benigaar, perhaps it has been too long since you have had to deal with magical matters so I will take the time to remind you of our agreed upon ways. The Ruling Council is here on an official matter of importance. You will address us with the respect of our positions and address the matter we have presented, promptly, and without questions. And then we will simply leave you as quickly as we came." He added the last with the tiniest effort at a polite smile.

"Oh, now, Calivon," the drag said, using his name, rather than his title, deliberately. "I would surely not want you to leave in a hurry. It is my insistence that you all sit and we enjoy some refreshments." He indicated a side room, with a conference table and a big pitcher of some kind of beverage, in the middle of it.

Refreshments in a small room with one door in and out, Sandra thought with alarm, as the group moved reluctantly that way. Maybe they would have to bargain for their own release!

CHAPTER 41

A Rescue Gone Wrong

Location: Drag Headquarters in Middle Earth

"Enough!" Calivon declared, stopping them all from entering the room. He knew it was better to stay in the big space they were in, close to the portal if they needed to leave in a hurry. "Benigaar, I must insist on your cooperation and that you release these two to our keeping right now."

"I will not," Benigaar said simply. "But thank you for coming. Let me escort you the few feet to the portal for your return to your world on the topside."

"Do not be contrary as your race so often chooses to be. It is tiresome. You will release them," said Calivon strongly, locking eyes with the bold drag.

"Ha! You DARE to try your magic here!" said Benigaar, shaking his head as if to clear it. "You really believe any of your attempts at influencing my mind will work here?"

Laile now was waving her arms about and Grosson seemed to be trying to increase his size.

Benigaar now turned to them. "You two as well? You dare to try magic where you know it cannot work?"

Things were obviously going bad fast and Wistle did what a desperate fairy in love was prone to do. She called out.

"GHOST! JASON! ARE YOU HERE?" she screamed it as loud as she could. Sandra and Divina quickly joined in. "GHOST! JASON! ARE YOU HERE?" They screamed it together, several times, until they thought they heard a muffled shout in return from down the hall. They dashed that direction but were quickly held back by the drags at the counter.

"Let us go!" Wistle screamed. "You hold the king of fairies!"

"You will release them," Calivon was saying.

"We will not!" said Benigaar, cackling at them with amusement. "And there is frankly nothing you can do to make it different."

Calivon stood there, as angry as he had ever been. He seemed to realize that the drag was in the power position and indicated with a nod toward the portal to the group that they should move back that way. Divina was the first in, ready to be away from the mean drags. Laile and Grosson walked over with Calivon and stepped in, but Wistle and Sandra did not budge. The drags had to threaten to pick them up for the two to move that direction at all. Both knew, if they left, they would likely never see their friends again. Before they even got to the portal,

Benigaar reached out and sent it and the Council members on their way. Now it was just the two young women with the menacing drags.

"I don't have a good feeling about this, Sandra," Wistle said, as the three menacing drags closed around them.

"Such a prize as you two might make me willing to release the others," Benigaar was saying.

Sandra, you are a Leezle, the most powerful ruling family of the magical world, use your ring. The words of her mother were as loud to her as if her mother was standing there with them in the room. *Use it*, she urged her again.

Sandra took Wistle's hand and gave her a look as she twisted her ring and hoped beyond hope that the magic it held would not be masked like the others and that it could make, not just her, but Wistle, invisible as well. She wasn't sure it had worked until she heard the drags shouting.

"Where did they go?" The drags screamed out at once, turning around the room to see where they might be hiding.

"Search for them!" Benigaar demanded. "No magic works here so this is some kind of fairy trickery! Somehow they must have orbed. Look high!" The drags cranked their necks up, staring at the ceiling while Benigaar stomped into the conference room sure he would find them hiding there. Sandra used the moment to hold her locket and wish them to Jason. They landed inside the cage where Jason was standing and staring at a door where all of the noise had been coming from.

"Jason, we're here," Sandra said quietly and urgently. Jason whirled around, but could see nothing. He was completely confused. Was his mind now playing tricks on him?

"Ghost!" Wistle had let go of Sandra's hand and instantly became visible again.

"Wistle?" Jason said, now seeing her in his cage.

"WISTLE!" Ghost said softly, but urgently, from his cage across the room, looking nervously at the door. "How did you get here?" And then adding, "Never mind - get out of here!"

"Sandra did it," she said, grinning as Sandra twisted her ring and appeared beside her. "Nobody else's magic worked here but Sandra's," she said the words with a new sense of awe and pride.

"Sandra?" Jason was still having trouble taking in that she was standing there in front of him.

"Oh, Jason," Sandra exclaimed in return, alarmed at his pale, gaunt face and thin figure. "I'm so sorry it has taken us so long."

"Never mind that," Jason said, now fully engaged and understanding that this was his dreamedabout rescue. "Who else is coming and how are we getting out?"

"No one else," Wistle said briskly. "Just us girls this time and very little time. Sandra can you get us all out?"

Sandra assessed the situation and made a quick decision. "I think so. Jason, hold my hand. Wistle you hold Jason's. I'll get you out of this cage into the room and then do the same for you, Ghost.

Then I'll get us all to the portal."

"We can't leave Thogo and Danger behind," Jason said quietly.

"Who?" said Sandra.

"Thogo and Danger," Jason said, nodding his head toward the other two cages. Thogo was looking at her anxiously and Danger even had a hint of anticipation. "We can't leave them behind, Sand. It will be even worse for them. They're as innocent as we are."

Sandra looked at the two others noting that one was very large and one was a drag. She wasn't sure how much power she had, but she knew from the look on Jason's face she had to try. She grabbed her locket, grabbed Jason and Wistle and got them into the room. She then popped into Ghost's cage and delivered him to Wistle who hugged and kissed him right in front of Jason's startled face. Then she popped in and got Thogo.

"They're coming!" Ghost said urgently as they heard clatter outside the door. "We have to go!"

"Not without Danger!" Jason said. Sandra popped into his cage, grabbed a wing and got him out too. The drag rose to almost as large a size as Benigaar.

"Go! Go!" Danger shouted. "I am the brother of Benigaar and mightier. I will be safe and can hold them off. I call you friends and am in your debt. Now go!"

Jason reached out and shook the drags offered talon and then grabbed Sandra's hand.

The door opened and the guard drags ran in shocked to see the cages empty but the doors still locked.

"Hello boys, surprised to see me free from the bars?" Danger said moving forward, with his wings fully spread offering the group some protection to escape as the two drags cowered.

Danger went toward them with a terrible roar.

"Hold on to each other, everyone!" Sandra said. She twisted her ring and they all disappeared. Then she wrapped her fingers around her locket and wished them to the magic portal, praying her magic was strong enough to move so many.

But Benigaar was no dummy. He stood waiting there with two others. Sandra's powers seemed to be waning and as they dropped at the portal their invisibility wore off.

"Ah, so there you are," Benigaar said, coming toward them. "I'm impressed. No magic works here, yet, it seems, that is no longer true is it, Miss Claus? We will need to have a little discussion on how you got around our magic blockers. For now, however, let's take care of all of this before you make more trouble."

Sandra was fighting a feeling of panic. She needed to get them out of there but there were so many and she could feel that her magic in this dark place wasn't quite strong enough for such a big rescue. It was shocking to all of them that it had worked at all.

"Sandra," Jason said. "We can do this together. Tell me where you want to go and I will think of it too. Your magic and mine can do it."

"And mine!" said Wistle.

"And mine as well," Thogo said.

Ghost just grinned. "I'm happy to add a prayer to the mix," he grinned in Ghost style.

"We'll take it," Sandra said. "Hold on everyone! We're going straight to Happiness Hall at the North Pole right NOW!"

She shouted the words as the drags leapt at them. The drags had worked for hundreds of years, maybe even thousands, to block magic from the outside in their world. They had stolen the technology from wizards eons ago but they had perfected, and strengthened, it all on their own. It was perhaps their greatest achievement as a race. But they had never dealt with Christmas magic and they had never dealt with magic born of pure kindness. The combination was mightier than the drags restraints and the drags found themselves blinded by an incredible bright light as they leapt at the group, right before they fell in a heap where the group of escapees had just been.

The escapees were tumbled and spun roughly, clinging to each other's hands tightly as strong, magical, forces pulled at them. Finally, they found themselves sprawled out on the floor just outside Happiness Hall. It took only the briefest moment to realize they had pulled it off. They shouted and hugged each other. Even Thogo, the big rock being that he was, jumped up and down. A rare sight indeed. They had joined their magic together and made magic happen.

"Thanks, mom," Sandra said out loud, not forgetting who had really made it all possible. A light wind whipped up and kissed her cheek.

CHAPTER 42

Home!

Location: North Pole Village

"SANDRA!" Em shouted loud enough to alert the whole North Pole right before she flung herself into her favorite Santa's arms. She had no interest in the others – just seeing Sandra.

"I'm so glad to see you but you know we haven't been gone long," Sandra said, as elves from all over came running.

"Jason!"

"Ghost!"

"Wistle!"

"Sandra!"

Amidst the pile of elves greeting them, Jason managed to introduce Thogo. "Elves, this is my friend Thogo. Thogo, this is the elves of the North Pole. Everyone, Thogo could use an elf pile hug, too." The words were barely out when they all piled all over the big rock guy. After months locked away in a cage with no touch and very few nice moments, the normally brusque monument welcomed all the attention.

"Ah, gee, you guys," he said. "Thanks for the great welcome."

"Ho Ho Ho!" said a booming voice that even Thogo recognized. Santa came in view and the elves squealed their delight with him. "Santa, look!" the elves cried out stepping back and pointing at their guests. "Sandra did it!"

"Well, of course she did," Santa said, looking over at her. Sandra mouthed to him, "It was hard."

He gave her a nod. "I bet she had a lot of help from Wistle." Santa said.

"I did," said Sandra. "And from Jason and Thogo and even Ghost." She smiled with appreciation at her friend who had his arm around Wistle. The fairy hadn't moved from his side. They were finally safe, and free, after months of being scared, and she was soaking it in. "We have a big story to tell but, first, we need to feed these guys some real food."

Jason looked at her with appreciation. He desperately wanted some time with her but not as much as he wanted to eat and clean up. Santa himself wanted to take the three who'd been rescued to lunch and the impromptu welcome began to break up. Even Em and Squawk went with Santa when they heard corn on the cob was on the menu at the *Eat, Drink & Be Merry* diner. Noelly had recently introduced them as a new taste delight and now, pretty much all the elves, wanted it all the time.

As usual, Sandra took great glee at seeing them so happy and especially when they were so happy eating something actually good for them.

"You need to fatten up Jason," Sandra heard Santa say as they walked off.

"I know, sir, I know," said Jason as he looked back at Sandra with appreciation in his eyes. He mouthed to her "thank you" and she nodded with tears in her eyes. She couldn't believe he and Ghost were back. Plus, the magnitude of what they had just gone through was beginning to hit her full force and tears ran down her cheeks.

That was how Gunny found her, facing away from him, when he came walking up. He'd been working in the barns and just heard the news they were back.

"Did you do it, Sand? Did you get 'em both back?" He realized he was holding his breath a little, feeling scared of the answer. What if she hadn't rescued his brother? What if she had rescued Jason?

He walked to her and spun her gently around by the shoulders. She nodded her head as she burst into sobs!

"Ah, brave girl, it's okay. What happened? What are the tears for? Did someone get hurt?" He held her back from him to look her over to be sure she wasn't injured before wrapping her in his arms and letting her cry.

"Gunny it was so scary!" she finally managed to sputter out, wiping her eyes, and her nose, on Gunny's shirt. He smiled. He didn't care. Having her close was worth a little snot. "You were right. They were going to keep me and Wistle. They sent the others away and then my mom told me to use – ”

“Wait, wait, wait, what? Your mom told you?” Gunny asked, thinking he had missed something.

Sandra nodded her head in his shoulder before pulling back. “Yes, my mom. She wasn’t there but it was her. I knew it was and when I tried the ring like she said, even though magic doesn’t work below for anyone who isn’t from below, mine did.” She ran through what happened, without taking a breath, until she got to the part where they landed safely there.

“Gunny, I really didn’t think we were going to make it,” she teared up again and Gunny pulled her in for some more consoling.

“Sandra, I would have come for you. No drag in the world could have kept me from you,” he said with such conviction that it made Sandra feel a little bit scared for the drags. She re-alized, again, how safe he made her feel. He hated to break the magic but he had to know.

“How is my brother?”

“Anxious to see you, brother,” Ghost said coming up and throwing himself on his brother’s back like a monkey. Gunny wrestled around and threw his arms around him.

“Little brother, I am so glad to see you!” Gunny whooped it up like he was back on the ranch during a cattle round-up. “And Wistle,” he said as she came walking up too, hanging back, wanting to give the two brothers their special moment together. "Come on over here for a Holiday hug. I have nothing but respect for you, fairy or not. Thank you."

"I couldn't leave my guy down there," she said shyly looking at Ghost, while Gunny looked over at Sandra with wide eyes at that piece of news. She just grinned and shrugged.

"Now, now, brother there's nothing wrong with fairies. At least this one," Ghost said reaching out and taking Wistle's hand to pull her in for that hug. Weirdly, now that he was free, he couldn't make himself stop smiling or stay away from Wistle. Even weirder for everyone, was how smiley Wistle had become. It was an odd turn of events but they all felt the look suited them both. They're goofiness was catching and Gunny reached out and took Sandra's hand, who squeezed it in return and smiled herself. *For the first time in almost a year*, Gunny thought to himself, *there is pure happiness in the air*. He felt perfectly content.

Until something super important popped into Sandra's head.

"Oh, Christmas crackers!" she exclaimed. "We've got to call St. Annalise and let Christina and everyone there know about Jason and Ghost!"

She turned to run off but changed her mind and skipped away instead.

CHAPTER 43

Shower Me with Fun

Location: St. Annalise

"Cappie! Cappie?" Sandra shouted down the dock as she ran to the *Mistletoe*. "Squawk?" She hadn't had time to stick around at the Pole and catch up with Jason because she had important, not-to-be-missed, business on St. Annalise. She had left early with Em in tow and forgot to call Cappie ahead. Now she wondered where she was at.

". . . *squawk!* . . . you're home! . . . *squawk!* . . . so happy!"

"Squawk! I'm so happy to see you," Sandra said, genuinely thrilled to see her dear bird. "Come on over here and let me love you up."

The big bird flew to her outstretched hand and Sandra kissed him right on the beak, much to his enjoyment.

". . . *squawk!* . . . love you . . ."

"Love you more," she said.

"eeeee eeee eeeeee" Rio heard Sandra's voice and greeted her happily, dancing on the water.

"Rio! I love you too. I will be right in!" Sandra promised.

"Over here," Cappie called out, waving from a couple docks down on the deck of Thomas' tug. It gave Sandra a moment's pause to see Cappie there, looking so happy, but she shook the feeling off and kicked off her shoes as she headed to her berth on the big tugboat. *It was so good to be home,* she thought, as she chucked off her clothes and slipped on her favorite island swimsuit. She put her hair back in a high pony tail and dived over the side to swim over to Thomas and Cappie. She took her time, enjoying the beautiful, clear water and playing with her favorite dolphin. Cappie met her at the side of the *Lullaby* with a big towel in hand and an even bigger grin on her face seeing her beautiful ward.

Neither Cappie, nor Thomas, waited for Sandra to dry off before squeezing her in a big family bear hug.

"Mmmmmmm," Sandra said, wallowing in the wonderful feeling of being loved unconditionally.

"That is the best welcome home ever." Cappie and Thomas stood there smiling, until Thomas ran to get them all some refreshing pineapple juice and sparkling water with lots of ice, knowing it was Sandra's favorite combination.

"Are you by yourself?" Cappie asked. "No Em?"

"Oh, she's here. She just stopped off at the barge first for some things. It's so good to be home," Sandra said, drying off while looking around and seeing something new added to Thomas's big deck. "Cappie, that looks like your rocking chair?" she said, feeling puzzled and slightly disturbed.

"Oh, sweetie, it is," Cappie said gently. "I, well, I had Thomas move it over here because I'd been spending so much time here lately."

Well that made sense, Sandra thought. "Oh sure, of course," she said feeling relieved. "I have been gone a lot."

"Well, it's really more than that, dear," Cappie was saying haltingly as Thomas rejoined them and immediately assessed the situation. He set the tray of drinks down and jumped in to the conversation, rocker first.

"It was my idea to move it really because, you see, dear Sandra," he said, taking Cappie's hand. "Well, I very much hope that Margaret will consider this her home too once we're married. Or even now. I'm quite impatient really." He grinned like a school boy in love as Sandra took in the news she had never, ever, ever, considered in all of her life. Not even when Cappie had said yes. She had just always been sure Cappie would call the *Mistletoe* home with her and, in this minute, with the location of that one rocking chair, her world had been rocked.

"Of course," she managed to sputter out to their now concerned faces. "I mean, duh. Of course, Cappie would move here with you, Thomas. I'm so happy for you both." She reached out for another big hug to hide any sorrow on her face. The truth was that she was happy for them both.

She was just sad for herself.

"Of course, dear, I will absolutely not move if it isn't what you want," Cappie was now scrambling to say. "I mean I've been wanting to talk to you about it but there just hasn't been a single good chance for a chat. I'm so sorry you learned about it this way." She was in distress over causing the person she treasured most sadness, which helped bring Sandra to her senses.

"Nonsense, Cappie," Sandra said, as she pulled away from the hug. "I mean it. Truly. Where's that pineapple juice, Thomas? It's time for a juice toast. Let's sit over here on the far side of the tug in the shade." She moved to the shade, held her glass in the air and clinked it against theirs. "I believe this toast should be, may we always sail side-by-side and may the currents keep us close."

"There is no current in all of the oceans that could pull me far from you, my darling girl," Cappie said in return and Sandra knew it was true.

"Okay, so what I want to know most, what Squawk and Em have been talking on endlessly, is have you decided on what flavor of wedding cake you're going to have?" Sandra said, lightening up the mood, and asking a question that was of dire importance to two of the most important individuals in her life.

"Well, one layer is going to be coconut, for sure, because Squawk would never forgive me if it wasn't," Cappie said.

"And cocoa fudge, for another, because Em and the elves would boycott the wedding if we didn't have a cocoa cake," Thomas said.

"You are too good to both of them," Sandra said. "And honestly, you should pick what you like."

"Oh, we have," Cappie said. "We love both those flavors. And for the top layer of the cake we picked our very favorite flavor in honor of our very favorite Santa Claus. We picked – "

"Candy cane!" Thomas blurted out smiling. "For Christmastime and you."

"Candy cane! I love it!" Sandra said, grinning. "Such an honor and such a perfect combination of flavors. Now, please catch me up on everything else I've been missing out on while I've been gone and I'll tell you both about the big rescue."

The three had talked non-stop for well over an hour when Em came running, breathlessly, up to the boat.

"Sandra! We need to see you, please," she called out as she leaped on to the *Lullaby*. "You too, Cappie." The little delgin winked at Sandra. Cappie missed the wink - which was hard to believe since Em didn't do anything subtly – and expressed concern jumping up out of her seat.

"Is everything okay, Em?" Cappie asked.

"Oh yes, Cappie. I just have something important to show you."

"I hope we don't need to go far," Sandra said, playing along with Em. "I don't have any shoes."

". . . *squawk*! . . . flip flops coming . . ." Squawk called out. He gathered a pair from the pile Cappie and Sandra kept on the deck of the *Mistletoe* and flew over.

"Squawk, you are the best," Sandra said, as she shoved her feet in the mismatched pair he dropped on the *Lullaby* deck. Color didn't matter, love did.

"Okay Em, I think we're set. What would you like to show us?" Cappie asked, starting for the other side of the *Lullaby* automatically to look over at the *Mistletoe*. They had been lounging on the far side away from the *Mistletoe,* and in the shade as Sandra had suggested, and now the two women moved to follow Em. As soon as they did, a big group of Cappie's friends from the island, all shouted "surprise" from the deck of the *Mistletoe.*

"It's your shower, Cappie," Em said proudly. "We set it all up while Sandra kept you busy."

"Em, don't tell everything you know," Sandra said, smiling at the little smiling delgin.

". . . *squawk!* . . . I knew too . . . *squawk!*"

"But you can't come," Em said happily. "Girls only."

"You can hang out here with me, Squawk," Thomas said quickly to quell a fight.

". . . *squawk!* . . . save us some cake! . . . *squawk!*"

"We'll see," Em said primly at the same time Cappie said, "of course."

"*eeeeeeeeeeee eeeee eeeee*"

"Yes, Rio, you can come. You're a girl," Em said matter-of-factly.

"Can I go?" Cappie said smiling.

"Yes, Cappie! It's for you!" Em said, taking her hand and leading her over to the dock and to the tugboat full of smiling women and elves. Cappie reached out for Sandra with her other hand.

"A shower!" she said happily. "I would have said no if you'd asked and now I'm just delighted."

Sandra doubted Cappie was as delighted as she herself felt having pulled off the surprise.

"We got you pillows," Em said as they walked.

"EM!" Sandra exclaimed as Cappie laughed. Elves could never keep secrets!

CHAPTER 44

Unannounced Visitors

Location: St. Annalise

"Sandra, wake up. Sandra."

"What? Who? What? What time is it?" Sandra turned groggily to look at the clock. "It's 3:15 in the morning. Go away."

"Cassandra Penelope, you will wake up." Gunny was speaking bolder and louder now.

"Gunny? Go away!"

"I wish I could but Santa sent me for you. The Esteemed High Council of Magical Beings is on their way and demanding to see you."

"What?" She sat up straight in bed feeling fully awake at the news. "Now? At this time of the morning? With no warning? Why?"

"They are demanding to see you and Wistle. Zinga is waking her up now too."

"How did you get to St. Annalise so fast, by the way?" Sandra asked, still not completely awake, as she got out of bed.

"Through the new magic portal on the South Pole Village barge," Gunny said proudly. "It works! I'm the first one to come through but they are right behind me with Santa. What I don't get is why. This must be about the rescue, but why should they care?"

"I'm so excited about the portal working!" Sandra said from the bathroom where she was pulling on some shorts and a sweatshirt. "If I know Calivon, and I think I do, they're coming here because we succeeded at the rescue when they didn't. Even though there was a successful outcome, he doesn't ever like to be shown up. Least of all by me who he thinks is a Leezle."

"You *are* a Leezle," Gunny said, thinking she still wasn't yet fully awake.

"Be quiet Gunny! Of course I am, but he doesn't know it, and must never know what he only suspects. He's totally afraid that I'll take his place as ruler of the magical world but I have no interest in that at all. I love being South Pole Santa. I never want to be anything different than that." She untied her hair and ran her fingers through it. "Okay, how do I look?"

"Unnaturally beautiful for the middle of the night," he said sincerely, moving toward her. "I miss spending time together. I need to know where I stand now that Jason is back." He reached out and put his hand on her arm.

She hesitated for just an instant. "Gunny, I – "

"Are you ready, Sandra?" Wistle said, orbing into the room, looking quickly from one of them to the other. "Uh, did I interrupt something?"

"Yes, me telling her she was incredibly beautiful and had nothing to fear from these jokers." "Well, you are beautiful," Wistle said wryly to Sandra. "I think he might be lying about the rest, though."

"I want to like you, Wistle," Gunny said. Wistle shrugged and grinned and Sandra ignored him.

"Exactly what I was thinking too, Wistle," Sandra said, feeling a little scared of seeing Calivon like this on her home turf. "Santa will help keep us safe - and why should we be scared anyway?

All we did was rescue our friends?" They all headed to the half-finished barge to greet their visitors.

"Yes, but exactly how did you rescue your friends?" was the first question Calivon asked when Sandra said as much to him. He had arrived with the usual mix of Laile and Grosson and added in Zeentar and Reesa this time – the full traveling Council membership. They all seemed somber and more severe than their usual slightly less somber and severe selves. Well, except for Laile who, thankfully, like usual, was just a little bit nicer than all the rest. "I mean, magic doesn't work below so how did you get in to where the captives were held, release them all from their cages and get them topside without being caught by the drags?"

Careful Cassandra, her mother whispered in her ear. Sandra felt stronger knowing her mom was there. *Do not let him know of your special magic. Guard your locket away.*

"While you distracted them in the portal, we were able to slip away, get inside and let them out. We are in your debt, for your assistance." Sandra bowed her head ever so slightly in deference to him, despite her true feelings of disdain for the not-to-be-trusted leader.

Calivon was not dissuaded from his line of questioning by her compliments or bowed head.

"How, then, did you get out from their jailed area without being apprehended?"

"She, we, had help from another captive." It was Jason who answered this time. He had entered the room not looking like the Jason held captive or even the Jason Sandra knew. He looked like a Jason who was king. His clothes were of nothing she had seen him in before. Expensive in appearance, fitting tightly to his physique but it was his manner that exuded his power. He stood tall and was fused with confidence. Wistle curtsied and bowed deeply as soon as she saw him, and much to Sandra's surprise, even Reesa bowed her head briefly to him. To Sandra, and the rest of the room, he looked handsome and powerful.

Jason knew Sandra's secret of being a Leezle and she knew he would never tell. Together, with Wistle, they would get through this grilling by the Council. He gave her the briefest nod and one to Gunny as well. It was the first time Sandra had seen him since he had gone to get some food and rest after the rescue. The Supreme Fairy Council had insisted on seeing him immediately after that, to be sure he was really free, Sandra suspected, and he had been whisked away before Sandra, or Christina, got to catch up with him.

"And you are?" Calivon said with a little malice. It was almost impossible to believe Calivon didn't know full well this was Jason, and very rude to not address him with the respect due the new king of fairies. In that role, Jason was almost the equal of Calivon himself. The fairies would argue he was Calivon's superior. The rightful ruler of all magical beings. It was likely that tension that encouraged Calivon's behavior. Jason rose above it.

"Jason of St. Annalise Island, your royalness," Jason said. He added graciously, "Here to thank you, in person, for your generous efforts to have me released." He bowed deeply to Calivon, Grosson, Zeentar, and Laile each individually.

"We accept your thanks," said Laile, smiling. She, alone on the Council, seemed happy to see him.

"Ah, the purported new fairy king," said Calivon. "The Council is honored to welcome you." His words did not match the tone of his voice. "So, please, Jason of St. Annalise, this very small island that we are on actually, tell us of your rescue."

Jason did not so much as glance at Sandra. To do so would have implied they had something to hide, or had collaborated on. With this suspicious Council, it could not seem like they were hiding anything, or Sandra could be found out as the last of the Leezles and put in great danger.

"There were four of us held by the drags – unjustly, I might add. As far as I could ever tell, three of us were just passing through Middle Earth and one, the one of their own kind, was being held for political reasons. It was Danger, a drag himself, and the brother of Benigaar, the drag warden of the institution where we were kept, that assisted with our escape."

"And did this Danger escape with you as well?" Calivon asked.

"No, your royalness. He chose to stay back and engage with the others, giving us valuable time to get to the portal." He carefully did not elaborate on how they got to the portal.

"And at the portal, what did you do? Did you escape through it?"

Sandra was about to speak up and say "yes" so he would not know of her magic power when her mother gave her another clear warning. *He knows you did not*, she said.

"No, your royalness," she spoke up before Jason could say otherwise. "We could not use it. The drags had cut us off from it to recapture us."

"Is all of this true?" Grosson now was talking directly to Thogo who had also entered the room.

"It is." Thogo said as Sandra breathed her relief that they all were telling the same true story.

"This then leads us to the part of this elaborate story that I am perhaps the most interested in," Calivon said, leaning forward. "You managed to get into the jailed area, get your friends out – and their friends even – without almost any trouble at all, and you discover you cannot use the planned portal to return to topside earth. What now, in this place where magic is impossible to use from all of those - like yourselves - who are not from Middle Earth, did you do?"

"Well, that bit about magic from above not being effective below, turned out not to be true," Jason said simply. "The key, it seems, is joining magic together so the whole is greater than each of the parts. I think I actually learned something about that in one of the classes I didn't skip at the academy." He smiled thinking about it as did Sandra and Wistle. The three had many wonderful shared memories of St Annalise Academy.

"So, we are to believe this story?" Calivon questioned. "And before you answer, I should warn you that, while we were there, I tried magic, as did Laile and Grosson, and I can assure you that we are powerful magic makers. Are you sure this is your story?"

"It is and it is not a story. It is the truth," said Jason, a little tersely, growing tired of the questioning. His fairy king side was getting stronger all the time and patience was not a strong fairy attribute. "With respect sir, did you three work your magic as individuals or as a concerted effort all together? I suspect it was the first."

"Your story then is that you four – " said Calivon.

"Five, sir. I was there too." Ghost said this from his place next to Gunny on the sidelines.

The Council members barely looked his way. "We are expected to believe that you five, put your magic together, and it not only worked in a magic-blocked space but worked so well it brought you to the North Pole?"

"Exactly. That is what happened. We are thankful that it worked out so well."

"Show me," Calivon said.

"Show you?" Jason replied.

"Yes, please. Show me. Show this Council how you five did it. Make yourselves go somewhere.

Anywhere."

Careful, Sandra's mom said to her.

"We are not circus dogs," Jason said. "We are not, I certainly am not, here to entertain you."

"Who do you care about here?" Calivon asked, which gave Sandra a very bad feeling. "Ah yes Sandra, but we need her for this. I'll use Reesa instead."

Before the haughty fairy could object to his plan she was gone. The room gasped.

"What have you done?" Jason demanded, stepping forward to the front of the room where Calivon sat.

"I have simply sent her somewhere as is my right as the elfin king and ruler of the magical realm," Calivon said callously. "You may get her back, or she can stay there until you do get her back, but I believe it's a quite uncomfortable place so you five may want to hurry. She is under my control and as such, cannot change her circumstances on her own."

Jason looked at him with fairy king fury as Sandra considered what they should do. To find Reesa, she would need to use her locket, which would expose her as a Leezle. *There is no way around it*, she said in her mind to her mother as she reached for it.

"You have made a grave mistake Calivon of the Elfins," Jason was saying. "You have gone too long unchecked by another and you have apparently forgotten that I am not just Jason of St. Annalise but the king of both the Shan and Shanelle tribes of the ancient kingdom of fairies. I have had a lot of time to think about what that means.

"I've had months in fact to accept my role. Months to explore it in my mind, to receive the magical downloads that seemed to keep coming and coming whether I wanted to accept them or not and to understand the meaning of this." He rolled up his sleeve to show the crown tattoo on his wrist. Wistle curtsied again. "I also had many months, since my nineteenth birthday, I believe, to understand the meaning of this as well." He rolled up his other sleeve to show another, different but complimentary, crown tattoo on his left inside wrist. Now Wistle dropped to her knees in a deep bow.

"The crowns of myth and prediction," Wistle said in an awe-filled whisper.

All the members of the Council, including Calivon, seemed shook by what Jason had shown them and all bowed their heads slightly to him. All but the defiant Calivon.

"Tattoos? You show us tattoos of myth? Of a fairy myth that is widely known? You would not be the first to have the crowns of the two tribes tattooed on your wrist for a chance at the crown."

"In deference to your role here," Jason said steadily to just Calivon. "I shall ask you kindly for the return of Reesa, the royal representative of the fairies to this Council, who should have never been subjected to your games. Think carefully on this Calivon of the Elfins. Our tribes do best when we work together, not apart."

Calivon laughed at his words and with that Jason crossed his wrists touching the two tattoos together. A large fairy orb appeared to the whole room. It acted as a sort of crystal ball and the whole group could see that Calivon had put Reesa on a very perilous, slippery, and slim outcropping, high on a windy cliff with a turbulent ocean crashing on sharp rocks below. For once, the regal fairy looked terrified.

"Reesa," Jason called out gently.

"Jason?" Reesa said, looking around to all sides. "Are you here to rescue me? Upon my return, I shall strike down that elfin monster --"

Sandra saw Calivon flinch and move uncomfortably in his seat.

"That is for another time," Jason said evenly. "Be assured we will see to a reckoning regarding this incidence. For this minute, however, you must trust me. You must believe I am indeed your king and therefore, would never let you fall. I am sworn to protect you."

"Trust has never been my best feature, Jason," she said in true Reesa fashion.

"Perhaps now would be a good time to start calling me 'your highness' so you can practice your trust for I'm about to ask you to take a step forward right off that cliff and for that you must believe I will not let you die."

Reesa stood there and without another word she did indeed step forward off that cliff . . .

. . . and right into the fairy orb in front of them all in the hall! The whole of the audience there, with the exception of Calivon, broke out in applause and cheers. Reesa stepped out of the orb and curtsied deeply to Jason.

"My king," she said.

"You trusted me," Jason said in return.

"It seemed like my best option," Reesa said. "If it didn't work out, I, at least, never had to call a false king 'your highness' and, if it did, I would know for sure it was true. Thank you, my king." She curtsied to him again.

Sandra and all of the rest of the hall were simply staring at him and still cheering. Calivon was fuming. "Order, order," he called out to the hall.

"Calivon," Grosson said. "We have seen enough. The Council will depart with our thanks to you Sandra and Wistle, for your bravery in rescuing Jason of St Annalise and the human."

Ghost and Gunny laughed out loud, despite themselves, at his words. Magical beings never seemed to get how cool being human was but that discussion was for another day.

"Calivon, for continued order in the magical realm, you must make your apology now to Reesa and Jason of the kingdom of fairies or you may prepare one for later. It will be your choice, of course, but it must be done." Calivon looked at Grosson and the others and then directly at Jason and Sandra with an anger level she felt she had never seen.

"Grosson, it is clearly you that will need to make the apologies," he said, at last. "No one addresses the ruler of the magical realm with such words of ridiculous instruction." With that, he stood up and walked out, as the crowd parted to let him through.

The rest of the Council followed shortly with Santa as their guide. Jason turned to look at Sandra. She saw emotions flicker across his face but none long enough to clearly name. Just one.

The look of concern. It matched the look on hers as well.

". . . *squawk*! . . . Jason did good . . . *squawk*!"

Sandra laughed. For once, even Squawk was impressed by their island friend.

Jason swept out of the room and ran to catch up with the Council members not willing to let them alone with Reesa still. Sandra went to follow, as well, but felt a quick hand holding her back. When she looked down there was no hand, however. Just the outline of three fading marks in a circle. Her family symbol! A sign from her mother.

"Love you mom," she said, as her friends crowded around. There would be no more sleep after this dramatic night.

CHAPTER 45

A Reunion at Last

Location: St. Annalise Island

"Jason! Jason!" Sandra had finally managed to separate herself from the others and had gone looking for the guy she needed to see. She headed toward his home on the island, taking the shortcut they always used by the beach. He had spoken with Christina but hadn't actually seen his mother yet and Sandra felt sure he would head there now that he was back on St. Annalise. She kept calling out his name, anxious to see him and concerned the Council might have insisted he go with them and he'd be gone away from her again. Her heart beat fast at the thought. Seeing him, talking to him, was her top priority.

Jason's too, apparently, as he came walking briskly toward her and without so much as a pause took her in his arms and held her there like he might not ever let go.

"Sandra, I missed you so much," he whispered to her. "Every single day. I am so, so, so sorry for everything I know I put you through. For what I put everyone through."

"It's okay, Jason," she said, thinking how much time she had spent wanting him to hold her like he was and thinking how wonderful his strong arms felt. "It really is okay now that you are here and safe." She meant it. Life would be okay again now that they had Jason and Ghost back. She pushed back from him so she could see his eyes and reached out for his wrists to look at both of the tattoos. He didn't flinch as she carefully pushed his sleeves up and studied both intricate crowns.

"Even I have heard the story of the fairy crowns of myth and prediction," she said, with awe, careful not to touch them as she remembered how her touch of the first one had pained him so much. He remembered it too and was thankful she didn't. The pain had been severe but he would have endured it if she had felt she needed to reach out and touch either one. He preferred pain to her not touching him at all.

"Do you remember the story?" she asked him suddenly, still holding his hands but now looking at him intently. "We studied it in our Magical Beings class."

"I'm pretty sure I skipped that day." He said with an apologetic shrug. "What a total loser I was for not going to class more and paying attention. I don't deserve to be the king of fairies. I don't blame anybody for doubting my worthiness."

"Are you kidding?" Sandra said. "I don't think I've ever seen anyone more royal in their bearing and their response then you just were to Calivon and the others! You are already an incredible king. No one will ever doubt it again.

"I will never doubt it again." She added the last part quietly, dropping his hands. Jason pushed down his sleeves quickly so he could hold her again without the risk of the tattoos being touched in any way by her.

"Sandra, I doubted it. I didn't want it. Of course you would wonder about it and hope it wasn't true. I understand that. I also understand, very well now, that it is true. Maybe that's why I had to be held in that horrible drag prison for so long."

"Oh Jason, I'm so sorry it took us so long to find you! We wanted to come earlier and we tried but we just didn't know where you were."

"No way are you apologizing, Sandra. Or anyone else here. No way. And especially not my mom." Jason said this firmly, stepping apart from Sandra and pacing a bit in the sand.

"I left as a total jerk. Not telling anyone and thinking I needed no one. It would have totally served me right if you all had left me there to rot away, but I'm so glad you didn't. I'm not that same guy anymore. I will never be able to thank you enough for rescuing me."

"And I need to thank you for not telling Calivon about how we got you out. Jason, it's important he never learns," Sandra said with a sense of foreboding in her voice. A shiver went down her spine and she shuddered. "I think he might hurt me if he ever finds out exactly what happened."

"No one will hurt you, Sandra," Jason said powerfully. "Do you understand that? No one will ever tell and no one will ever hurt you." He went to pull her closer but she backed away and looked at him with tears in her eyes.

"I know you mean that, and I trust you, but of all people to say that, you are the one person in the whole of the world that has hurt me before," she said, not with malice, just with simple truth. The words pained him worse than the pain of her touch on his tattoos. He visibly winced and reached for her again wanting to soothe her, tell her how much he loved her, how much he had thought about her, of them, how much he had wanted to come back and tell her he was wrong and they would figure it out. He would tell her now. She stayed out of his reach, though, speaking before he could.

"I thought the pain of our break-up would never leave. Never. Each day went by and you never reached out to me, never called or wrote." He went to object but she held up her hand to put him on pause. "Yes, I know why now, but, at the time, it just made it all feel like the whole of the world was closing in on me. Little by little, though, with the help of my friends, and Cappie, and Santa and the elves and the children of the world, I found my way back to, not just okay, but happy.

"And then we found out why you didn't ever reach out to me or Christina or anyone else and that was worse, I think, because then the guilt came rushing in. How could I have not sensed there was something wrong?" She looked at him pleadingly, now begging him with her eyes to forgive him, and when he moved toward her she again held up her hand. If he held her, she couldn't finish.

"And Gunny was gone then too. And then Ghost went in to find you and he was lost. So much loss all because of me being too proud to find out where you were when we didn't hear from you." She looked down now, as if thinking of what she would say next, and Jason took that opportunity to enfold her in his strong arms, whether she wanted him to or not.

"It was never you who caused all this Sand, it was only me. Mixed up, jerky me, who deserves none of what he has been blessed to have been given. Not my mom, not the academy, not being king and most of all not the love you gave me. But now, I want to claim it all. All of it, Sand. I want to call Christina 'mom' like she deserves from her sullen son. I want to learn all I can from everyone I can. I want to be king of the fairies – they need me and I know it now. And more than all of that, all of that put together, I want you to love me again. Could you dare to risk it again?" He was scared to ask the last for fear of what her answer would be but he had to know.

She said nothing for a long moment, listening to his fast-beating heart and feeling his strength against her. At one time, she knew what her answer would have been without hesitation. She had longed for the kind of words he was speaking now. This wasn't then, though, and a lot had happened in the time in between. She sighed and leaned up to kiss his lips lightly.

"Please give me time," she said, looking at him with love and hesitation mixed together. "There is so much to take in, you're just back, and Christmas is less than two months away. If it is meant to be, it can handle a little more time."

He went to object, but thought better of it, knowing she was right – and wrong. "We are meant to be," was all he said as she took a step away. She needed space to think.

She decided to lighten up the mood. "Either way, Jason, king of fairies, I am in awe of your magic." She said this, smiling at him now and he joined in.

"Oh, girlfriend of mine," he said, shrugging at her when she raised her eyebrow with skepticism.

"If you thought that magic was special you should see the magic I have planned to use on you." He smiled now with the old mischievous Jason look he used to get, and despite herself, she blushed.

He saw it and said even more cheekily. "Exactly," he said with a suggestive smile.

"Jason!" she said, not totally objecting, but still feeling embarrassed. "I will see you later. And keep that magic to yourself!"

"I'm saving that all for you," he called after her, feeling hopeful as she looked back smiling. "Oh, and Sand, I'm spending the next couple of months going back and forth between the fairy realm and with my mom and doing whatever she wants. I owe her that and more. I know you're going back up to the North Pole. Will I see you again before Christmas?"

"Probably not, but your mom is going to be so happy to see you." It made Sandra happy enough thinking about the two of them that she darted back down the path and kissed him lightly full on the mouth.

"I head back up to the Pole early tomorrow morning and, you're right, I won't be here much," she said.

"Hey, I'll write you a list about what I want for Christmas," Jason said grinning. "Just for you, though. I really wouldn't show it to the other Santa, if you know what I mean."

"Jason Annalise, king of the fairies, you are truly on the bad list!" she sputtered.

"That is my favorite list," he grinned and she grinned too. He stood there looking at her with a dopey smile rarely seen on a royal king of fairies or even the sullen plain ol' Jason of old.

She laughed and waved at him. "Maybe we have a chance," she said quietly just to herself as she walked away smiling.

"A fat chance," Gunny said to himself from the dark spot behind a tall hedge he had pressed himself into when he had come upon them. He had been looking for her and instead found them.

His very least favorite combination of people. He wasn't proud of himself for listening to their conversation but these were desperate times with the fairy boy and his impressive magical ways now home. A regular human guy like him had to do what he had to do if he wanted any chance at all with the one girl he was crazy about. Things were complicated now, but Sandra hadn't told Jason yes when he had asked her straight out for her heart again.

Hope lived.

CHAPTER 46

Cocoa and Corn-on-the-Cob

Location: North Pole Village

Gunny wasted no time on *"Operation Wipe Out Thoughts of Jason."* He woke up the next day later than he planned after spending too many hours tossing and turning. He knew Sandra had headed back to the North Pole so he headed right for the new portal to get there himself. He tried to look nonchalant about it all but he couldn't help but break out in a big smile when he found her.

There she was sitting at one of the long tables in the main village square, surrounded by elves, with all of them, including Sandra, slurping down a double tall cocoa and munching on corn on the cob. At ten o'clock in the morning. It was the new fave food for elves at any meal. They loved it with butter, they loved it without. They loved it because it was sweet and they looked funny eating it. They didn't even like plain ol' corn off the cob but they had discovered corn on the cob and they all loved it! To them, it was fun food and fun food meant good food even if it was a vegetable.

"Hey, Gunny!" Dear Lovey saw him first and gave him a wave.

"Come sit over here by me," Redwood called out waving with his long, branchy fingers. "Thanks, Redwood," Gunny said. "If Em doesn't mind scooting over, I'd really like to squeeze in next to Sandra here." He was only sort of requesting it of Em as he squeezed in between them.

"Gunny, you need to diet!" Em said, objecting and giggling with corn in her teeth. All the other elves giggled along with her and all of them had corn teeth.

"Squawk, you mean you love corn on the cob now, too?" Gunny asked the big bird who was chomping on his own ear of corn as he sat on the table across from Sandra.

". . . *squawk*! . . . corn's the best . . . *squawk* . . ."

"Well, then, hand me one of the ears too, please, Em, and the butter. I like mine with lots of butter. And you better give me one of those bibs y'all are wearing 'cause you just know I'm going to get some of that melted butter all over my nice work shirt here."

Sandra smiled at him, feeling super happy about starting out her busy day with a pile of corneating, cocoa-drinking elves and now a good-mood Gunny added into the mix.

"Gunny, look! Quisp is here, too," Sandra said with emphasis so Gunny wouldn't miss her. The little fairy had made a rare visit up from the South Pole to the North Pole when the South Pole elves had come up for the trip to Iceland and she was still there. Sandra had come to love the little wisp of a fairy. She had the tiniest orb Sandra had ever seen and it was easy to miss her.

She often liked to hide in Sandra's hair, which is where she was now, but she shyly peeked out at Gunny when she heard her name. He gave her a big smile before she hid again.

"It's so good to see you again, Quisp," Gunny said graciously, since he barely had seen her at the South Pole. He just barely saw her now, too. She was excruciatingly shy and very sweet for a fairy. He loved how all magical beings had their own personalities just like humans. Being human meant you were an individual and not like anyone else and that, it turned out, was the same for all beings he'd met so far. He suspected it was the same for all beings, no matter whether they were human, magical, animals, birds or even fish. Even though it meant that sometimes you ran into a few, not-so-nice personalities, he liked that everyone was different. It definitely made life more interesting. He smiled at the thought and turned his attention fully to Sandra.

"Tie this on for me?" he asked. He flashed Sandra one of his most charming smiles, handed her the two ends of the big bib, and turned his back. *Operation Wipe Out Thoughts of Jason* would be won in slow, small moments he knew. He just needed to make sure they happened. He kept moving the two tie ends out of her reach until she had to reach way around him to where she was almost hugging him from behind. She finally realized what he was doing and swatted at him, until he handed them both to her with a sheepish grin. She grinned back. He had a way of making her both annoyed and happy all at the same time.

"That was quite a grilling by the Council last night," he said to her. "Thanks for filling me in on how things went at the rescue. I'm glad none of that came up." Like Sandra, he didn't trust Calivon. He worried what the elfin ruler would do if he knew, as the rumors persisted, that a Leezle still lived. "I worry about you, Sandra," he added quietly.

"I'm fine Gunny, really," she hastened to assure him. She felt better with the Council members gone and some sleep. There was too much good happening in her life to worry about anything that wasn't. "I'm concerned about Santa though, Gunny," Sandra said as low as she could as the elves chattered away. It didn't work.

"WHY?" All the elves at the long table seemed to stop mid-chew and question her at the same time.

"What's the matter with Santa?" Redwood asked speaking for the whole table. "Is he sick?

Should we be worried?"

"Now, now." Gunny said, jumping in. "First of all, you all are very nosey since Sandra and I were having a private conversation. And secondly, Santa is fine."

Sandra interrupted him. "No, he's not," she said quietly as Gunny stared at her and the elves all started swaying with worry. She hurried on so they didn't start crying. "I mean he's not ill or anything dire like that, of course." She paused to be sure the elves all heard her and no one looked like they were about to cry. "The thing is, and I don't want to sound immodest, but all the children's letters are coming to me! Children are becoming so kind that they are hardly thinking about their Christmas want lists anymore and just sending in their kindness lists. I love the lists! I know Santa does too, and he's happy about them, but it seems to be taking away from Santa instead of just adding to the goodness here and in the world like I was trying to do. That makes me sad and I know it is making him a little sad, too, even though he would never say so. And the worst part is, I'm not sure how to change it. What do you all think? Is there anything we can do?"

"I don't like Santa being sad." Violet said, sniffling.

"Me neither!" came from around the table.

"Me either," said tiny Quisp, though Sandra was the only one who could hear her since she was still hiding in her hair. "We need to do something."

Sandra smiled at her words. Quisp was a special little fairy. Most fairies would not care at all about something bothering Santa.

All of them, Sandra and Gunny and the elves, sat there silently with no real answers. There were some sniffles from the elves and still some corn chomping. Redwood was fairly new to sad thoughts and started coughing real hard in obvious distress. The others around him patted his back, consolingly.

"I'm alright, I'm alright," the gangly elf said, looking a little sheepish and turning redder then he normally was. "I just snorted some corn up my nose. Guess I shouldn't have tried to listen and chew and think at the same time."

The idea of corn being in his nose made the elves all snicker with silliness which broke the mood. Now, they were thinking on some ways they could help Santa.

"Would you like me to paint him a picture, Sandra?" Violet asked.

"Of course I would," Sandra said, smiling. She loved elf ideas.

"I don't like Santa being sad either," said Tack. "I'll work on finishing up the new robot so he can try it out."

"I'll do a card for him," Dear Lovey proclaimed. "And make it extra special with glitter."

"Glitter!" the elves shouted together and then up they stood, all together, and headed for the factory to get their ideas going. Sandra didn't have a long-term answer yet, but, in the short-term, the elves knew exactly how to get Santa to smile.

CHAPTER 47

A Santa Saver

Location: North Pole Village

It was November already and there was so much to do every day. From sun up to sun down, every man, woman, and elf at the North Pole were on the run. The letters to Santa, specifically, might have slowed down but they were still coming in. They just were coming in more and more addressed to Sandra, along with the kindness lists.

Both Santa's tried to ignore the trend. Santa put a good face of positivity on and Sandra tried to ignore the tug in her heart that worried about him. Sandra had directed the elves in the mailroom to put all the letters addressed to both of them in Santa's pile, which helped to keep it all looking more even. The volume of letters was higher than ever, no matter what Santa they were addressed to, since there were more children than ever. That meant there were more toys to make and that kept everyone busy. Too busy to fret.

With the little bit of time Sandra did find for herself, she tried to spend some of it getting in a few laps at the pool with Dear Lovey and using the gym equipment. She was just leaving the gym one morning when the words "breaking news" appeared, flashing, in all caps, on the big screen TV in the gym lobby area. It looked like Beatrice Carol was about to speak. Sandra stopped for a moment to hear what the busy reporter was chasing down now. She suspected the news was grim, as breaking news so often was, and if so, she would just go on her way. Often though, Beatrice Carol was reporting on acts of kindness by children. Sandra hoped that was what this would be about too. She reached for the controller to turn the volume up.

"We interrupt this broadcast to bring you the latest in a strange turn of events," an announcer said as Beatrice Carol brought her microphone to her mouth to speak. The words "breaking news" now moved from the middle of the screen to the bottom. Beatrice Carol pointed to the sky.

"I am here in downtown London where we are witnessing what appears to be magical words appearing in the sky. In fact, it seems these messages are not appearing just here in London but above cities all around the world," the reporter was saying. "No one see's how they are appearing and the theories are running rampant. Let's look at this one above us here." The camera moved to show the writing in the sky as Beatrice Carol continued.

"'Santa is sad' it reads." The reporter read each word off slowly as Sandra gasped and leaned against a lobby couch for support. "Other versions have been appearing everywhere today around the globe. Check out some of the views from our sister stations." The screen jumped around to show other words written in the sky. They looked like cloud words.

Santa is sad read the one above London, England.

Please write Santa said another above Sydney, Australia.

Santa needs letters read one over Johannesburg in South Africa.

Please love both Santas was the appeal over New York City in the U.S.

Santa loves you was the sweet message in Spanish over Panama City in Panama.

Send in your lists was the message in French above Paris, France.

"These mysterious messages in the sky have been appearing randomly around the globe,"

Beatrice Carol continued. "We actually watched this one appear out of nowhere! There is literally nothing there spelling the words and yet, there," she pointed skyward, dramatically, "they are."

As she continued to point, the camera panned the crowd around her.

"Who is writing these?" Sandra asked, staring at the screen.

"Who is writing these messages?" the reporter echoed the question that not just Sandra, but everyone, was asking. "How are they doing it? There is no plane. No drone of any sort. The words are simply coming out of thin air. Equally mysterious is that they don't leave quickly like a message written by a plane would. These words have now been there, just like that, easy to read, for more than an hour.

"Let me see if any of our bystanders here think they know what is happening. Sir, who do you think is making these messages?" the reporter asked a man near her.

"Why, I think it's a bunch of fuss about nothing. Those probably aren't even words but just clouds that look like words."

The reporter looked at him like he had come from another planet and moved on. "How about you?" she asked of a nearby woman staring at the sky. "What, or who, do you think is writing these messages?"

The woman with kind eyes looked at Beatrice Carol and the camera and paused before she replied. "I don't really know," she said finally. "But I hate to think that Santa is sad. My family loves Santa. We will write and tell him tonight!"

"Well, news viewers, what do you think? I have reached out to the North Pole who assure me this is not some kind of publicity stunt. But if it isn't them who is writing these messages and why? Do you think Santa is sad? When's the last time you wrote Santa? Does your family love the happy, old, guy? Children, tell us this, do you still love Santa? I know him personally and will reach out for comment directly from him. Meanwhile, this is Beatrice Carol with the World Wide News Network."

Sandra clicked the TV off, completely puzzled just as Breezy came running in, breathless.

"Sandra, come quick! Santa called an emergency Claus Council meeting and he wants you there. He's mad!" She said the last two words a little quietly, like she had never said them before, and looked quickly around to see if anyone else might have heard her.

Oh goodness, this can't be good, Sandra thought. At least she didn't have to ponder what he wanted to talk about. She was pretty sure she had just seen for herself what it was.

# # #

"I want to know who is doing this?" Santa boomed out as Sandra and Breezy slipped into the room. He was pointing to the screen on a Claus Council Room TV showing the writing appearing around the world. Thankfully, the sound was turned off. "And I want to know now!"

Like usual, there was a big overfilled bowl of candy in the middle of the table but, unlike usual, none of the elves were munching on any. Instead they were pressed back into their seats, eyes wide, a little taken aback by Santa's strong words. It was so unusual for him to express any stress or outright anger.

"Breezy, do you know?" Breezy just shook her head. "Tack? Waldorf? Zinga, surely you didn't arrange this?" He turned to every elf at the table and they all shook their heads wordlessly.

"I do not need a public relations campaign!" Santa said, loudly, feeling as frustrated as he ever had. Yes, the number of his letters was at an all-time low, and yes, it seemed the children would never turn their attention back to his old traditional ways, but if that was their choice then that was their choice. He would learn to live with it. This sky writing was, well, it was humiliating and he wanted it to end.

"Beatrice Carol said she talked to the North Pole," Santa said, still talking loudly. "Who talked to her? What did you say? Breezy, I believe that is part of your job." He looked around at the table until his eyes landed on the nervous elf.

"No-no-nothing really, Santa," Breezy stammered out. "She called the press line and I told her we had no idea who was doing it because we don't. I didn't really know what she was talking about. None of us are sky writers and none of us, except Em, flies."

"I didn't do it!" Em said standing up and starting to spin. Nerves and anger usually sent her into a spin.

"Now, now, Em," Santa said. "None of us think you did."

Sandra reached out and slowed her little friend down till she sat back down on her own.

"Sandra," Santa now turned his attention to her. "Is this your idea? Did you recruit someone for this?"

Sandra fought feeling hurt that Santa thought she would do something to hurt him or do anything like this without seeking his counsel. But a part of her wished that she had thought of it. This was being done by someone that loved Santa.

"I didn't Santa, but I wish I had," she said with more strength in her words than she felt. Even she was a little scared of how angry Santa seemed. The elves and Santa all stared at her, thinking they hadn't heard her correctly.

"That's right," she said, now standing up and moving to the TV screen. "This is clearly being done by someone who cares about you. Someone who loves you like we do, so you're right to think it's one of us.

"I wish I knew who it was so I could thank them." Santa went to protest but Sandra hurried on.

"Santa, you've been sad and we've been worried. The world's children have been all caught up in the latest greatest which happens to be me, right now, and haven't been paying enough attention to the old and the true, and, let's face it, the very best." Santa went to protest again but now it was the elves who spoke up.

"The very best!"

"You are Santa!"

"Sandra is right!"

"No other Santa comes close!"

Well that was a little more than she had expected, Sandra thought, smiling. *Oh, the honesty and loyalty of elves!* She continued as Santa enjoyed the moment.

"Someone, obviously, has been worried about you and the children," Sandra said. "Sure I want them to be kind and good and send in their examples but if they don't start getting their letters in to you right away, we aren't going to know what they really want for Christmas! This is sort of becoming an emergency situation this late in the season! So yes, I wish I had ordered the sky writing."

She looked over at Santa almost daring him to continue to shout. He spoke more calmly now.

"I understand what you are saying," he said with as much patience as he felt he could muster. "But surely there was another way to handle it."

A knock came to the door and Zinga scrambled to answer it. She read the note handed to her and handed it to Sandra, who smiled.

"Well, Santa, you can stay grumpy and keep all of us here, or you can dismiss us so you, and the rest of us, can get back to work answering the seventy-seven bags of letters that just arrived already!" She couldn't help herself. She jumped up and down as the elves all cheered!

Santa though was quiet . . . before he broke out in the biggest grin they had seen him wear for weeks, maybe months!

"Pass me that bowl of candy there would you, Waldorf? I'm going to need some sugar to get me through those bags."

The elves all cheered as Sandra grabbed a Yellow Buzzer (the newest candy treat that "buzzed" your mouth like a bee sometime while you sucked on it but you never knew exactly when) from the big bowl before every piece was taken by the rest!

CHAPTER 48

A Bird in Distress

Location: St. Annalise

Sandra had been working for weeks without a single day off or any trips to St. Annalise. Letters now were pouring into both Santas, requests to meet both Santa's were coming in and fan mail for both was piling up. The two Santas were working constantly to get in as many guest appearances as they could manage and children were swooning once again for Sandra – and for Santa! Everywhere they went, there were long lines to meet each of them. It made them both happy, and even Santa had to concede the sky writing idea hadn't turned out to be a terrible idea after all. It did seem he had been suffering from a bit of an unexpected public relations problem.

He was terribly frustrated, however, that no one had claimed responsibility for the sky messages.

Sandra had set all of that aside. The children from the first drawing were finally due at the Pole that week and she had had no real time to get home to St. Annalise and see how the progress was going on the barge or check in with Birdie on ideas for the children while they were visiting North Pole Village. Not to mention, she was the worst maid of honor ever, since she had barely had any time to focus on Cappie, and the wedding, since she and Em had thrown her the surprise shower. Oh, and it was her birthday that week. Jason's too.

It really was all too much, so she decided to change it. Too busy was never healthy and it called for a break. Without over thinking it, and telling only Breezy and Birdie, she decided to give herself a birthday present and popped into the new magic portal. She arrived in minutes on her beautiful barge.

"Well, lookee, lookee, who we have here," said a delighted Gunny, who was working nearby with his brother. It was either Ghost or Crow but Sandra couldn't immediately tell. She was just glad to see the smiling brothers. "I do believe Sandra Claus has come to hear our Christmas list, Crow." *Well, there was that answer*, she thought. She grinned at them both.

"You can put those items right on a list and send it off to the North Pole care of Santa Claus, who, by the way, is the top guy again! You would not believe how many long lists and nice words have been coming in for him since we talked about it that day with the elves, Gunny. He's been very happy. Me too." She smiled thinking about it. Gunny had returned to St. Annalise to work on the barge that same day after their "corny conversation" as he thought of it, and they hadn't had any chances to talk since then. With the push for Christmas on, conversation was a luxury this time of year.

"So Quisp did good then?" Gunny asked. "Her sky-writing plan worked? I wasn't sure it would." "What?" Sandra stammered out. "It was Quisp? You're saying our little tiny Quisp wrote out all those messages?" She was shocked thinking about it but then realized she hadn't seen the tiny fairy for weeks. Sandra thought she had returned to the South Pole outpost.

"She's tiny but she apparently can be mighty," Gunny said. "She whispered to me that day we were around the table that her name was Quisp because her fairy power was 'wisping.' To be honest, I didn't really know what that meant but she said it was like making clouds. She was embarrassed because, she felt, and the fairies felt, it was such a silly fairy power but she thought she could write something in the clouds for Santa. And she did. Turns out, she had one of the best fairy powers of all, I'd say."

"Quisp," Sandra repeated, so impressed with the little fairy. She would have never guessed it was Quisp but it just proved again that no one should judge another on appearance, or size, or anything else really. Quisp was the littlest fairy of all but she had done something really awesome for Santa. Sandra could hardly wait to thank her - and keep her secret.

"If you two don't mind, please do me a favor and keep this between just us," she said as the two nodded. They didn't need to know all the details. It was enough that Sandra asked.

"So, are you here to help?" Gunny teased, handing her a hammer. She looked at it skeptically. "More to hinder then help, I fear. I would really love a tour of what all has got done since I was here last and I know that will take you away from your work. Sorry, Crow," she said, trying to flash him her most apologetic smile.

"It's all good," Crow said. "He'll be nicer this way, anyway."

"I'll see you tonight at dinner with Birdie," Sandra said as they turned to leave. "Gunny, is the ceiling done in the main hall? I can't wait even one more minute to see it!"

"Miss Claus dot dot dot! Here you are! Birdie said you would be here," Redwood sputtered as he ran up at breakneck speed and made a gangly stop in front of them. Gunny had requested Redwood for working on the barge since, this year, he hadn't yet fully learned how to mass produce toys. Plus, he was a skilled woodworker and the barge was full of beautiful woods. The big elf now collected himself. Pulled on his shirt a bit to straighten it and addressed Sandra again.

"All the elves are looking for you Miss Claus dot dot dot," the formally-polite elf said to Sandra.

"Why, Redwood? What's wrong? And please, as I keep mentioning, call me Sandra," Sandra was moving to follow him as Crow set down his hammer at the mention of Birdie's name and Gunny pointed her toward the door.

"It's Birdie," Redwood said. "Her mom's here. She made Birdie cry." The tall elf said as he wiped away his own tear. Crying always made elves cry.

"This is the fastest way off the barge right now," Gunny said, taking her arm and heading toward the far door that Crow had already run off through. "The other way has all sorts of things in the way that you have to go over and around."

"Birdie's mom is here?" Sandra was trying to sort out what she was hearing. Selena Snow, was a tribal princess of her African nation and rarely left the continent. Sandra had only met her twice before and both times she had gone with Birdie to Africa to see her. Only Birdie's dad had visited them on the island prior to this time.

Sandra went running across the island from the barge and found the mother and daughter in a surprisingly loud conversation outside one of the St. Annalise Academy main doors. Sandra thought of Birdie as always being gracious and serene. Her mother, too, had seemed the same but neither was showing those qualities at the moment.

"You ignored my letters and made me come here." Royal Selena Snow of the Secret People was saying, while stomping around Birdie who was standing still and looking sullen. Sandra thought she had never ever seen Birdie take that kind of pose.

"Oh, here you are, Sandra," Selena Snow said to Sandra as she ran up. "Please talk some sense into my daughter. She is a princess of the land, as you know, and her mother, the grand princess, has summoned her. I have, in fact, been summoning her for months." Sandra remembered the letter Birdie had been reading when they met after her tour and suspected that it was about whatever her mother was upset about now.

"She must respond. Instead, she refuses, for months, until I must come here myself and still she dares to refuse me. This is not to be tolerated. Where is Christina Annalise? Is this the behavior I should expect from this school we have sent her to?"

"This has nothing to do with Christina Annalise!" Birdie said firmly with emotion. "She is a wonderful mentor for me. This is about me and my right to make my own decisions. I knew if I returned to discuss this with you that you would insist I stay and I like my life here, mother. Here with my friends, and the elves, and Sandra, and serving the children. And I like the boyfriend I have." She smiled woefully at Crow, who seemed to know to stay separate from her. Maybe it was the withering glance that Birdies's mother was giving him.

"Your boyfriend? Your *boyfriend?*" This news of Crow seemed hard for Selena to grasp. Now she stared at the handsome young man until Crow began feeling like he wished he had stayed on the barge. "Does your *boyfriend* know of your betrothed?"

The whole of the large group gathered around them gasped as Birdie looked crestfallen. "Birdie?" Crow asked, looking confused. Sandra went over to her best friend. "Bird?" she asked. She too had never heard anything about Birdie being engaged. It hardly seemed possible since she almost never went home.

"I am not marrying someone I've never met," Birdie said with the firmest voice Sandra thought she had ever heard her best friend use.

"You have never met him by your choice but your engagement is not a surprise. You have known! Your twentieth birthday approaches and the formal ceremonies will begin on that day." Selena Snow turned to the gathering and added, "All of this she knows. All of this is a requirement of our lineage. It is how I was wed to her father and how my mother met my father as well. This is not an option."

She turned back to speaking to her daughter directly. "I should not have had to come here for you, Ambyrdena, princess of our people. Your role is one of great opportunity."

"Opportunity? It is obligation, mother, not opportunity," Birdie said with restrained fire in her voice. "My 'role' requires of me to sacrifice who I am for who it was determined I would be at my birth. My role. What about my happiness? I honor the ways you have chosen mother, I do, but I am very determined to live a different way. I am happy mother! Please be happy for me."

"You will be happy again, Ambyrdena, but this is not a choice I am here to present, it is your destiny." She looked around and her eyes landed again on Crow, who now had come forward and stood next to Birdie with his arm around her. "Perhaps it was good she had a chance to know you, but it will make this transition easier if you bid her a goodbye without tears or drama."

"Unless she asks it of me, I will not," Crow said. "I can't. She means too much to me."

"We love each other mother," Birdie said. "Surely you understand love."

"Of course I do, Amyrdena! I love your father but that wasn't so when we were joined. It came to be as it will for you and your chosen husband. Now, where can I stay tonight? We will rest before leaving in the morning for home."

"No, your highness," Birdie said addressing her mother formally. "I understand you believe in what you ask of me and it gives me great sorrow to bring you any distress. I would dare to hope you would feel the same for me, as my treasured mother, and want for me whatever I want for myself. My home is here now with all of these people who I also call family."

"Surely, Ambyrdena, you understand these feelings of love for this, this, boy, are likely fleeting?" Birdie felt Crow's arm tighten around her protectively with those words.

"My feelings for her are true and strong," he said with a tinge of anger and pride flashing in his eyes.

"It's okay," Birdie assured him. "You may be right, mother, but to that I say that Crow is just part of the life I choose to live. I contribute here! I make a difference! I love these people and this life in the same way that I love you and father – fully and with all my heart."

"We love you too, Birdie!" the few elves that were still on St. Annalise cried out together, wiping at their eyes. The discord and idea of losing Birdie was creating big elf tears.

". . . *squawk*! . . . me too! . . ." The big red bird came and landed on Birdies shoulder, knowing he was always welcome. Birdie reached up and stroked his favorite spot just under his chin. Sandra noticed even the island birds were flying about now. They all knew Birdie because she alone could speak with them. Birdie, and the birds, all loved their bond.

The mother and daughter stood there with a canyon of difference and silence stretched out between them. Cappie had arrived at the standoff and now helped to break the tension.

"Sometimes things are best decided after some rest," she said warmly to Selena Snow. "We would be honored to have you as our guest on the *Mistletoe* tonight if you would be willing to grace us with your company."

She added, "Ambyrdena stays there as well."

Selena Snow, nodded graciously, looking at her daughter and turning to Cappie. "It would be my honor and I thank you. Would it be possible for me to join you there now? I find myself in need of some time to rest and think."

"Of course," Cappie said, turning to show her the way. "Join me for the walk across the island and we can discuss our choices for dinner."

"Ambyrdena, enjoy your evening with your friends," Selena Snow said as a sort of royal command, Sandra thought.

Sandra walked immediately over to her best friend who clung to her, and cried. "Sandra, what will I do?" Birdie asked with sorrow in her voice.

"Start by filling me in and we will figure it out," Sandra said, consolingly.

"There is nothing to figure out," Selena Snow called back. "Her path is clear. Tonight is her last night here."

CHAPTER 49

A Deal is Struck

Location: St. Annalise Island

After a full day of crying, lamenting, and talking with her friends without any resolution to the problem she faced. Birdie got to the tug late that evening. But if she thought the late hour meant she could avoid her mother she was wrong.

"Ambyrdena," said a voice she knew as her mother's coming from the back deck. "We must talk. Alone. Here together as we have always been able to do. A mother and daughter who love each other."

Birdie knew it too. Above everything else, she did love her mother but she wasn't at all happy with her at the moment. She walked over to where her mom sat primly with a blanket around her and sat down across from her.

"I've made a decision," Selena Snow said at last.

"As my mother or my ruler?" Birdie said tiredly, knowing they had to have this conversation.

"Both, I suppose. I will give you a reprieve," said her mother.

"A reprieve? What does that mean?"

"I will postpone your return," she said, and Birdie's heart soared with hope. "For one month." Birdie's heart sank again. One month was nothing.

"During that month, I ask that you not see this Crow. Could he go away, perhaps? Instead, you will spend time with your betrothed."

"Mother, that is not a reprieve at all! I told you already that I will not return to Africa right now."

"You will not have to. I will send Sam here."

"Sam? I had almost forgotten his name." That wasn't really true. Such a simple name was hard to forget but Birdie was feeling stubborn.

"He is not as displeasing as you seem to think he is or re-member him as," said her mother.

"Remember him? I remember almost nothing about him. I've only heard stories of him and had forgotten I was promised until your letter last month arrived. Until then it seemed like part of a tribal story about somebody else's life."

"Well it is not about someone else's life, it's about yours and it's important. And it's something that, normally, as your ruler, I would not consider a compromise on. As your mother, howev-er, your happiness is of great importance to me." She patted the seat beside her for Birdie to join her but Birdie stayed where she was. Her mother pressed on.

"If you will agree to Crow going and Sam arriving and allow him to court you with an open mind to considering him, I shall agree to your decision at the end of that time."

Birdie found this to be both a frustrating and tempting offer. She had absolutely no interest in meeting this Sam, let alone "being courted" by him and she had no interest in being separated from Crow. However, she also recognized her mother could enforce a marriage protocol or at least make her life quite unhappy, and the offer her mother proposed was unprecedented. Plus, a month was not that much time to be free of it forever.

"Yes. I will do it, mother," she said, yawning. "I will agree to see if Crow will step away and to then spend time with Sam."

Her mother felt some hope surge in the same way Birdie did but for opposite reasons.

"But I also have my own terms. It will have to be after Christmas," Birdie continued. "We can't just drop things around here. Truly, mother, we're busy. It can be for the month of February." It was the shortest month of the year and therefore, perfect from Birdie's perspective.

"It will be for January," her mother said firmly, knowing what her daughter was thinking.

Birdie didn't want to argue. "Okay, agree.

"And secondly, you must not counsel or guide this Sam in anyway. If we are to get to know each other in a short time, than I will need him to be his true self, as I promise to be in return.

That is the only counsel I want you to give him: be your true self."

Selena wondered to herself how her daughter had grown to be so wise. She wanted to think she had had some influence on her but it seemed her treasured daughter had been wise since the moment she was born.

"I agree to that point as well. I will send him to arrive on January first. It will be the perfect way for you to start the new year and your new life." Birdie was too tired to argue and simply ignored her words.

"Then we have an agreement – provided Crow agrees – and, now, I am going to bed," Birdie said. She now walked over to her mother. "Tweet, tweet, mama," she said and kissed her on the cheek.

"Tweet, tweet, my love," Selena said in return, loving that her daughter had used their affectionate good night from her childhood. For the first time since she had arrived, it seemed to her, that all would be right again in the world. After meeting Sam she knew her daughter would do the right thing.

Birdie was thinking the same thing. She would indeed do the right thing. She would meet this Sam, send him away, and stay right there on St. Annalise. That was the exact right thing for her.

CHAPTER 50

Kids at the Pole!

Location: North Pole Village

Sandra only enjoyed two fast days at home on St. Annalise but it was enough to renew her and push her through to Christmas. She had finally got the tour of all the work Gunny and the others had completed on the barge. The elves had been a big help, but this close to Christmas, most were all back at the North Pole helping with the final push on toy production. Only a few stayed to help Gunny with the many things that needed done there on the barge.

It was probably for the best that the elves were gone. The barge was coming together with just about as much finished as not finished. The elf quarters were being finished next and getting those done without input from the elves would make the whole process go much faster. Sandra was pretty sure she knew what they would like. She ordered lots of bright colors and fun designs put on the walls, with spots of glitter-reflecting light here and there that would sparkle bright when the sun hit through the portholes.

Most of her time at home, she had spent with Cappie and Thomas going over all the details on the wedding and reception, and what still needed to be done. Happiness oozed out of the couple and was contagious for all of those around them. Sandra was sure that even Selena Snow had returned to Africa happier than she had been when she arrived.

Adding to Sandra's happy calm was the two hours she had spent at the beach surfing. Even better, surfing with her friends. Spence and Birdie and Jason all made time in their schedule to drop all the busy things they had going on and hit the waves with Sandra. It felt like old times. She realized how much she missed it and resolved to be sure she got in more wave time after Christmas. January was Slumber Month for the elves so she knew she could get some needed free time then to call her own. Surfing was one of her very favorite ways to spend it.

She had particularly loved the time spent with Jason. It wasn't about being a couple, or not, but rather about spending time together as genuine friends, with their best friends, doing something they all enjoyed and had in common. It was easy, relaxing, and the perfect way for them to spend their shared birthday. Cappie had baked a cake that night and the whole of the island had popped by to give their good wishes. Except for the troubling situation with Selena Snow, almost every minute Sandra had spent at home had been perfect. She knew she and Jason, and even she and Gunny, had things ahead to figure out, but she gave her head a shake just to clear the thoughts.

Those matters were for after the holiday.

Now with Birdie and Spence in tow, they were loaded in the Pole to Pole Portal – the PtoP as they had taken to calling it – and headed back to North Pole Village to meet and greet the children who were arriving that day. Santa and Mrs. Claus had agreed to host the parents so that Sandra and her friends could focus on the boys and girls. There were exactly six of each.

"Sandra! There you are!" Breezy called out as soon as the portal arrived at the Pole. "They're here."

"Who's here?" Sandra asked, confused.

"The children," Breezy said. "The reindeer express arrived early. Barney is giving them a tour in the barn."

"Why in the flying reindeers are they already here? Since when does the express run ahead of schedule?" Sandra asked, feeling flustered at the news. The group wasn't due for another four hours. Despite having a full year to plan, Sandra suddenly didn't feel ready. "Oh, never mind. It doesn't matter now. Birdie, can I look at your agenda again?"

Sandra actually had one of her own but Birdie handed hers over to her clearly nervous best friend. Now wasn't the time to point out the obvious.

"Okay, so the line-up is tweaked just a little since they are starting with a tour of the barn and we were going to do that last. Instead, it's now first, followed by a tour of downtown, a tour of the sports center, a tour of the toy factory and then a thirty-minute meeting with Santa.

"Tomorrow, we'll give them a tour of the elf neighborhoods, a tour of the park and finish with a special performance by Buddy and Ellen before they head out for home. Everybody got that?"

Spence and Birdie nodded, excited, but feeling a little anxious.

"That sounds boring."

It was Em, being Em, who stated the obvious. She had come running to find Sandra and listened to the line-up Sandra had just reviewed.

"What?" Sandra looked at the stubbon little delgin.

"Well, not to be rude, Sandra," said Breezy. "But Em is right. It sounds boring. Who wants to tour everything? The children are here to have fun."

Oh Oh Oh, how right they are, Sandra suddenly thought. *Oh the simple wisdom of elves. What had she been thinking? Not about the kids, for sure, but really about being efficient and that was not what this tour was about. This tour was supposed to be about kindness and having fun.*

"You two are one hundred percent right," Sandra said, kneeling down to talk to them on their level. This was important and she wanted to get it right. "So, what should we have them do?"

"Anything they want," said Em in her matter-of-fact way.

"Well that seems a little bit chaotic but I understand what you're saying and I have an idea,"

Sandra said. "Breezy would you go round up twelve elf volunteers that would like to spend two days hosting our guests? They will each need to be willing to take their personal guest anywhere they would like to go, get them to meals, and most importantly of all, make sure they have fun.

Do you think we have any elves willing to do that?" Sandra asked, knowing she had a whole Pole full.

"I will do it, Breezy!" Em said, as excited as Sandra had seen her in weeks.

"I will too, of course," said Breezy. "So now we'll just need ten more instead of twelve. I think I'll start with the rest of the Northern Lights and ask the others individually. Okay Sandra, we gotta go!"

Off the two elves ran, chattering the whole way, as Sandra and her friends went equally fast in the direction of the barn.

"Make sure they check with Tack!" Sandra called after them. Tack was a task master this time of year and even Sandra didn't dare interrupt his production schedule.

"So, what do you two think?" Sandra asked her friends. "Should we try this plan out instead?"

"What I want to know is, what were we thinking?" Birdie asked in response. "Of course the children are going to want to have fun with the elves. This is a much better plan!"

"Hey, don't even ask me," said Spencer. "I said all along that I didn't know what to have them do. Plus, no hitting me, but I like tours."

The two girls groaned at him good naturedly as the trio walked briskly to the barn to meet the dynamic group of kind kids, as the elves had taken to calling them, waiting there for them.

Barney had many very fine qualities and talents but one of them, it turned out, was not tour guide. The group found him with the children, all crowded into an empty reindeer stall, with Barney talking on how to clean a stall!

"Hello, everyone!" Sandra called from across the arena area.

"Look! Its Sandra Claus dot dot dot!" the children all seemed to say together.

"Whew," said Barney as they all scrambled to leave the stall. It had been the longest hour of his long elf life.

Sandra gave him a wave and went around with Birdie and Spence to officially meet each child, though she felt she already knew them so well from their letters. They were each even better than she had imagined. She noted to herself that her nervousness had been time wasted and she wouldn't do that again. *Nervous meeting children? What was that about?* The thoughts ran through her head as she greeted each of the delightful, kind-hearted kids who, themselves, seemed rather nervous. And then they seemed rather distracted, looking at something behind her.

Even before Sandra turned around she could hear elf tittering coming from the big hay bales that were stacked against the tall wall. Elves were so out-going most of the time, but often very shy in the beginning, of any new experience, and though they could hardly wait to meet the kind kids, it would take a little coaxing to get them out of the hay.

"So, kind kids, as the elves love to call you all, which, I think, is such a perfect group name," Sandra said, grinning at them all. "We had a whole schedule set up for you to tour and learn while you are here and then we realized that you only have two days and what we most want in those two days is for you to have fun! So we threw out our boring, non-elf-approved agenda and decided to pair you up with elves for the two days. Does that sound like fun?"

"YESSSSSS!" the children said with such enthusiasm that Sandra knew it was the perfect solution. *Thank you, Em and Breezy*, she thought again in her head. Now the elves were starting to peek their heads out of the hay more and the children were all pointing and laughing.

"Okay, so do I have any elf that would like to have fun with Bella?" Birdie asked, taking over for Sandra. She was reading off a clipboard so she could write down each pairing.

"Me!" came shouts as two elves jumped out of the hay. It was Breezy and Em. "There are two elves for each child," Breezy said primly. "It could have been three but I got stern."

Birdie just smiled. She was sure it could have been five elves per child for a plum assignment like this. She thought Breezy had done great keeping it to just two.

"Well, then, perfect," Birdie said. "Bella, please meet your wonderful escorts for the next two days, Breezy and Em. Now who wants to go next?"

It took a full hour to get it all sorted out and, in the end, one child had three elves because there was an odd number of elf volunteers but the only part that really mattered was they all looked spectacularly happy. Even Tack and Zinga, two of the busiest elves that time of the year, had volunteered. Elves simply couldn't resist getting the chance to spend time with the kids they devoted their lives to serving. Sandra's favorite moment might have been watching the child assigned to Ellen and Buddy marching down the street to Buddy's latest rendition of "Jingle Bells."

She turned from watching the last of them go and faced her friends. "Well that was harder and easier than we expected!" she said. "Thanks for the help, you two. Care to get a cup of cocoa at our favorite stand and watch some of the fun from the town square?"

"You don't have to ask me twice!" said Spence. "Although, Gunny said he had cocoa and corn on the cob together the last time he was here and I am definitely going to pass on that."

The girls laughed as they linked up their arms with his. "Me too!" they said in unison.

CHAPTER 51

Happy Christmas Eve!

Location: Around the world

Over the course of the two days, the Kind Kids did all sorts of things that Sandra and Birdie and Spence never considered and some that they had. The three got a lot of ideas for the next year when they kicked off the official Academy of Kindness on St. Annalise.

Almost all of the children wanted to do the same things, but they did most of them at different times. They also were clearly loving all the attention. When Sandra asked them at the end of their visit what they all liked most, every one of them said spending time with the elves was their favorite part. That gave the elves sniffles of joy, but none of them actually broke out crying.

During their time at the village, the children got to meet with both Santas and give them their Christmas lists and their list of kind things they had done at home that helped get them there.

That was Sandra's favorite part, for sure. They also got to ride Em, which they all loved. They got to watch a Pole Pong game – with their parents as pongers, which made them all laugh -- and go swimming with Dear Lovey. Plus, they joined a karaoke session with Ellen and Buddy and toured the toy factory to see their favorite toys being built.

The other thing they got to do was have a slumber party in the elf barracks. It sounded to Sandra like they had stayed up all night singing Christmas carols, telling crazy stories about Christmas and toys, and eating way too much candy. Basically, it sounded like the perfect night!

All the elves took a rare break from toy production to line up and see the children and their parents off. There were a few tears but mostly they were just happy children who all promised to keep being kind and gave genuine thanks and hugs to everyone. It tugged at Sandra's heart and she reached for a tissue from the box Zinga was holding.

"I know how you feel," Santa said, reaching for one too. "I can't even remember what this place was like before you got here, Sandra." Sandra burst into a happy grin at his kind words. She was part elf and smiling big came to her easily. The moment was so perfect and she was so happy again that Santa had selected her.

"I'm so lucky to be South Pole Santa with you, Santa. I could never thank you enough," she said, reaching over and hugging her mentor.

"Ah c'mon now," the big guy said, not wanting to show his teary elf side. "Time for all of us to wave good-bye and get back to what we do!"

"Good-bye!"

"Good-bye!

"Merry Christmas!"

"See you Christmas Eve, Santa!"

Sure enough, on Christmas Eve, both Santa and Sandra found two of the children waiting up for them. Normally, the Santa's would have given them a bit of magic powder to put them to sleep but because these children knew them personally they both had fun letting the children help stuff stockings at their homes.

After three years of working together, the two Santas had gotten a rhythm down on delivering gifts and, not surprisingly, liked working together. They weren't sure they would ever split up the world like they had originally planned but instead work together to deliver faster, everywhere. They did try to honor any special requests for one Santa, or another, for any children that made that request. Most children didn't care which Santa came, so long as their house didn't get skipped or passed over. Sandra had come up with a signature she liked to leave so that children at her assigned homes would know she had been there. She left a small seashell in the toe of each stocking she personally filled.

The two Santa's worked very differently. Santa used his magic to go down chimneys or make chimneys first, when needed, and pop into each home that way. Sandra used her locket to simply wish her way in. She liked her way much better and, in truth, it tended to be faster. Plus, she could use her ring to be invisible for those times when kids were still up.

In the air, Sandra loved his flying reindeer, including Rudolph at the lead and Sandra found herself with her own full group of helpers. Em, of course, was her transportation. This year Squawk had opted to use the special cage Spence had designed so he could come along, too.

Sandra loved having him there and he turned out to be a huge help to her.

". . . *squawk*! . . . two boys in the next house . . . *squawk*!" He would share with her information about each home and check the list for her so they didn't miss a single delivery.

And she had one more special helper with her. Once they had gotten airborne, out popped Quisp from Sandra's sparkly hair.

"Quisp!" Sandra had exclaimed. "What are you doing here? Are you okay? I haven't seen you in weeks. We're delivering presents right now." She was worried Quisp might have hid in her hair and not known.

"Oh, I know," she said in her tiny voice. "I wanted to help."

"What would you like to do?" Sandra asked, feeling a little puzzled on how the tiny fairy could help.

"I can add some fairy dust, if you like, to any gifts for kids that believe in fairies. They'll know it is fairy dust when they see it."

"That is wonderful," Sandra said, knowing some children would love that very special extra touch. "And Quisp, I know it was you that did the sky-writing for Santa. Thank you. But never do it again, okay? We wouldn't want you to get hurt or discovered."

"Okay," she said. "I did it because I love you, Sandra, and I love Santa."

"We love you back, sweet, little Quisp," Sandra said with huge affection. She had grown to care about several fairies she realized. From tiny to mighty. One real important fairy king was included in that mix. Thoughts of the past, however, could wait till a future time. Now was the present, and it was all about presents! The best night of the year!

"Em, straight ahead please! Squawk, is that Desmond's house?"

". . . *squawk* . . . it is . . . *squawk*!"

Sandra had suspected the bright little boy would be awake and he was - just barely. He was there waiting for her next to the stockings. She decided that he deserved to see her and she stayed visible.

"Sandra Claus dot dot dot!" he exclaimed when she appeared. "It's me, Desmond dot dot dot.

You know, from the beach. " He added the last part seriously.

"Oh, of course I know that, Desmond dot dot dot. I could never forget a friend like you," she assured him. The little boy just nodded, knowing that was true, which made Sandra grin even more.

"I put out the treats," he said motioning her to a plate and glass. "I know you like carrots so I picked those and I had to get new ice water for Em cause you got here so late and the ice all melted."

"Well, how nice of you," said Sandra crunching on a carrot. "Would you like to meet Em?"

"Would I ever!" Now the little boy was completely excited.

"Full size or elf size?" Sandra asked him.

"Full size, please," Desmond said in return.

Sandra walked to the nearest window and popped it open. It was a warm night there in San Diego, California. "Em," she called out, and just like that a big delgin head came in through the window. The little boy jumped back.

"She's big!" he said, clearly surprised by Em's true full size.

"She is, indeed," said Sandra. "But very nice and she really loves children who like to meet her.

And she loves ice water too. Would you like to help her with that?"

"O-okay," Desmond stammered, reaching for the glass. He was willing but not exactly sure what to do.

"Just take the ice and put it on your hand. She'll lick it all up from there," Sandra said.

The little boy scooped it up and held out his hand so Em could just barely get it. She reached over and nudged his face in thanks and he bravely reached up and petted her long green mane before he hugged her neck.

"I love you, Em," he said as Sandra's heart melted into a thousand pieces. *There is no better job, there is no better job*, rang through her head over and over.

At every house the same refrain was in her head. Along with *"I am the luckiest person I know. I am the luckiest person I know."*

Ten full minutes before midnight, in their last time zone, the two Santa's and their hard-working transportation had finished up. It was their fastest time yet!

"C'mon, Sandra," Santa said. "Let's head for St. Annalise Island!"

"You got it Santa," Sandra said. "Em, follow that sled!"

CHAPTER 52

The Best Christmas Ever

Location: St. Annalise

It took some coordinating, but for the first time ever in North Pole history, all the elves, except a very few Sherlocks for security reasons, were gone from North Pole Village on Christmas Day.

Instead, as soon as the two Santa's had left for their Christmas Eve deliveries, all of the elves, and Mrs. Claus, had used every magical method possible to get to St. Annalise Island and by noon on Christmas Day, they all had arrived.

Sandra and Em had beat most of them there and even managed to get in a little rest. Santa swung peacefully in a hammock for a couple of hours before the elves found him and elf piled in for a big Santa hug. "Merry Christmas Santa!" they exclaimed as they clamored to squeeze in.

"Ho Ho Ho! I'm so glad to see you all," Santa said, feeling like it might be one of the best Christmas days ever. "Careful now, careful. This hammock can barely hold me let alone me and too many elves." He went to try to sit up and the whole bunch of them, including Santa, landed in the sand below!

"Santa! You got sand on my outfit," said Goldie in a little elf huff that was unusual for her. All the elves were brushing each other off and Santa could see they were not dressed in their usual red and green working outfits.

"Look how wonderful you look in your dress-up clothes and glitter glasses," Santa said, seeing how handsome and pretty they all looked.

The elves all beamed. Nothing was better than a compliment from Santa and nobody cared about the sand now.

"We wanted to look our very best for the wedding," Perriwinkle said.

"*hiccup*! Do you like my top hat Santa? *hiccup*!"

"Why yes I do, Hiccup," Santa said, a little worried that it might be too hot in the tropical sun.

"Look!" Hiccup said, taking it off to show it off. "It doesn't have a top so air can get in. *hiccup*!"

"I custom designed each outfit and wanted each elf to have something special," Diva said, beaming and looking extra spectacular in a shiny silver dress – with flip flops. "Twirl around everyone, so Santa can see you."

It was a special site to see so many elves twirling in glitter and shine, some in dresses, some in pants, some with hats, some holding parasols for shade, all of them wearing huge smiles. Santa realized again how much joy Sandra had brought to the North Pole and the world. Most of the elves had never left the Pole and now most of them had taken two big trips just this year. Positive change was coming, not just to the whole world, but to Christmas and the North Pole too.

"Santa, I made you a special suit too," Diva said a little more shyly than normal. She wasn't entirely sure if Santa would welcome that kind of surprise or not. The elves all seemed to be holding their breath a bit. Santa didn't generally like change much more than they did. He did a little better with it overall but he would never be considered any kind of "champion for change."

"You did?" Santa said, taken a little aback. He was most at ease in his red and white suit but even he had to admit that it was a little too warm to wear on St. Annalise comfortably. If the elves could dress up, so could he. "Wonderful! I need to look as dapper as all you for this very special occasion. And elves, Merry Christmas! I am so proud of all of you."

"Merry Christmas Santa!" They all shouted at once. They loved this day always but this year was extra exciting.

"So, shall we go find where this wedding is happening?" Mrs. Claus said walking up to the group with a warm smile on her face.

"YES!" The elves all shouted out. Now they all jumped up and down, sand and hats flying everywhere. Most had never been to a wedding and couldn't wait to be at this one.

"You look beautiful, my dear," Santa said reaching for Mrs. Claus hand. "Let's go get me looking as good as the rest of you."

Sandra too, had realized that morning that this wedding of Cappie and Thomas was the first wedding she had been asked to as well. That made it even more special than it already was. When she and Em got back from their Christmas Eve deliveries they had gotten a couple hours of sleep but Sandra had woke up early and found Cappie already awake on the back deck of the *Mistletoe*. She had held out her arms for Sandra to slip in next to her on the big seat. Cappie hugged her tight.

"Oh my darling, darling, girl," Cappie said, holding her close. "You know I will always love you with the whole of my heart wherever I go, right? And that when you need me, I will never ever be far away?"

"Of course I know it Cap," Sandra said quietly. She loved Cappie with all of her heart and wanted this to be the best day ever. "No one, not even Thomas, could possibly ever change who we are together. We're family and now Thomas is part of this special family of ours – along with Squawk and Rio and Em – and, well, pretty much every other person and elf we know." The two laughed. "We're lucky, Cappie. We have lots of people we love and who love us back."

"We are lucky darling girl! Me, especially, for having you. I never would have wanted to lose your parents, you know that, but what a privilege it has been getting to be part of raising you," she squeezed Sandra tighter as if to never let her go and Sandra took in all the love.

"I wish they could be here today," Sandra said wistfully, knowing Cappie would know who she meant.

"I feel like they are," Cappie said. "I don't know why exactly, but for some reason, I have felt like they have been around. I have found myself talking out loud to your mother just in case and fully expected to get an answer." Sandra looked at her then, and Cappie pushed on, knowing what Sandra's look was about.

"No, I didn't get an answer. She seems to save those for you. It's been puzzling me, though, the last few days. Have you felt any different about them lately? Like they were close by?" Cappie asked it as casually as she could but she felt more intensely about it than she was indicating. She couldn't quite put her finger on it but there had been an energy around the *Mistletoe* lately. Like somebody – or something – was hanging about.

"I haven't felt them lately," Sandra said, wishing her answer was different. "But honestly, Cap, I've been so busy with Christmas, I hardly know what way is up and what way is down. I'm sorry I couldn't help more with the last minute wedding touches."

"Nonsense!" Cappie said. "We had almost everything ready weeks ago thanks to all your help and Birdie's help and even Ems. Christina has been indispensable the last two weeks and she's so happy having Jason home again. I really think this year might go down as one of my very favorite Christmas seasons ever!"

"Because you're in love," Sandra teased, sitting up and smiling at her. Cappie didn't argue but just smiled in return.

"Merry Christmas!" Birdie said bounding on to the deck with Em right behind. Em threw herself into Cappie's lap and hugged her.

". . . *squawk*! . . . Merry   Christmas!   Merry Christmas! . . . *squawk*!" Squawk wasn't about to be kept out of any Christmas or wedding fun.

"*eeeeee eeeeeeeeeeee eee!*"

"Merry Christmas, you all!" said Sandra, beaming and thinking that, like Cappie, it might very well be the best Christmas season ever. "Merry Christmas Rio! Leedy Aliota!" She added the elfin language version of Merry Christmas, as she loved the words.

"Hey, what's all the noise over there?" Thomas hollered over from the *Lullaby*. "You'd think it was Christmas day and someone was getting married or something." His smile was almost too big for his face. Cappie's was too.

"Merry Christmas, my bride!" he said to just Cappie. "Let's get this party started. This groom has been waiting long enough!"

CHAPTER 53

Wedding Bells!

Location: St Annalise

"Dearly beloved, we are gathered here . . ."

Sandra heard the minister but her mind was miles away. Cappie looked stunning in her long, island-style white dress. She might have been a capable, sea-going, tugboat captain and completely devoted guardian but when she chose to, usually only on very special occasions, Cappie could get as gussied up as anyone, and today she looked more stunning than she ever had in Sandra's lifetime.

Her dress caught in the island breeze and fluttered around, making it even prettier. Thomas, too, looked his best in a fine tropical style shirt that wouldn't fit in at many weddings but was perfect for this beautiful ceremony being held on one of the grassiest parts of the island, with one of the most stunning views of the ocean. It was a perfect spot.

Of course, Sandra was standing up as Cappie's maid of honor. Cappie had let her pick any color she wanted to wear. After a lot of consideration, Sandra had decided on a light green color that looked beautiful against her hair, represented the island setting, and still felt a bit like Christmas. Her hair looked magnificent with the island sun highlighting the sparkles in it. She had left it in her full Leezle, Christmas Eve, glory but chose to wear it up to help ensure it didn't take away from keeping attention on the bride and groom. Sparkly hair, for some, had a way of being distracting.

Cappie had asked Christina and Birdie to be her bridesmaids and had added on Em, too, who beamed like the sun shone only on her. It made Sandra's heart so happy seeing how proud the little delgin had looked coming down the aisle escorted by the very tall Gunny. What a sight! But somehow it had worked. The happy look Gunny wore helped people not to laugh at all at their disparity in heights as they saw him taking it all in stride.

Thomas had asked Spencer to be his best man and Spence looked almost as handsome as Thomas that day standing there next to him. Spence had been honored to have been asked and kept smiling at Sandra every time she looked over. Making it even more special was that Squawk sat quietly on Spence's shoulder taking his role as "second best man . . . *squawk*!" very seriously. Cappie and Thomas had wanted the big bird to be part of such a wonderful event and he was doing his part to behave. He, too, had fussed and preened all morning and his feathers looked clean and full. Sandra could not have loved him more in that moment.

She marveled again to see how handsome Santa looked in his tropical shirt too. It was a completely different look to see the Christmas icon with a trimmed beard and sunglasses. Followed by Jason as the other groomsman, standing there next to Gunny, and both of them looking happy being up there together. That was just another little, mini-miracle, moment of the day, as far as Sandra was concerned.

Originally, Cappie and Thomas had talked about having a very small ceremony with just a few people gathered on the *Mistletoe*. Sandra was so glad that the couple had changed their minds.

Once they thought about it more, they knew that, for such an important occasion, they wanted all the people they loved and who loved them to be there.

Sandra looked out again to the large gathering of islanders they had called friends for years and years and elves who had seemed part of their life for much longer than they actually had been. The elves were all dabbing at their eyes as Zinga and Dear Lovey handed out tissues down the rows. Gunny's family, too, had been invited which had taken special clearance from Christina Annalise as only by her okay could people be invited and actually find the very remote and hidden St. Annalise Island. Sandra loved seeing them all there celebrating this very special occasion. That made two Christmases in a row they had all been together. *But this one is a lot better than last year,* she thought, glad to put the last one in the past. Her eyes lingered on Ghost and Wistle holding hands in the audience and looking so happy together. Mango sat quietly with them. The whole moment washed her in a light of incredible gratitude and happiness. There was nowhere in the whole of the world, not even with her parents she realized in that moment, that she would rather be.

Even as she thought it, her mother whispered in her ear, "We wouldn't have missed this." And her father whispered in her other, "Merry Christmas, Cherry Top!" She smiled so big she was afraid she was going to outshine the bride at that moment! Cappie had been right! They were around!

It wasn't a long ceremony and Sandra realized how much her mind had wandered when she heard the officiant say happily, ". . . I now pronounce you husband and wife. Thomas Jackson you may kiss your bride!" With those words, Thomas reached over and dipped Cappie down for a big, dramatic, kiss and the whole of the gathering burst into cheers and applause. And just when it seemed the moment couldn't get even a tiny bit better, it did. The fairies of the island, led by Wistle, orbed over the happy couple and sprinkled them with glittering, effervescent fairy dust in indescribable colors. It floated out to the whole of the wedding gathering. It was the most perfect, magical, moment Sandra thought she had ever experienced. She deliberately thought to herself, *"save this memory for all time."* It was a memory she knew she would love coming back to over and over. This was happiness wrapped up in wedding finery and it was wonderful!

Cappie reached over and hugged Sandra extra hard. Sandra took the opportunity to whisper to her. "You were right, Cap. Mom and dad are here. They told me so just a little while ago."

"I just knew they wouldn't miss this," Cappie said in return.

"Love you, Mrs. Jackson," Sandra said, smiling in return.

"I love you too, Cappie," Em said, wrapping her arms around Cappie's legs.

"Thank you Em. I love you too," Cappie said, as others closed in on her, and the men gathered around to shake Thomas' hand in congratulations. Finally Thomas worked his way free.

"Excuse me, but my *wife* and I have some official papers to sign. Then we will meet you all at the wedding reception on the South Pole Village for the first ever celebration to be held on the barge. Join me, my dear?" he held out his hand to Cappie, who slipped her hand in his, as they headed off with the officiant for official business.

As far as Sandra was concerned, this was the best day ever. First, it was Christmas, already the most wonderful day of the year (well, tied with Christmas Eve). Then, it was Thomas and Cappie's wedding day. And finally, it was the day of the official reveal of the main floor of the South Pole Village barge! She could hardly stand how excited she was for this big reveal. Thomas and Cappie had wanted some time of their own after the ceremony. They asked Sandra if she could think of a way to entertain their guests so they wouldn't have to hurry back to the reception and they thought what she had come up with – along with Santa – was the perfect solution.

"Ladies and gentlemen. Elves and magical beings, it would be my great honor if you would follow me to one of my very favorite places and let me introduce you to the beautiful South Pole Village," Sandra said. Gunny and Birdie stood smiling with her. They had worked very hard to help make this day happen. The rest of the group shouted with glee. It was, by far, shaping up to be the best Christmas ever.

CHAPTER 54

Welcome to South Pole Village!

Location: St. Annalise

"Thank you all for coming," Sandra said, needing to talk loudly to be heard over the crowd of excited attendees. She stood on a picnic table so everyone could see her. Gunny and Spencer stood near a tall, portable, ramp waiting for their cue to push it up to the barge and let everyone aboard.

"I am so happy, along with Santa, who, as you all know, has made all of this possible, to welcome you to the South Pole Village.

"This village barge is so perfect for me in my role of Santa. It can be docked here at St. Annalise, the place that most holds my heart as home in all of the world, or it can move around to anywhere in the world and especially down to sail about in the South Pole Seas where we can best serve many of the world's children.

"I have Gunny to thank for envisioning what I could not manage to think of for myself. He was able to somehow know this barge would be perfect for me." She beamed with thanks over at Gunny who soaked it in. Though Sandra missed it, Jason visibly flinched at the words of praise for his tall competition.

"It is such an honor to stand with Santa but being South Pole Santa has only been made possible through the support of so many. It was Gunny and Birdie who helped oversee the construction of this large barge, for instance, while I've been running about doing all the really wonderful things that come with being Santa. That has left me with little time to do anything but direct how I would like it laid out and designed.

"My other best friend, Spence, has been critical to the barge coming together as his smart brain, working with other smart elf brains, has invented so many of the latest and greatest innovations that will be installed on the barge." She waved at Spence who actually waved at her and the rest of the crowd. He enjoyed his moment.

"And Christina Annalise, where have you gotten to?" Sandra scanned the crowd looking for her until she spotted the headmistress standing with her son. "Christina, I don't know if this ever would have been possible without you agreeing to allow us to bring this massive project to the shores of this beautiful secret spot we call home. Thank you." Sandra held her hands to her heart to emphasize her love for Christina.

"Of course, every successful person is made so through the love of family and in my camp I have always had Cappie along with the wonderful friends that I've mentioned, plus I've had Squawk." She held out her hand for the big bird to come land on.

". . . *squawk!* . . . love you! . . . *squawk!*"

"I love you too, my handsome friend," Sandra said and he preened.

"And I've had Rio, my loving dolphin friend, who obviously can't – "

"*eeeeeeeeeee eeeeeeeeeeeee,*" came loudly from the water between the barge and the shore. As the big, beautiful, green dolphin leaped out of the air and made a big splash.

"RIO!" Sandra said, laughing happily. "That, my dear friends gathered here, is my very precious, very clever dolphin friend, Rio, getting in on the party too. Feel free to toss her some of your fish tacos from dinner later."

Rio slapped the water with her fin in response.

"Before I conclude this little talk, thank you to everyone gathered here because if you are a friend of Cappie's, you are most certainly a friend of mine and we love you."

Em pulled on her dress. "What about me?" she asked, and the crowd laughed.

Sandra laughed too. "I could never forget you, Em!" she said. "Everyone, this is Emaralda, Em for short and she is a delgin. My special delgin to be very clear. She and I deliver gifts with Santa to children all around the world."

The audience applauded at that and Em actually curtsied. She never ceased to surprise Sandra.

"Every elf I've ever met has been special," Sandra continued sincerely. "Elves, you have brought so much joy and happiness and," the elves all dabbed at their eyes, "love and laughter and yes, even some tears to me. This barge would not be here today if these brave little, hard-working elves hadn't agreed to come somewhere totally new – which they normally hate to do – and been willing to put their toy-making expertise to work on this giant project. I love all of you."

"We love you too Sandra!" the elves called back in unison.

"Okay, and last but never ever least, before we pull up this ramp and let you explore this fabulous barge, I want to thank my mentor Santa Claus for seeing in me the ability to do the coolest job in the whole wide world and giving it to me. Santa, you have been my hero since I was very small and you remain my hero today. Thank you for showing the world what it is to be kind and generous."

"Ho Ho Ho Sandra! You have even taught this old Santa some new ways to be kind and generous. I could not be more proud, or surer, of having made the right selection for second Santa." Sandra heard Gunny cheer the loudest at his words and appreciated the support from her friend who came in second.

"Okay, well, today you are all the first people in the whole of the world to get a glimpse of the South Pole Village. She's not done yet but all of her top deck and rooms are completed thanks to my very dedicated team and that's where we'll be celebrating today. Feel free to wander about and ooh and awe over its wonderfulness." She stopped and smiled feeling pleased just thinking about it.

"At the North Pole there is a wonderful place called Happiness Hall. It is one of the most special spots at the Pole. It's where I was named South Pole Santa, and consequently, another one of my favorite places in the world. For our showcase hall here, I struggled with what to call it. I didn't want the confusion of having two Happiness Halls even though I loved the name. I joked with Gunny that I might name it 'Happier Hall' but, of course, that wouldn't have been right. I toyed with 'Celebration Hall' but while celebrations are almost always happy not everything that happens at Happiness Hall is a celebration. Most often, but not always.

"I wanted that same happy feeling to be part of this hall and part of its name. I thought for months on what other word I could use to replace happiness that also represented me, until I finally realized what it was. It was obvious in the end. The word for me that holds happiness and could be used interchangeably with the word happiness is mistletoe. There is simply no place I have been happier then on our merry tug. So, without further ado and with the wonderful fanfare of Buddy and Ellen leading the North Pole Marching Band in a spectacular performance on to the barge, I hope you all will find you love Mistletoe Hall as much as I have loved Happiness Hall."

The cheers and applause were deafening and joy was everywhere as Spence and Gunny pulled the big ramp up to the barge. Buddy and Ellen, with the North Pole marching band, all of them decked out in special wedding day uniforms, went marching grandly up the ramp playing a wonderful new rendition of "Santa Claus is Coming to Town." Clicker snapped photos as the guests lined up, cheerfully marching in place themselves as part of the glee-filled day. It was an even grander moment then Sandra had anticipated.

It was right then that Cappie and Thomas came walking up and the crowd parted to let the newlyweds go on up the ramp first where they stopped at the top to welcome each person onboard with hugs and smiles. Sandra stood watching and Santa came to stand with her.

"Sandra, you truly make this old Santa very proud," he said more emotionally then he usually let himself be. Sandra's eyes welled up in tears. She couldn't take too much more great stuff on this day. "May I be your escort into this wonderful Mistletoe Hall of yours?"

"Oh Oh Oh, Santa! I wouldn't want it to be anyone else," she said beaming with love at him.

"Thank you again for picking me to be South Pole Santa." It would be a fabulous night of dancing and merry making and incredibly happy moments on the best Christmas ever but this would be one of the moments she most cherished from the day.

"Merry Christmas, Santa!" she said. "Merry Christmas, everyone!" she shouted out in happiness to the whole of the island as she and Santa marched cheerfully up the ramp and onto the South Pole Village barge.

It's All in the Family

Location: The Mistletoe

Sandra returned to the *Mistletoe* by herself after the very long day. In two of the very biggest days of the year – of her life, really – she had gotten very little sleep and it was catching up with her fast now. She plopped down in the chair closest to the rail on the back deck and gazed out at the beautiful night sky.

Cappie and Thomas had caught a reindeer express ride to Florida, where they were catching a plane for a surprise destination honeymoon that Thomas had arranged. Em and Squawk both had been so tired after all the wedding festivities they had fallen asleep on the barge. On this night, despite her exhaustion, Sandra had felt the need to come home to her berth on the *Mistletoe*. It was here that she had always felt at home, and here that she would now have to get used to having all to herself as

Cappie began her new life just a couple of docks down on the *Lullaby.*

She was at peace with the change and knew that it meant she was growing up. There was a time it would have been far too upsetting to even think of a home without Cappie in it but now she knew they would both be okay. They would always be close, no matter how far physically they actually were from each other, and most of the time they would be just a couple of docks apart.

All in all, as exhausted as she felt, life was feeling pretty close to perfect.

She sat thinking over all her blessings and how thankful she felt. It had been a tough year but a really wonderful Christmas season. Things weren't resolved yet for Birdie, and she had no idea what was going to happen with either Jason or Gunny but neither of them was missing anymore. The wedding had been perfect and she was content. Past content, really, to plain ol', spillingover-all- sides, happy. After a few years of almost too much excitement, it felt like things were finally calming down a little bit and that was a good thing.

A shooting star went streaking across the tropical night sky as she sat there trying to get energy enough to get up and go in to change for bed. As tempting as it was to sleep on the deck, as she had her whole life, she didn't want to sleep in her dress. She needed to go in, change, and sleep for hours and hours.

"Gotta make a wish," she said out loud, forcing herself to get up from her chair. She knew what her wish was without a second thought since she had been making the same one most of her life. She took one last look at the beautiful night sky and started for her berth when she completely stopped, feeling fully awake now, and her breath caught in her throat. There, plain as day, in the bright light of the full moon, on the deck of the *Mistletoe*, stood her parents.

The End

Mango's Favorite Dog Bones

Recipe created by Betsy Chan, Bloomington, MN

2 large egg whites, beaten
1/2 cup peanut butter
2 tablespoons olive oil
1/2 cup cold water
1/4 cup finely chopped carrots
1/2 teaspoon ground cinnamon
1/4 teaspoon ground flaxseed, optional
2 teaspoons finely chopped dried parsley flakes (or fresh parsley, if available)
2/3 cup old-fashioned rolled oats
3/4 - 1 cup whole-wheat flour, plus extra for dusting surface (may substitute all-purpose flour)

Preheat oven to 350 degrees F. Line 2 cookie sheets with parchment paper, or spray with nonstick cooking spray.

In a large bowl, combine all ingredients <u>except</u> the flour, until well mixed. Slowly add flour in 4 or 5 parts, mixing until a soft dough forms.

Knead dough on a "dusted-with-flour" surface. Sprinkle more flour to the dough if it's too sticky, until dough is smooth and easy to handle. Return dough back into bowl. Lightly flour the surface again, and plop a handful of dough onto it. Lightly flour a rolling-pin and roll (or press) dough down to about 1/8" thickness, then use a dog bone-shaped cookie cutter (or any shape) to cut into the dough. Another variation is to use a butter knife to cut dough into strips, squares or any creative shape you like! Repeat with the remaining dough until all is used.

Transfer the shapes onto prepared cookie sheets. Bake in pre-heated oven for 20-22 minutes for small shapes or 22-25 minutes for medium shapes, or until golden brown.

Remove sheets from oven and let dog bones cool completely before giving them to your favorite dog(s) to eat. Store in an air-tight container. Bone-Appetit! Woof, woof!!

Acknowledgements

Thank you most especially to **Brieanna Vennard** and **Tina Fischer Mitchell,** my trusty book team, who are always there to help lift me up and keep me moving forward. You are talented and wonderful!

Thank you to **Betsy Chan, Diana Kwong, Wendy Parris, Krysta Rasmussen** and **Brittany Rien**. You all know the wonderful parts you have played in adding to this book.

Don't Miss!
Books in the South Pole Santa series by JingleBelle Jackson

Book 1: The Search for South Pole Santa – A Christmas Adventure

Book 2: Sandra Claus... – A South Pole Santa Adventure

Book 3: The Santanapping – A South Pole Santa Adventure

Book 4: Unwrapped – A South Pole Santa Adventure

Book 5: The final book in the South Pole Santa series. Coming Christmas season 2016!

Thanks for being wonderful and reading *Unwrapped*! If you enjoyed this book, I would welcome your review. Find more about Sandra and her madcap elf friends at www.jinglebellejackson.com.

Oh Oh Oh!